REVELATION

REVELATION

BOOK THREE OF
THE DEVOLUTION TRILOGY

JOHN CASEY

PHiR Publishing
San Antonio

PHiR Publishing
San Antonio, TX
phirpublishing.com

First edition: December 2022

ISBN: 978-1-7369081-6-7
Library of Congress Control Number: 2021905949

Printed in the United States of America

ALSO BY JOHN CASEY

DEVOLUTION
Book One of The Devolution Trilogy

EVOLUTION
Book Two of The Devolution Trilogy

RAW THΦUGHTS
A Mindful Fusion of Poetic and Photographic Art
(with photographer Scott Hussey)

MERIDIAN
A Raw Thoughts Book
(with photographer Scott Hussey)

THE BARN
A Novella Mystery
(co-authored by Doug Campbell)

For my parents, John and Caroline Casey

"Hell is empty, and all the devils are here."

— William Shakespeare

WHAT CAME BEFORE...

In DEVOLUTION, Michael Dolan was introduced as a stoic perfectionist and former special operations pilot working a staff job at the Pentagon who accepts an improbable CIA request to help prevent impending terrorist attacks in Europe. The Agency had reached a dead end and was in desperate need of an agent who could be quickly embedded within the terrorist organization without raising suspicion.

After being vetted and receiving a bare minimum of training, Dolan found himself back in Paris, France where he'd experienced a terrible mishap years before while attending the Sorbonne University on a military scholarship. Dolan's French girlfriend at the time, Claire Fontaine, died after falling from the balcony of a hotel room. Dolan never fully recovered from the tragic and questionable circumstances of her death. He was close friends with Sharif Lefebvre back then, son of an Algerian oil industry mogul who later became the leader of the al-Mulathamun Army (AMA), a newer terrorist organization in Africa with historical ties to al-Qa'ida. The CIA believed Sharif might be involved with Lefebvre's shadowy plot to attack American interests in Europe using a weapon of mass destruction. Their plan, codenamed Operation EXCISE, tasked Dolan with rekindling the friendship in order to collect and report on Sharif while maintaining his cover as an employee of a multinational intelligence-sharing organization led by the French government.

Meanwhile, François Martin, a wine industry engineer and past colleague of Sharif, established a base of operations for the terrorist cell and finalized plans to attack in both France and Germany. As the story evolved, Dolan became intimate with Anne Bernard, Sharif's ex-girlfriend and onetime best friend of Claire. As difficult truths about himself and what really happened to Claire began to surface, Dolan realized the CIA had been keeping him in the dark about many aspects of the mission and found they were spying on *him* using his cell phone. Faced with mounting obstacles and with no one to trust except Anne, Dolan decided to go dark and try to take out the cell himself, one terrorist at a time.

Lauren Rhodes, leader of the CIA black unit SCALPEL, did everything she could to keep the mission on track while holding threats from leadership to close the unit down at bay. She left Washington for Europe to help Tony Stone, SCALPEL's field operative in Paris, in a desperate attempt to salvage the operation after Dolan went underground.

Ultimately, Dolan concludes his rogue mission in dramatic fashion. But there are unanswered questions and business left unfinished.

The story picks up two years later in EVOLUTION. After the climactic end of operation EXCISE, Dolan cut ties with the CIA and settled back in his hometown, Boston Massachusetts. There, he finished his graduate degree and began teaching as an assistant professor at Boston University. Just as he had come to terms with much of what happened in Paris and Berlin, the Agency came knocking once more. Terrorists had launched a bioweapon in the Middle East, thousands were dying of a horrifying virus with no cure, and Dolan was targeted for assassination by the AMA. CIA Deputy Director for Operations Phil Dittrich saw it as an opportunity to capture the assassin in the hopes he could be pressured into revealing information leading to the location of Hakeem and Sharif Lefebvre.

Dolan agreed to join SCALPEL once again on the condition that he would be, unlike last time, fully read into SCALPEL as a full team member. Dittrich and Lauren agreed. Dolan completed a condensed training course and was brought on board as an official counterintelligence officer. His training was administered by a longtime, old-world spy and psychologist named Howard Welker who accompanied him to Germany. There, they joined Mike Collier and Stan Bolden from Berlin Station in an elaborate plan to use Dolan as bait to lure the assassin out.

Early in the operation Anne Bernard showed up unannounced, having learned of Dolan's presence in Berlin from a social media post designed to manipulate the assassin. The team decided to use a meeting between the two as part of the operation to identify their target. Though it worked, both Anne and Dolan were nearly killed in the process. A Russian spy named Yuri Kuznetsov saved them but killed the assassin, thus scuttling SCALPEL's objective of capturing and interrogating him. The team then moved south to Frankfurt, where it was believed an AMA cell was planning to execute the next phase of attacks.

In the meantime, Deputy Director for Operations Phil Dittrich was leading a large and complex joint operation from Langley codenamed Operation CLEARCUT to find Lefebvre, locate any remaining bioweapons and put an end to the AMA. While SCALPEL began to uncover plans by the terrorist cell in Germany to attack the Frankfurt Airport, CLEARCUT launched a raid from Israel into Syria where they believed Hakeem and Sharif were hiding. It turned out, however, that Sharif was actually in Germany leading the cell, and the compound in Syria was largely a dead end.

By then things were evolving quickly and Dolan was right in the thick of it. After taking out two cell members at an abandoned warehouse, he chased Sharif across southern Germany. Dolan ultimately forced him off the road, captured him and brought him back to the CIA's safehouse in Frankfurt for rendition back the United States. From information Dolan gathered at the warehouse, SCALPEL was able to greatly reduce the impact of the AMA attack on the airport and prevent any spread of the virus.

Though Hakeem Lefebvre was never found, their mission was considered a big success, and largely because of Dolan's efforts. This was not lost on Deputy Director Dittrich, and Evolution ends with the understanding that after a period of time, Dolan would be installed as the leader of a new, more capable and lethal black ops team that would replace SCALPEL under a new codename.

Thus begins REVELATION.

CHAPTER ONE

"We have confirmation on the ground, it's him. He just entered the building with his Information Officer, Ahmad Korichi."

Michael Dolan wanted to say *something*, or to high-five somebody, but the serious atmosphere of the room precluded such a response. There would be time to celebrate when the strike was completed successfully. The CIA officer continued to brief the small, select group on the situation as it evolved. He used a laser pointer to highlight the position of their two Agency operatives about half a kilometer away, adjacent to the Seal Team situated behind a ridgeline a short distance to the north. He then pointed to the eleven al-Mulathamun Army terrorists assembled, including Hakeem Lefebvre and Korichi, inside the large mud-walled, thatch roof farmhouse. Their heat signatures on the video made them appear as fuzzy, bright white ghosts. There were four armed guards, one at each corner of the building, and a hundred or so workers spread out across the four hundred hectares of sorghum fields to the south and east. As they watched, one of the guards left his post and went inside the house. The real-time infrared and visible spectrum video was provided on side-by-side screens courtesy of a National Reconnaissance Office satellite and a U.S. Air Force General Atomics MQ-9 Reaper that took off from Niamey, Niger three hours earlier. Two Boeing twin-engine, heavy-lift CH-47F Chinook helicopters were positioned in a field four and a half kilometers to the west, rotors turning and prepped for immediate dustoff and extraction. A backup team of fourteen waited onboard one of them, if called upon.

"What now then, can we take them out?" The authoritative voice came from a large display to the left of the satellite and Reaper feeds. It was split into quadrants, reminiscent of a zoom meeting.

"Mr. President, confirmation of Lefebvre's presence was the last, and most important requirement to be met," replied Phil Dittrich, the Agency's long-time Deputy Director for Operations. "With the guard covering the northwest corner of the property now inside the house, we just got lucky. We can begin ingress undetected. The workers in the fields are sufficiently far away. There should be little to no collateral damage. With your approval, we are a go."

The President nodded approvingly. "Good. We've been searching for Lefebvre for years. It is time put this behind us, and to avenge the deaths of all those the AMA are responsible for. You have my approval."

"Thank you, Mr. President," Dittrich replied.

They made the unusual decision to strike shortly after sunrise. Though there are significant operational challenges associated with a daylight attack, in this case there were good reasons for doing it that outweighed the inherent risks. The farm hands slept in a large outbuilding next to the house. And though they were civilians, there was a high probability they would join the fight in the event of any trouble. If that were to happen, DEVGRU and the rest of the strike team could very quickly be dealing with over a hundred men instead of eleven. A nighttime strike would require a larger team and a more complex plan that would result in numerous casualties. Having them spread out and far from the house gave the team a window of time that was sufficient to get in and out without having to engage them.

After observing the property for several days via satellite, it was also apparent security was much tighter at night—Lefebvre knew an assault was much more likely in the wee hours of the morning. As a result, the CLEARCUT team, formed two and a half years ago to track down and take out Lefebvre after the AMA launched a bioweapon attack in Amman, Jordan that killed thousands, decided to flip the script.

The Vice President, Chairman of the Joint Chiefs of Staff, National Security Advisor, Secretary of Defense, Director for Counterterrorism, the Director of National Intelligence, and the President's Chief of Staff were with the President in the White House Situation Room. Three-star General Scott Thornton, Commander of Joint Special Operations Command (JSOC) was on the screen to the right of the President. A Navy Captain walked into view behind him to give an update on the status of forces on the ground. The general gave him instructions and turned his attention back to the group. "I've just given the green light; Operation SUNSET is a go."

As he spoke the Seal Team could be seen breaking for the farmhouse, finding cover behind bush fig and gmelina trees as they went. The two Agency operatives fell in behind them. Joining the team was one member of the King Abdullah II Special Forces Group of the Jordanian Armed Forces, whose Commander was looped into the VTC and visible directly below Thornton on the screen. Three additional monitors on the wall displayed helmet cam footage. Audio from their communications was piped into the room, but for now it was quiet as they made their way past the workers' quarters near the single-story house using hand signals. Everyone in the room held their collective breaths as Seals took key positions with lines of sight on the guards. Two seconds later, they exhaled as all three collapsed to the ground in unison.

The silence in the room was broken as situation reports and rapid commands came across the comms network. The team then split into two groups, silently converging on the front and back doors of the house.

It was a beautiful thing to watch, Dolan thought. Choreographed and practiced, of course. Seal Team Six, more commonly known as DEVGRU within JSOC, practiced this raid numerous times back at The Stage, the CIA's Top-Secret training facility at Harvey Point in North Carolina. So far, everything was going according to plan. None of the farm hands seemed to be aware of what was going on, and all indications were that Lefebvre and his men would be taken completely by surprise. If anything went wrong, they'd flex their plan accordingly. Every conceivable outcome had been strategized, every variable and eventuality considered.

Dolan took a moment to marvel at the resilience and tenacity of Hakeem Lefebvre and his core group of followers. In the aftermath of their foiled plot to deploy the deadly Marburg Virus at the Frankfurt Airport in 2021, the CIA and other intelligence organizations from various countries uncovered and shared a vast amount of intelligence that led to the unravelling of the terrorist group. AMA cells and supporters were killed and captured across Europe, the Middle East, and North Africa. But nothing they found, no one they caught and interrogated ever divulged or pointed to the whereabouts of Lefebvre and his inner circle. Their biggest prize to-date, Hakeem's son Sharif, was captured by Dolan and renditioned to the United States immediately after the failed attempt in Frankfurt. Though he demonstrated a willingness to reveal everything he knew, he held fast to the claim he did not know where his father was. Sharif admitted knowledge of the existence of three key hideouts, properties Hakeem had prepped to escape to, but was aware of the exact location of just one—the compound in southern Algeria he escaped to from Marseille. A second in Syria was uncovered by CLEARCUT and hit by an interagency team of U.S. forces in coordination with the government of Israel, and with a bit of unplanned help from the Russian Federation. But the third had remained a mystery until recently. After eighteen months of interrogation and multiple polygraphs, they believed Sharif was telling them the truth. It was apparent Lefebvre didn't trust his own son with certain information. He was notorious for being secretive and stovepiping information within his terror organization. His strictly-enforced communications protocols and operational security practices bought him two and a half additional years, hiding on a sorghum farm in Niger at the edge of the Saharan Desert. But not a day more.

Again, the room was silent as they waited. "Three, two one," came the countdown over the speakers, followed by the sound of both doors being breached simultaneously. At that moment, both Chinooks took off and headed toward the farm. Flashbang grenades were tossed inside the house. Then, what looked and sounded like total chaos ensued. The video was difficult to follow, constantly moving and jerky. There was a barrage of gunshots and yelling as the team moved inside the dimly-lit house from both doors. Their order was shoot to kill. Women and children who do not pose a threat were to be subdued. DEVGRU appeared to have taken them by complete surprise. Though there were rifles leaning against the walls, they were out of reach and none of the eleven terrorists were armed. Exactly thirteen seconds after the doors were breached, it was over.

"Is that it? Did we get him?" asked The President.

Dolan, Dittrich and the others at Langley watched, waiting for the Navy Captain to tell General Thornton what everyone already suspected.

"Yes, Mr. President," Thornton replied. "We got him."

"Yes!" yelled The President enthusiastically, banging a fist on his desk. Congratulatory exuberance came through the speaker from the Situation Room.

"Sir, it's not over yet," Dittrich interjected. "We still have to get our team safely out of there. The field workers are now running towards the house, and some are armed."

"I understand," he replied. "What is the ETA on the helicopters?"

"Thirty seconds, sir," said General Thornton. "We will need to deploy suppression fire. Any workers who engage our team are considered enemy combatants."

Dolan watched the Reaper video feed. More and more of the workers were now running through the fields towards the house. As both Chinooks came into view at the edge of the screen, the Seals exited quickly from the back of the house, two of them carrying a body. The first helo remained high as a door gunner began firing in swaths, just ahead of the nearest farmhands. Most of them stopped abruptly. A few with rifles pointed them skyward and began firing at the Chinook. All bets were off at that point, and the door gunner began cutting them down.

The second Chinook landed with the cargo ramp open. Most of the team ran up the ramp and into the back, some of them carrying boxes and other items of intelligence value. They were followed by the two carrying Lefebvre on a stretcher and last, three Seals who were providing cover fire. They took off the second all were on board, the ramp still closing as the huge helicopter lifted and sped away in an impossibly large cloud of dust, temporarily obscuring the immediate area on the video feed. The first Chinook turned and rejoined aside and just behind the second, and they disappeared off the edge of the Reaper's feed at just over one hundred and sixty knots. A few seconds later, the farmhouse erupted in an accelerant-fueled, fiery explosion that sent up a mushrooming plume of smoke. Workers in the field who were not already fleeing turned and ran. Though they'd been effectively wiped out for some time now, with the death of Hakeem Lefebvre the AMA was now officially erased.

"Mr. President, we have him and our men and aircraft will land soon at Niamey," General Thornton announced. "Zero casualties. Once on the ground we'll process Lefebvre, then hand him over to Jordan."

"Fantastic, thank you General," responded the President. "I want to thank everyone involved. We've just concluded the largest and most complex manhunt in history, even more so than for Usama bin Laden. This was the best outcome, and everyone here played a pivotal role. Congratulations, and thank you all."

General Thornton, Dittrich and others thanked the President. After a bit more discussion General Thornton ended the secure VTC, and the screens went blank. As the fluorescent lights flickered on in the room at Langley, Dolan got up from his chair and walked over to Dittrich, still seated.

"Sir, did I hear him right? We are giving Lefebvre's body over to Jordan?" asked Dolan.

Dittrich stood up. "Yes, they wanted his body. As you know, their participation in the raid was our idea. No one was hurt more by the AMA than Jordan and when this hits the news later today it will play to our advantage. As for the body, we will have the photos, fingerprints, and DNA. So, we won't need it and frankly, we don't want it. Our original plan was to dump him in the Atlantic, like what we did with UBL in the North Arabian Sea. But Jordan has other ideas, some kind of ceremony planned and that's fine with us. Let them. We got what we wanted."

"Sure, OK," Dolan responded. "So, what now? This is all I've had on my plate for months, and now it's empty. I don't want the team to become restless."

Dittrich took him by the arm and led him to a corner of the room. He lowered his voice as he spoke. "I want you to investigate something that is quite sensitive, politically speaking. Very few people know who tipped us off to Lefebvre's location, in part because it happened so recently, in part because it's highly classified, but also because they asked us to keep it quiet. It was Turkey."

"Turkey? That *is* surprising."

"Yes. They have no known intelligence presence in Niger outside their embassy, same situation in Algeria. They haven't been a significant part of any collaborative or coalition efforts to eradicate the AMA. This would indicate to us it was a coincidence, that they got lucky. But there is a third option, that something else is going on. Oh, and this is important—it's so sensitive, I can't even let Ankara Station know. At least, not yet. I'll send you the details."

"OK, I'm on it," Dolan replied.

"And Michael, keep this very quiet. Our relations with Turkey are far better right now than they've been in over a decade. Do not stir the pot. Fact-finding—that's all we're doing here. For now."

"Understood," Dolan replied.

They shook hands and Dolan left the briefing room, wondering whether this 'fact-finding' mission would lead his team to uncover something worth following up on, or if it would ultimately lead to nothing. It was entirely possible a Turkish diplomat or intelligence officer stumbled fortuitously upon Lefebvre's location in the course of some other, unrelated effort. Though the odds of that were bad, it was still the most likely scenario. But something felt off and Dolan couldn't shake it. His gut was telling him something different. And his gut was usually right.

CHAPTER TWO

For the past few years, nearly everything had played out according to Dittrich's plan. Just two months after preventing the AMA's bioweapon attack at Frankfurt Airport in late September 2021, SCALPEL was disbanded. Lauren Rhodes, SCALPEL's longtime leader, was reassigned to Canberra Station in Australia. Thomas Freeman was given a very good job helping research and design the next generation of hi-tech spy gadgetry with the Intelligence Advanced Research Project Activity (IARPA). In Berlin, Stan Bolden and Mike Collier were read out of the program, as was Chief of Paris Station Jean-Luc Le Pen. Howard Welker went quietly back to his business process management company as if nothing had ever happened. Finally, Dolan was read out. But what no one else knew was, he was immediately read into a brand-new black program codenamed REVENANT.

REVENANT didn't replace SCALPEL; it was more accurate to say that SCALPEL was subsumed by it. Everything that SCALPEL had been—its mission, scope and resources, would be absorbed, strengthened, and expanded. But the new program couldn't be launched immediately. There was a waiting period of two years, during which time Dolan completed his Doctorate at Boston University. He continued to teach there as an assistant professor and on the side, was called away by the Agency from time to time for advanced training and to participate in certain critical operations. Three of those ops prevented significant casualties and severe damage to the general security of the United States. And as had been the case in his first two missions, Dolan was again uniquely responsible for key intelligence breakthroughs and the killing or capture of several high-profile terrorists. During this time, a legend of sorts began to build inside the walls at Langley. Analysts and desk officers began hearing about Dolan's exploits and successes. Headquarters staff were whispering in certain small circles about a counterintelligence officer named Michael Dolan who was quietly taking the clandestine world by storm.

As part of his transition to lead the new team, Dolan was offered a full professorship at American University in Washington. It was a perfect cover, but almost unheard of in the annals of academia, particularly at an esteemed university. Dolan had been an assistant in Boston for just over two years. It was his doctoral thesis on International Cooperation in Pandemic Prevention and Mitigation that had propelled his career, and dizzyingly fast. A world-renown mathematician happened to read it and was so impressed he decided to use it as the basis for a new model that was uncannily accurate in predicting the spread of epidemics. It was fast becoming an international standard. Once the *Miltner-Dolan Model* was published, Dolan's academic credibility was instantly and firmly established. At that point, any worry the Agency had about his cover concerning perceptions about his meteoric rise simply vanished.

The relative fame proved to be both a hindrance and a help. Dolan was receiving an inordinate volume of requests for information, speaking engagements, and offers of collaboration. As a professor he could now hand much of it off to his assistants and students, but he still found himself spending a lot of time culling through it all to make sure those that were worthwhile received attention. He was in a narrow, though international academic spotlight. It wasn't ideal for his role as the leader of REVENANT. But if he played his cards the right way, he could use it to his advantage. That spotlight gave him the latitude he needed to do what he wanted, when he wanted, and without having to explain everything. He could create a cover wherever REVENANT's mission needs took him with relative ease.

While completing his thesis research for Atlantik Brücke in Berlin, Dolan had several opportunities to spend time with the love of his life, Anne Bernard. He visited her in Paris a few times, and she spent time with him in Germany on several occasions. They grew incredibly close. Though everything about their relationship was wonderful and positive and good, Dolan began to sense that it would end in ruin. For her, for him, for both. Anne was nearly killed in Berlin because of his work with the Agency. He'd accepted a way of life that would always put her in harm's way. It was a fact he couldn't ignore. As his research came to a close, they discussed these concerns at great length. And though they knew it would be difficult, they decided to maintain a long-distance relationship. It would be a temporary arrangement, and they shared a hope that one day they could be together without a dark cloud of uncertainty and danger constantly on the horizon. They'd seen each other six times since then, each a vacation to different, exciting parts of the world. Dolan couldn't help but feel that their arrangement, while wondrous and fulfilling, was beginning to wear thin for Anne. That it wasn't enough.

Both Bolden and Collier were read in to REVENANT but reaching the end of their assignments in Germany, and it remained to be seen where they would go next. Dittrich assured him, however, that they would remain part of the team. Le Pen retired and was replaced in Paris by a new Station Chief, John Fitzhenry, who was added to REVENANT upon its official standup. Freeman wrapped up his work with IARPA and was sent back to his old office in Clarendon. He was joined by Howard Welker, who sold his BPM company and was once again a full-time CIA officer. It took some convincing, but in the end, Dolan won him over.

Additionally, REVENANT was given three new resources. Andrew Andino, who never passed up the opportunity to let everyone know his last name meant 'manly,' was a very good counterintelligence officer stationed in Athens. He was well-liked and a former protégé of Welker's. Omar Haddad joined the team from Jordan. After the AMA attacked Amman's public water supply, Haddad was assigned to investigate how it had been done and for getting the young Syrian attacker, Issam Yassefe, to break under interrogation. Additionally, he helped broker and frame the agreement on Jordan's participation in the raid in Niger and subsequent transfer of Lefebvre's body to their government. It was a delicate, high-risk arrangement, given the need for extreme secrecy. Though it would never be acknowledged publicly, it was rumored Jordan planned to cut Lefebvre's body into four parts, burn each part of him separately, and jettison the ashes into the Red Sea, the Mediterranean, the Persian Gulf, and the Gulf of Aden. The interoffice joke was that their plan was overkill, but the Jordanians just couldn't kill him enough.

What no one ever joked about, however, was their team's codename. REVENANT, meaning 'ghost,' was appropriate in more ways than one. First, they were a black program and as such, everything they did was deniable. Their very existence was deniable. They *were* ghosts. Second, Operation SCALPEL had been disbanded and REVENANT was born of its ashes, a stronger and more powerful reincarnation of its former self. Back from the dead. Dittrich pushed hard for the codename 'Phoenix,' but ultimately, he gave in to Dolan who suggested it was too much of a cliché. In any case, Dolan argued, REVENANT better approximated his personal vision for the new team. Invisible, mysterious, and dangerous. Lethal.

Dolan revisited these things in his mind as he drove to REVENANT's headquarters in Clarendon. It had been an amazing sequence of events that led him to where he was today. Things could have easily gone in a completely different direction given how many times he had bent or broken the rules. In every case, however, he believed without a doubt he'd made the right decisions. His conscience was clear. In the end, and despite Lauren Rhodes' attempts to railroad him out of the Agency, it was Dittrich's belief in those decisions and in his abilities that led to his new role.

Though he'd pulled an all-nighter and it was now four in the morning, any fatigue he felt was beginning to wane as a new day began. In any case, he wouldn't be able to sleep until he'd read Dittrich's email. He exited the elevator, keyed in through the door and went straight to his office, flipping on the lights as he went. Though it was greatly satisfying and cathartic in a way to close the book on Lefebvre, he felt no compulsion to sit back and enjoy it. He was eager to move on to the next important thing, whatever it might be. And this task was at least related to the AMA. It was very strange that for over two years a coalition of western, Middle Eastern, and African governments searched for Lefebvre, and it was a country completely uninvolved in that effort that eventually found him. Though Lefebvre was dead, it could be that the book shouldn't be closed quite yet. There could be one last chapter to write.

As he read Dittrich's message, that thought took on a more concrete form. Lefebvre's location had been passed directly from Adem Avci, the President of Turkey, to the President of the United States during a phone conversation between the two that was scheduled at

Avci's request. Avci would not reveal how he came about the information, citing protection of sources and national security concerns. He assured the President that it was irrefutable, directly sourced intelligence. There was an immediate, mad scramble to position a reconnaissance satellite overhead and to deploy two CIA assets in Niger to confirm. Two days later they were able to positively identify Lefebvre and his longtime friend and lieutenant, Korichi.

Avci's rise to power had been nothing less than spectacular. He was born in Bergama to a wealthy family and educated at Oxford and Yale. After school, he joined the Turkish Navy and served four years as an officer. Then he returned home and enlisted as a political staffer for a prominent parliamentarian. Three years later he was selected as an aide to the Mayor of Ankara, was married and quickly gained favor and local influence. That influence led eight years later to his own run for the mayoral office, which he won handily, defeating his former patriarch in a tempestuous, though one-sided race. As the mayor of one of Turkey's largest cities, his reputation grew as a strong and economically savvy leader whose poise and diplomacy under fire was unmatched. He served two terms in Ankara before jumping into the presidential race, again trouncing the incumbent. But his campaign was not without controversy. When he entered the race, he was well behind in the polls. He enlisted the help of a longtime friend, banking and IT genius Yusuf Solak, to launch a social media assault against his opponent. After just a few weeks the race tightened. Solak focused on using Facebook, Twitter, Instagram, and other apps created by his global IT company, Red Fig.

Red Fig was best known for its mobile applications including several games, some of which proved very popular. The most successful, however, was a social media app called eL8, pronounced 'elate.' It cost ninety-nine cents in the U.S. and its purpose was, admirably, to increase happiness. It did so by learning about the user's habits over time and suggesting small changes to daily routines to catalyze self-improvement. It also connected users with like-minded people whose goals and ambitions were similar. It took the world by storm—to date there had been over six hundred million downloads worldwide, over a hundred million in the United States alone.

The incumbent, whose large initial lead in the polls grew steadily smaller, accused Solak and Red Fig of using social media and other means to interfere with and manipulate the election. He was unable to produce any hard evidence of it, however. Then, just four months from election day, Avci's wife died tragically during a shopping trip to Istanbul, struck by a vehicle when crossing the street. She was three months pregnant. The driver, unbelievably, was never apprehended.

Avci was devastated, almost to the point of dropping out of the race. Ultimately, he decided to see it through and credited his good friend's emotional support in giving him the courage and strength to do so. His razor-thin lead in the polls swiftly reached double digits. All accusations of election fraud by the incumbent fell on deaf ears due to the 'sympathy effect,' as the media dubbed it. Solak and Avci maintained that her death had nothing to do with the surge, assuring the public it was Avci's political platform and the people's confidence in his ability to lead the nation that had swayed public opinion. At the age of forty-two, Adem Avci became the youngest president in the history of Turkey.

He inherited a government that over the previous decade had soured relations with the west and in the region. This was due in part to Islamist-centric policies carefully put in place by his predecessor that were unpopular with the West and the Turkish military, which views itself as a guardian of Turkey's secular political traditions. Siding with Russia after their invasion of Ukraine on certain international issues complicated things further. Though thought by many to be a closet Islamist, Avci demonstrated right away he was a gifted diplomat, repairing relations with the United States, France, and even making headway with an unlikely three-way diplomacy-infused peace deal between Turkey, Azerbaijan, and Armenia that built on the ceasefire and Russian-brokered progress made in November of 2020. Many of the domestic policies of his predecessor went largely unchanged, however, and were even enhanced to some degree. Those things went unnoticed, overshadowed by his regime's considerable efforts at improving and strengthening relations with the European Council and taking measurable steps to increase and improve regional security and trade.

The Turkish economy was booming. Unemployment had gone from roughly twenty percent in 2020 to less than nine, and confidence in his leadership was polling at an all-time high. He had come to be revered within his own country, well-liked in the surrounding countries and was gaining respect across the globe. This was best evidenced by his face gracing the cover of Time Magazine as Person of the Year after only a few months in office. Handing Hakeem Lefebvre to the United States on a silver platter was yet another feather in his cap.

A long and detailed report attached to Dittrich's email provided Dolan with considerable context. It would take some time to consume all the information. Scanning it quickly, he saw there was no evidence Turkey had interests or assets in Niger that might have led directly to the discovery of Lefebvre's hideout. Diplomatic relations between the two countries were solid, but limited.

There was a large section in the report that detailed the exploits of Yusuf Solak. Though not nearly as well-known as Bill Gates or Mark Zuckerberg, Solak was increasingly a leading figure in the world of mobile app development. Red Fig was one of the fastest growing corporations in big tech. Through rapid and strategic acquisition of several key Chinese and Indian IT companies, it had grown quickly into a competitive world player.

Close friends from childhood, Solak and Avci attended Oxford together. There, Solak was quickly singled out as a math and analytical genius. He famously scored an eye-popping 195 on an IQ test at the university administered specifically for him by Mensa. When Avci continued to Yale, Solak returned to Turkey to begin building his empire with the vast fortune left to him by his father. Seemingly uninterested in pursuing a career suited to his mathematical abilities, he began with an import-export business that stretched across Europe and North Africa. Then, fifteen years after establishing Blue Olive Exports, he sold it and invested everything in software development. Red Fig took off rapidly and was now the fourteenth most valuable company in the world, with three hundred and sixty-two apps for sale on both Apple and Android operating systems, and another seventy-six in development.

Adem Avci's status and standing on the world stage was helped along by many things, but the launch of Hypotherion stood above them all. As big as Red Fig's social media applications success was, it was their blockchain division that was making headlines. Solak teamed with his country's government to launch the Hypotherion crypto Bank and Exchange. Hypotherion was similar to Bitcoin, though there were key differences. At the time, it was the first government-controlled crypto bank and much of the financial world scoffed at the idea. But no longer. The premise for Hypotherion was completely new, and arguably magnanimous. Their goal was to use Hypotherion and its bank to fund very low-interest loans to third and second-world federal governments. The loans could only be used to improve infrastructure or recover from significant hardship, such as national disasters. Anyone could mine the coins, but once a Hypotherion coin was found it went directly to the exchange—miners did not get to keep it, but it remained tied to them. The miner would receive 'altruism stars' that, after a period, are annotated with the name of the country that the money associated with their coins had helped. When a country repays its loan, a miner's altruism stars become available again to help other countries, and new annotations are added. Since its launch, Hypotherion had made loans to thirty-one countries and the Hypotherion exchange had grown significantly, gaining enough relevance and credibility that the United Nations and World Bank held talks with President Avci about how it might be incorporated into their global banking and lending paradigms. Not inconsequentially, there was significant background chatter about Avci, who'd been instrumental in removing any and all roadblocks to Hypotherion's success, being the hands-down favorite for the next Nobel Peace Prize.

As he scanned, Dolan wondered why there would be so much detail about Solak. As he read, it began to make sense. At one time, Blue Olive Exports was the single largest funnel for trade between Niger and Turkey with several warehouses and an office building in Niamey. Those properties were never included in the sale of the company and are still listed as commercial assets of Red Fig. Niger wasn't known for software development, and it would be difficult to believe Solak had that type of work going on there. But who knows. He could have moved some work there to take advantage of tax laws and such. Regardless, they would have to dig a little deeper into Solak and his company's activities there.

He continued to read. And then, there it was. Dolan cursed the report's author under his breath—the most important nugget of information was buried near the end. Shortly after Avci's election, Solak was granted the title of National Technology Advisor. Later, he was appointed as the country's Minister of Industry and Technology. Though the analyst did not conclude that Solak could have been the source of the tip on Lefebvre's whereabouts, all the information necessary to make that leap was there in the report.

Dolan leaned back in his chair and stretched, looking up at the ceiling. Even if it was Solak who tipped off Avci, it was nothing more than interesting at this point. There were no red flags—just another Turkish citizen doing his duty. Unless of course he'd known about Lefebvre's presence in Niger for some time. Unless, for whatever reason, he had helped him in some capacity. Perhaps he had even kept Lefebvre hidden. Outing Lefebvre assured Avci and Turkey would gain considerable favor. Not just with the U.S., but internationally as well. It was possible, and way too juicy not to consider.

CHAPTER THREE

"OK team, let's circle our wagons. First off, I'm extremely pleased with everyone's work. Our efforts were critically instrumental in the overall success of Operation SUNSET." Dolan sat at the head of the conference table in The Pit. Thomas Freeman and Howard Welker sat to either side of him, facing each other. They were joined via secure VTC by Bolden, Andino, and Haddad. Collier was unable to make it, but Bolden could back brief him. Fitzhenry joined remotely as well from Paris.

"With the death of Lefebvre and his core group of followers, the AMA is now officially eradicated. Given we've spent the vast majority of our time and energy to that end recently, you may be wondering what's next. That's what this meeting is for."

"Good," quipped Welker. "I was already getting bored."

Dolan ignored him. "Though the AMA is gone, there are linkages that still exist—things to follow up on. Remember that for a long time, the AMA was doing everything it could to pull al-Qua'ida, what was left of ISIL, and other splintered terrorist groups into their fold. Some of those touchpoints remain unexplored. Another linkage, the one of interest to us right now, is related to the source who provided us with Lefebvre's location."

He went on to tell them how the U.S. government obtained the information, and the basics from the analyst's report. When finished, he paused to let it sink in.

Welker broke the silence. "So, the question seems to be, why did this come from Turkey? It doesn't make sense. Like there is something else going on here, beneath the surface."

Dolan nodded. "That's what I thought as well. There is more to this than is in the report. Deputy Director Dittrich wants us to dig around and find the answer to that question, Howard. Not the why, though, but the how. How it is that the CEO of a software development company with no good reason to have a business presence in Niger was able to find Lefebvre when in two plus years the combined intelligence organizations of fifty-something countries were not. I think Solak is dirty. I understand that's a stretch; let's call it a working theory. But it's the best I can come up with at the moment.

"We'll get what we can from Berlin and Paris on Niger and Turkey. Andy and Omar, I imagine we'll be able to find significant reporting on Ankara from Athens, less from Amman. Let's narrow our searches to, say, the last five years. Andy, I know that will be a lot to go through at your end so it might help to narrow your search further. Maybe focus solely on everything involving Solak, Avci, Red Fig, and Blue Olive."

"I know we've done some writing on Red Fig," Andino replied. "And there's quite a bit on Avci."

"There will be less of it at my end," said Haddad, "but if there's anything that's useful, I'll find it. If I run out of things to do, I can help Andy."

Dolan paused in thought, then continued. "Guys, this isn't just about the reports. It's the sources. This could get touchy so don't push it if people start asking questions. Bottom line, if your station has submitted a report you think sheds significant light on this, we may want to know where the information came from. *Who* it came from. We might need to talk to that person, and we are not going to be able to go through whichever officer wrote the report. This sounds sketchy and yes, it's breaking protocol but we are authorized to do it in certain cases, in the interest of national security. I can always beg Dittrich for forgiveness later. If this goes anywhere, and I'm not saying it will, but if it does our game plan could look a little different than what you are used to. As careful as you normally are, we will need to be even more so with this. For now, we are just poking around to see what we can see. But poking around can raise eyebrows, so cover your tracks. In fact, don't leave tracks at all. I don't want anyone at Amman or Athens Station, or even at Langley to wonder what you are up to. Stan, you'll have a lot more latitude since Collier is read in, and he's the Station Chief. He can give you additional resources. Fitzy, what do you think Paris can bring to the table?"

The newest member of the REVENANT team was also the most experienced, having served in the CIA for twenty-nine years. He spent most of that career earning his stripes in some of the lesser-stable African nations before transitioning to Switzerland as the Deputy Chief of Station, then to Paris. An old colleague and friend of Welker's, he was fatherly figure, quiet and unassuming. Bespectacled with thinning hair, a crackling voice and hunched posture, Fitzhenry had the look of a long-retired grandfather. Well known for being a devout Christian, he kept a worn, leather-bound heirloom bible on the corner of his desk wherever he was stationed.

His clandestine exploits were legendary. What forever solidified his status as a spymaster, however, was the story of his two years infiltrating a large gun-running organization in Cameroon. Just as he was about to take it all down, he was betrayed by one of his informants and was captured. After days of torture with no food or water and about to be executed by the local warlord, he sawed through his bonds with a shiv-shaped piece of wood and killed all seven of his captors with it as they slept. Then he loaded up all their cash, phones, laptops, and other intel into the warlord's personal Toyota Landcruiser and drove it all back to the embassy. He then helped coordinate an airstrike to destroy the compound along with an estimated twenty million dollars' worth of illegal weapons and ammunition. The intelligence he captured led to a takedown of the entire network, which stretched across three continents and seventeen countries. An amazing story of cunning, resilience, and grit. Some in the business wondered how he was able to reconcile such work with his faith. He'd been asked a few times by concerned leadership, always responding that he believed that it was what God wanted him to do. And leadership always believed it was the best answer he could have given.

Fitzhenry responded. "Well, as you may or may not know, Niger was a colony of France from 1922 to 1960. After gaining independence, the country experienced years of political instability that culminated in a constitutional crisis in 2009 when the military took over the country. But things have calmed down since then and relations with France have been quite good. Paris Station keeps an eye on the former colonies, but I must admit, our priorities have been focused elsewhere. I'm not sure we have much reporting you would consider useful there. But Turkey is another story. Give me a few days and I'll see what I can dig up."

"Thanks Fitzy," Dolan replied. It was a nickname very few felt comfortable using given his stature within the Agency. As long as he was a member of REVENANT, however, Fitzhenry would be following Dolan's lead. And no one seemed to have a problem with that. Not even Welker, who just two plus years earlier was showing Dolan the ropes. "Thomas, I'd like you to start combing through whatever data there is on the Red Fig warehouse and office building in Niamey. Let's find out what they are doing there, who is in charge, and what their personal relationships are with Solak, if any. And why the property was not sold off with the rest of Blue Olive."

"Sure thing Michael," Freeman answered with a wide grin.

He really loves his job, thought Dolan. They were lucky to have such a devastatingly gifted gray hat hacker on the team.

"OK. I will focus on reporting from Niamey Station. Howard, you can cover Ankara. Let me know if you turn up anything useful or interesting, and let's plan to meet every couple of days going forward until we have enough to formulate a better analysis."

"Sounds good," Welker replied.

One by one they acknowledged and dropped off the video call. Freeman walked out of The Pit and Dolan immediately began to mentally collate the rest of his day, which included partitioning time to review a course proposal submitted by one of his assistant professors. Which meant heading back to his office at American University. He realized at once there wasn't enough time left in the day to do everything he needed to do. Before he could reconcile it, Welker interrupted his thoughts.

"Hey there, I hate to disturb your moment of Zen," he said. Dolan smiled back. "Listen, I know we're just getting started but, in my opinion, the whole thing stinks to high heaven. If in fact it was Solak who handed Lefebvre to Avci, Avci now owes him. Big time. It strikes me Solak is way too rich, and way too close to Avci for him not to be influencing his decisions. At the very least, we should assume there is something we can use there. If Solak and Red Fig are benefitting financially from Avci being the President, we can put that in our hip pocket, should we need it. It's another thing we should be looking into."

He was right. The whole situation was so delicate and politically dangerous that having leverage could prove very useful. *If there really is any there there...* "A valid point," Dolan replied. "It's something Ankara Station might have identified already, or maybe there are data points within the reporting in general that we can connect, to paint a bigger picture; tell us what to look for. Thanks Howard."

Dolan stayed seated, expecting Welker to leave so he could finish organizing his thoughts, but he stayed.

"Are you good?" asked Welker.

At that, Dolan chuckled. "Is this the psychologist asking, or the friend?"

"Both, I guess. You seem distracted."

Dolan looked at him squarely. "Yes, I'm fine. As you might expect, it's not exactly easy working two full-time jobs. But yes, everything is fine."

"And Anne? Are you two still a thing?"

Dolan bristled but didn't betray his emotions outwardly. "Anne? Well, Anne and I are at a crossroads, I think. And I don't know where to go from here, honestly. I feel like if I don't make a decision soon, she'll make it for me." He looked down at the table and sighed. "I can't see a path forward that ends happily for either of us, to be honest."

Welker regarded him empathetically and got up from his chair. "You'll figure it out, Michael. Love is a difficult thing to manage in this business, we all get that. I would say, though, that regardless of whatever your business is, love is just a difficult thing."

With that, he turned and walked out. It was textbook Welker. Dolan was left alone then, wondering why he brought Anne up out of the blue like that. Could it be Dolan was off his game due to issues in his personal life without even knowing, and it was showing? Welker was exercising due diligence, both as a doctor and as a colleague. The result, intended or not, was a multitude of images of Anne that now invaded his mind, all of them propelled along on a wave of various emotions. Some poignant, others less so. And all of it obscuring and overriding the importance and immediacy of everything else needed to think about. He was pretty much helpless against it, a feeling he had very little experience with.

CHAPTER FOUR

Yusuf Solak poured coffee into an ornate kahve fincani porcelain cup for the President, then into another for himself. He made it extra sweet, with just enough mastic for that subtle piney flavor they'd both enjoyed since childhood. He placed the small, long-handled brass cezve on the table, sat opposite his good friend Adem Avci, and smiled.

"You've come a long way, Adem," he said.

"*We* have come a long way," Avci emphasized. "You know I wouldn't be where I am today without you, *kardeşim*." They had often referred to each other using this term, which meant 'sibling' or 'brother.' Once Avci was sworn in as President, however, Solak decided to forego the intimate informality. It was no longer appropriate, not even in private. And in public, he addressed him always as *Başkan Avci*. President Avci. Just like everyone else.

Solak acknowledged silently and sipped the strong, dark liquid. He was right—Avci would have been a successful politician, but he may not have become President without Solak's help. And even if he had, his popularity, his reach and influence would never have been where they are today. Because of Solak, Avci was probably the most popular man in the world right now. Everyone loved him.

Avci savored his drink for a moment. "Why do you always insist on making the coffee? You know I have people for that. I would argue, in fact, that Sidika makes it just as well as you. Maybe better. I cannot tell the difference."

At that, Solak's eyes widened. "You know why. It's our custom. Additionally, I'm here to help you however I can, and in doing so, to help our country. Little things matter. And no, Sidika does not make coffee as well as I. She's pretty good at reading the grounds afterwards, I'll give her that." He glanced to the corner where she stood, hands behind her back, and winked at her. Solak motioned with his hand, and she left the room dutifully, closing the grand double wooden doors behind her.

It was true, he'd always made coffee for the two of them and took pride in doing it well. Just as he did with every other important thing in life. And life had been good to him. He was now one of the richest men in the world and a primary advisor to one of the world's newest and most influential leaders. This more recent tradition, visiting with Avci twice per week in the library of the presidential grounds in Ankara, was an honor enjoyed by no one else.

Better known as the Beştepe Complex, the presidential palace boasted 1,150 rooms. Its library held over five million books, making it easily the largest in Turkey and one of the largest in the world. Though at first it seemed a strange place for their meetings, Solak quickly warmed to the idea. It was an extraordinary thing, to be surrounded by uncountable volumes of philosophy, theology, history, and art with one of the most powerful men in the world, his closest friend. And now that the attendant Sidika was gone, they had it all to themselves. Which is how Solak liked it.

"Listen," said Avci, "I'd like to get your opinion on something, this latest issue with Armenia. I think if we can convince Russia to let our forces protect the land corridor, instead of theirs, between…"

"Adem," Solak interrupted, "before we get into that, I have something more important. I mean, maybe those are the wrong words, but it is urgent, nonetheless. I want to try something new, something that could give you more leverage, more regional control as a rising luminary. Something that could better position Turkey to lead on the world stage. It's all big data and analytics, and not too different from the strategic and targeted influencing we used to build you up during the campaign. It will even help with Armenia. We can…"

"Yusuf, wait. It is my turn to interrupt you." Avci took another sip. "While I am forever in your debt for all your help, for what you did during the campaign and for everything since, I am at a point now where I want…no, I *must* do certain things myself. If people cannot respect and love me for what I say and for the decisions I make—if they need to be convinced or pressured to do so, well then that means I may be doing things wrong, or at least not as well as I could, and this is evidence that I must improve as a leader. It would mean what I have achieved was done so disingenuously, at least in part. How can I know for sure if you don't give me that chance? I understand the need for strategic messaging and political spin and all that but that's not what I'm talking about. I'm talking about the social media efforts. I must succeed on my own, going forward. For now."

Solak frowned, tilting his head questioningly at his longtime friend. "You know better than most Adem that this is the way politics works now. At least, for those who want to win, for those want to *keep* winning. And yes, I agree it is your voice, your vision, your leadership that the people hear and follow. What I do for you is to give them more of it, to make sure *everyone* hears of it. To echo your successes and your plans for the future of Turkey. Without some control of social media, without the ability to capture, analyze, and use big data, you will always be one step behind your competitors and enemies. Will you at least listen to my idea? It is different than what we did before, and it is revolutionary, if I can say so myself..."

Avci finished the last of his coffee, careful to leave the remaining, finely-ground Arabica sediment at the bottom of his cup. Then he turned the cup upside down on its saucer for Sidika to study later. "If I know anything about you, Yusuf, it's that you are a genius and much of what you've accomplished in life has indeed been revolutionary. How you were able to get the location of this terrorist Hakeem Lefebvre, that was truly amazing and useful beyond measure. The American President is now indebted to me. *To Turkey*." He made a fist when he said it, for emphasis. "I appreciate and value all your contributions greatly, and these are just some of the reasons why you are my Minister of Industry and Technology, not because you are my friend, though that is a bonus. But for now, let me be my own man. Let me earn it." He winked at Solak. "I will not stand in your way, however, if you feel you must do things in the cloud, or wherever your big data work takes you—do what you must but please do your best to...operate on the periphery of my agenda. I don't want our people or foreign leaders to think I've gotten where I am, that Turkey is where she is, because of anything other than good planning, hard work, skillful diplomacy, and righteous and innovative strategy."

Solak inhaled quickly, deciding halfway through Avci's long-winded denial to counter his friend's request. But just as he began, he stopped. Instead, he nodded and said nothing. After all, there were problems with telling him too much at least at this early stage. He would have to feed it to him over time, much as he did with the massive social media operation he masterminded for Avci's presidential bid. That effort was responsible for garnering at least seven percent of the vote he wouldn't have otherwise gotten. Probably more—it was a difficult thing to measure. And there were other things he had done, sacrifices he made, that had garnered him additional favor. Without Solak, it would have been a very tight race. It may have gone the other way, in fact. Instead, it was a landslide victory. But that was old news now, and with an eighty-six percent job approval rating, they had nearly all of Turkey in line. It was time to build on that.

"Kirmizi-beyaz?" challenged Solak. As Avci smiled and shook his head, Solak reached into his pocket and produced a small, flat, round stone painted white on one side and black on the other. Referred to by children in Germany as *Tag und Nacht* and *giorne e notte* in Italy, or 'day and night,' *Kirmizi-beyaz* actually meant 'red and white.' But Solak had always preferred the European version. Whenever they were at an impasse, one of them would flip their stone to determine the outcome. Solak's was thirty years old now and had been flipped thousands of times. He'd repainted it twice. Before Avci could say anything, Solak tossed it high in the air, catching it. Palm up, he opened his hand. Black.

He grinned. "I win."

"I didn't agree to it," Avci countered kindly, but seriously. "This decision cannot be decided by youthful games, Yusuf."

"OK my friend," Solak replied. "It is your decision. But I think you will change your mind later. In any case, you know I am willing to assist you with anything at all and at any time. You know what I am capable of."

"I know. Listen…" he placed his hand, palm down, on the table between them, "…the reality is, we are in a great place right now. Turkey is in a great place, and the trajectory is upwards. We simply need to keep doing what we're doing, and not lose sight of what 's important—the people. As you know, I am not against bending, or even breaking the rules when the welfare of our nation is at stake. You needn't worry, I will not hesitate to ask if there is something I truly need. But we'll give it a rest, at least for now. This is the way."

Solak finished his coffee. Unlike Avci, he swirled the small amount left in the bottom of his cup to capture what was left of the muddy grounds, then quickly tipped it back. Solak would never accept having Sidika, or anyone else, read his fortune. Avci watched him swallow the grounds with a hint of disdain. They had so much in common that to others, their differences were lost between the parallels. They even looked quite similar. Some in the press would kid on occasion about Solak being Avci's half-brother. At five feet, eleven inches, they were the same height. Both had lean, athletic builds, square jaws, and noses just aquiline enough to be considered strongly handsome. They were the same age and trimmed their short, jet-black beards the same way. They even wore the same brands of suits, though Solak was always careful to choose a different color tie whenever they were in public together.

But they did have their differences. Solak felt he understood more about risk and reward, for instance, and had risked much of his net worth on two occasions. Once on Blue Olive and again on Red Fig. Both times he won big. He didn't wager nearly as much of his personal wealth on Hypotherion, but if it had failed early-on it could have led to serious consequences for the future of his entire empire. If it foundered now, however, the government would more than likely mitigate or absorb much of the loss. But the chances of that were now miniscule.

His current endeavor, for which Hypotherion was the engine, was much larger and far more complex. With far more risk. Adem might not understand; it was likely he would reject the idea out of hand. It was too much for him to take in all at once, Solak knew. Adem had been more than willing in the past to play his part, even when the legalities were questionable. But this was different. In that moment, he was glad his longtime friend had cut him off. He would tell him certain parts of the plan, though, by degrees because it wouldn't succeed without Adem. Plausible deniability works in politics, but ultimately, he must be actively engaged in this. Not just a part of it, but intimately involved. The President was already revered by their people. He had brought hope and prosperity to so many, and with it a vision for the greatness of Turkey that would reshape the current world order. Solak would need more opportunity, more latitude to continue moving forward. Whether he knew it or not, Avci was on a path no human being had ever traveled; a metahuman path, of sorts. With Solak's guidance and help, Adem will move past the boundaries and limitations of the mind, to a new state of awareness, one that will tap into new abilities and untold power. His rule and legacy will be unmatched. It had been foretold.

In the end, the entire world will reap a great reward. There will be a short period of conflict, sacrifice, and even despair in certain regions. With time, however, it will all be overcome by an era of great opportunity, enabled by unprecedented economic progress and enduring regional stability. The most important consequence of his seismic plan, the *denouement*—was benefit beyond compare to the people of Turkey. It will be staggering; there was nothing remotely comparable, not in the history of man. The resultant bounty was nothing short of regional geopolitical and economic control of the Balkans, Greece, southwestern Asia, and parts of North Africa. A future kingdom whose borders would creep outward over time. And his great and gifted friend, Adem Avci, will rule over it all with Solak by his side. To effect such change required events that would never come to pass in the normal evolution of things. Solak's plan will trigger those events. In some ways, it will resemble a global revolution. Or better, a great awakening. A *revelation*.

CHAPTER FIVE

Dolan stroked the steering wheel of his beloved red 1966 Ford Bronco. He appreciated the little things in life and tried daily to ensure he never overlooked them. It was one of his morning drive routines to ponder everything in life for which he was grateful. Superficially, his Bronco was one of them. It was all about being present, remaining in the here and now, because that's where life happens. Something Père Aubertin taught him. As intelligent as he knew himself to be, he was continually amazed by what he'd found he still needed to learn. How best to take advantage of what he learned, for example. It requires a different type of thinking that is non-linear. There is a nuanced importance in understanding that the true value of knowledge lies in knowing how to apply it in the most useful way. It follows that contrary to the cliché, knowledge is not power. Power comes with the ability to apply it. His thoughts moved outward as he scanned the sea of red taillights. It was incredibly unfortunate that commuters here spent so much time stuck in traffic. He'd chosen long ago to accept it as a compromise and used that time to contemplate.

It was still dark as he made his way along the Key Bridge from his rowhouse in Georgetown and onto Route 66. In fits and starts he made it to REVENANT's second-floor offices in Clarendon and parked in the underground lot. He left the engine running for a few minutes as he considered the Deputy Director's request of his team. There was no question in his mind that Yusuf Solak and Red Fig were somehow involved. It was entirely possible there was nothing sinister in their actions or intent, but Solak was involved somehow, nonetheless. *How* was what REVENANT had to figure out.

"Good morning, Doctor Dolan," Welker greeted as he opened the door to The Pit. Dolan was still getting used to the title, and despite the veiled sarcasm he knew Welker and the rest of the team respected him for it. Not simply because he'd earned the degree, but that he'd been able to pull it off with roughly half his time preparing to lead REVENANT. It meant long hours and little sleep, but luckily, he'd never needed more than five or six hours each day, and he was rarely slowed if he only got three or four.

"Good morning," he replied, stopping just inside the room and surveying his team with pride. Thomas Freeman joined Welker at the conference room table while the rest of REVENANT appeared once again on the big screen. Gratitude came to mind once more as he took his chair. Despite the tragedy and difficulties of his past, there was no one he knew whose life had been as fortunate as his. Those things had made him stronger. Smarter. A better man and a better leader. And what they did here together, the impact of it, gave him great satisfaction. "I must be at American University in two hours, so we need to be efficient with time. I have nothing new from Langley, so let's go around the room and you can update me on what you've been able to dig up so far. Howard, let's begin with you."

"Well, not a lot, as of yet," said Welker. "I got in touch with Ankara. It's a difficult task, because even though they haven't been told yet, we must assume they are the one station that might be collecting based on a suspicion that Avci passed Lefebvre's location to the US. They won't reveal that, of course, until they've vetted their intel and finished their reports. And they will assume it's unlikely anyone else suspects what they do. So, I have to dance around that. What I did was tell them was I'm looking into Red Fig's possible interference in Turkey's last presidential election. It's a real concern of course, and as big as that company has gotten, there is the potential they could influence society in general, and perhaps even our own elections, à la accusations against Twitter, Facebook, Google, and others and our own federal elections. Heck, I personally know quite a few people who swear by Red Fig's eL8 app. I find it uncomfortable though, how much personal information you must give it access to, to make it work. But apparently, it does work.

"Anyways, they pointed me to a trove of reporting they did on Solak and Red Fig, and on the history of Blue Olive. I've parsed through it a bit and still have a lot to look at, but one thing did stand out. A Turkish source, a former Red Fig employee, told his handler there two years ago he had compromising information regarding Avci's wife, but that it came with a price tag. He wanted visas and plane tickets for him and his family to the United States in return. He'd been fired and it looked like retaliation. The reporting officer looked into the visas. They were turned down almost immediately, for two reasons. One, they deemed the source lacked credibility on the subject and two, the Agency wasn't really interested in compromising information on Avci's wife given he was the preferred presidential candidate. She was an energetic progressive, and analysts felt she offset Avci's traditionalist Muslim views and that it was a negative thing, politically speaking, when she passed. Speculation about what the dirt might have been ranged from designs she may have had to influence her husband's political platform to, get this, that the child might not have been Avci's. That would be fodder for anti-Avci conspiracy theorists of course, to claim he might have found out and had her killed. Apparently, they never found the driver or even the vehicle, which strikes me as strange.

"Shifting gears, to prove his worth he provided useful intel on Red Fig related to algorithms they were developing to push out strategic messaging through their platforms and apps. We didn't get all of it, looks like he was holding back on whatever he thought was most valuable. A few analysts at Langley showed interest. The problem was, again, what he was selling was only useful against the guy that we wanted to win. I don't understand the algorithm info. You'll probably be able to figure it out, Thomas. Whatever he had on the wife though, he kept it to himself. Anyway, I think it's worth looking into further. I have the name of his handler the date of contact from the report. I'm going to give the immigration office a call. With a bit of luck, I may be able to triangulate the source's name."

"Thanks Howard," Dolan replied. "A verified source with knowledge of how Red Fig operates could be helpful. Especially if he was high enough up in the food chain. The dirt on his wife, not sure that's anything that would help us, but it shows he was a motivated asset, which could still be the case. Let me know what else you find. Thomas, were you able to find out anything about the property in Niamey?"

Freeman scooted his chair forward eagerly, leaning in on the table. "Yes. Well, sort of. Everything regarding the property from the report you shared with us was correct, but as you know there wasn't a lot of detail. There is no information on Red Fig's website about it. There is nothing publicly available about it anywhere, in fact, except old info as it pertained to Blue Olive and their old import-export operations there. But I did find something on a government server in Niger. As a foreign-owned business, I figured there had to be records. What I found shows that the work being done there is in fact information technology related. Niger would not be a serious consumer of anything Red Fig is building there, though. In fact, I found no evidence of contracts with any African nation. What is more interesting than that—all the employees are

Turkish, and they all have current work visas, seven of them. That's it—seven employees.

"So, we have a two-story office building and a twenty-something thousand square foot warehouse for, at least on paper, seven total employees. It doesn't add up. When you put it together, even if they have some sort of tax exclusion, it appears there is no financial or strategic benefit for Red Fig to maintain a business presence in Niamey. So, why send Turkish citizens to Niger and maintain such a large property, when you could just do the work in Turkey?"

"That is interesting, Thomas," said Dolan. "Do we have the names of the seven employees, or any other information about them?"

"I have the names, but nothing else, which is strange. I did some preliminary work on those and get this, the first and last names of all of them are some of the most common in Turkey. All seven. There is no way, without more to go on, to find out who they really are. It leads me to believe none of them are bona fide."

"Sounds like an opportunity to do some surveillance," Andino chipped in on the VTC screen.

"We may have to, but we've just gotten started here," Dolan replied. "Thanks Thomas. Andy, other than volunteering to travel to Niamey, what have you got?"

"Well, as you might imagine, Athens Station watched the presidential election in Turkey very closely. The consensus was that Avci, like his predecessor, is a politically covert Islamist. Which is constitutionally problematic for that country. We also concluded, as did the desk at Langley, that he possesses many of the political leanings, skills, and traits a Turkish president would require to bring more stability to the region. That he was a better choice, significantly better in fact, than the incumbent. And so far, that has turned out to be true—in spades. Any plans he might have had to blur the lines between church and state have not materialized. Much of the reporting is quite positive on him. On his relationship with Solak, they've been friends since they were kids; it is inherently difficult to separate that from any sway Solak might have on his presidency. You would be hard pressed to convince anyone that he is not in a position do so, however, given his wealth, connections, and the influence he leverages via social media. Nonetheless, except insofar as he helped get Avci elected, there is no evidence in the reporting he has had any direct, personal impact on Turkish strategic or domestic decision making outside his ministerial duties. In other words, even though Solak is an omnipresent, powerful, and close friend and advisor, Avci seems to be his own man, politically speaking.

"All the same, Solak and Red Fig are just too big and potentially controversial to ignore. We have produced seventy-nine reports on the subject over the past three years, mainly about the company's influence via social media, both within and outside Turkey. I'll need more time to get through them all."

"OK, thanks. Good info. Keep at it." Dolan was disappointed, hoping Andino would have something more impactful. But it was still early. "Fitzy, what about Paris Station?"

"Well, like Andy we have a lot of intelligence on Turkey, but most of it is dated, and much of the recent reporting is more economic in nature. As you might imagine, I have a little less time than the average guy to dedicate to this, but don't mistake that for a lack of interest. I've set aside some time over the weekend to do more research. But if I may, I'd like to point out a few things that might give the work we're doing here a little bit of context.

"Andy, you may be aware of some of this, and you as well Michael, given your professorial exploits at American and work with the Joint Staff at the Pentagon. The Republic of Turkey is situated at the crossroads of Europe, Asia, the Middle East, and Africa. This alone makes them strategically important from a geopolitical standpoint. They are a secular, unitary nation and were a parliamentary republic as late as 2017. Their presidential system is new. They are charter members of the UN, members of the World Bank, the IMF, and NATO, and a founding member of the G20. Though accession talks have been stalled since 2018, we expect Turkey will be admitted to the European Union soon given the recent rapid and positive turn in their economy and diplomatic relations across the board.

"Their constitution is what they call *Kemalist*. Kemalism is an ideology rooted in democracy and secularism with state support of the sciences and free education. Islamism has been on the rise in Turkey for years, however, and it's our assessment that a contemporary candidate has no chance at winning the presidency in Turkey without being able to demonstrate both a strong Islamic faith *and* a commitment to secularism to prevent the possibility of a coup. The military sees itself as the protector of the constitution and its Kemalist statutes. They need little persuasion to overthrow the government if they feel the constitution is being subverted—they've tried six times and succeeded in two. That doesn't even count military memorandums issued in 1971, 1997, and 2007 that were essentially bloodless coup interventions. Their most recent, unsuccessful attempt was in 2016.

"Then there are the strategic issues of energy and water. There is the Turkstream gas pipeline with Russia and the BTC pipeline from Azerbaijan to Georgia. You may also remember the Nabucco project, which was supposed to supply Iraqi gas via a Turkey-to-Austria pipeline that would have lessened European energy reliance on Russia. After Russia's invasion of Ukraine, Nabucco seems like it was a great idea, in hindsight. With respect to water, Turkey controls the Tigris and Euphrates rivers, with Iraq and Syria downstream. When you add it all up, Turkey is in the middle of everything, which makes it impossible for anyone to ignore.

"It also makes it difficult for Turkey to fit in. Their constitution, their strategic alliances, their domestic policies—their very identity; everything is consequently and necessarily a complicated mishmash of those of the disparate countries and alliances that surround them. Making all of that work is difficult business, but this president seems to have a knack for it. Helped along by a surging economy and near-universal popularity, not only is he making it work, but he is also feeding off it. Thriving in it.

"So, why is all of this important, and what does it mean for REVENANT?" Fitzhenry removed his glasses and wiped the lenses while everyone waited. He put them back on matter-of-factly, blinked twice and continued. "Whatever happens in Turkey affects many nations, and what's been happening in Turkey recently has been good for most, if not all of them. As a result, trade deals favorable to Turkey and the region are being finalized. New alliances are being formed. World leaders have been clamoring to meet with Avci. He is untouchable right now. Not only do most governments think of him very favorably, but it is also likely there would be significant political blowback if any government attempted to push a strategy or messaging viewed as unfavorable to him or to Turkey. That consideration would extend to his cabinet, and therefore to his genius, multi-billionaire boyhood friend, Yusuf Solak. This is a potential minefield we are walking into. If we find anything actionable, whatever it is, and whatever we decide to do with it, we must have absolute confidence in our conclusions and be prepared for resistance, even from within our own government and particularly from the State Department. We must tread carefully."

Collier was nodding in agreement during much of Fitzhenry's commentary. "Michael, if I may," he interjected. "I agree wholeheartedly with Fitzy. We must be meticulous and discreet. Not that we normally aren't, we just need to take it up a notch. And who knows, this may all just be a dead end. But if not, it could be exceedingly difficult to operate. We will want to keep our circle tight. An interesting factoid—Berlin is home to the largest population of Turks outside Turkey, and there are significant concentrations in many of the major German cities. After World War II, hundreds of thousands of them were invited here by the federal government to help rebuild the country. There just weren't enough young German males left. It was supposed to be a temporary thing, but after the work was done many of them stayed. Ironically, we've seen a good number of them leaving Germany recently, to return to their homeland because of Turkey's improving economic situation. In any event, the German government pays attention to what's going on in Turkey and maintains close ties. Like Paris Station, our reporting is primarily focused on trade and financials. We have covered some Islamic fundamentalist groups based in Turkey that have made their presence known here, but I'm not sure any of that applies here. What does, however, is the Red Fig regional office right here in the city. We've had no reason to investigate them, until now. Let me see what Stan and I can come up with. We could try to penetrate their servers, see what we can see, but again, we need to be careful."

"Great, thanks Fitzy and Mike, very helpful. Stan, do you have anything to add?"

"I think Mike covered it," Bolden replied.

"OK," Dolan continued. "We have a lot to think about. I agree we need to be careful. Even if we think we've found something, we will have to double-check and validate everything. I also agree that we must keep all of this to ourselves for the time being. When we're ready I'll brief Dittrich, and the decision to do anything at that point will be his.

Keep up the good work, team. We'll meet again in two days. In the meantime, stay safe and take care."

Everyone said their goodbyes as the squares on the screen went black, one by one. Freeman and Welker got up to leave.

"Hey Thomas, hold on," Dolan said.

Freeman walked back to his chair and stood behind it. "Sure, what's up?"

"While we need to do a little more homework before we, for example, penetrate Red Fig's servers in Berlin, I think we can move forward safely in Niamey. If they are in fact doing coding work there, they should have servers we can hack into, right?"

"Well, just because they are doing coding there doesn't mean the servers are in Niger. They could be anywhere, Australia or here in the U.S. even. But if what they are doing is close-hold or super-proprietary, my bet is their servers are either there in in the building with them, or in Turkey. You want me to find out?"

"Yes. I want you to find out where the servers are, and what it is they are working on. Don't leave any tracks. If it's too risky, don't do it. But if you can figure it out without setting off any alarm bells, go ahead."

Freeman looked like a kid who was just given the keys to a candy store. "Understood. I'll get on it right away."

Dolan patted him on the back on his way out the door. "Thanks Thomas." Then he made his way to the hall, down the elevator and back to his Bronco in the underground lot. As he turned the key and grabbed the wheel, a dull pain coursed through his left hand. It was an occasional reminder of his fight with terrorist François Martin at the Potsdam property four years ago. A reminder of everything else that happened in Berlin and Paris. Both good and bad. The best thing that came out of that operation, aside from saving numerous lives, was Anne. He released the steering wheel, made a fist, then opened and closed it several times until the ache subsided. If he was going to be honest with himself, the most positive outcome had to be the cathartic self-realization he experienced right at the end of that mission. Absent that, his life would be no better now than it was back then. Perhaps worse. It was difficult to argue however, that without his love for Anne and her love for him, such an awakening might never have come to pass at all.

By the time he exited back into traffic, he was already working through his mental preparation for the class he'd be teaching in an hour. Anne remained, however, nagging at the back of his mind—he hadn't heard from her in days. He'd made no attempt recently to contact her, either. There were many difficult things for him to navigate through and resolve right now, but he should still make time to speak with her. Love. *Just another difficult thing.*

CHAPTER SIX

Dittrich tugged at his beard thoughtfully. "I'll be honest, I didn't expect this to go anywhere. I'd be lying if I said I was happy you seem to be onto something. At the same time, I don't want your team to be looking so hard that they create something from nothing. In other words, continue to proceed with great caution and double-check it all."

Dolan took a seat in front of his desk. "We are. Everyone understands the sensitivities." He waited to see if Dittrich would say something else before continuing. "I'm not convinced yet that we are actually onto anything. What we have right now are a several relatively odd and interesting, but incomplete pieces of intelligence. Not the least of which is this Red Fig property in Niamey. If there is a good reason for them to be working there, we haven't found it yet, and what we have turned up leads us to believe they are doing something very secretive. In and of itself, that isn't any kind of red flag. Big tech intellectual property is about as sensitive as it gets. But this particular team—they are off the grid. There are too few acknowledged employees to be working on anything of consequence, and their names are fictional. Bizarre business practices for legitimate research and development."

Dittrich sipped from a glass of water and placed it back carefully on a brown leather coaster. "Maybe. You'd be surprised how business is run in some cultures. Not everyone does things the way we do. And let's not forget that until the past few years, the Turkish economy was not doing so well. Their recent unlikely and considerable success is the international feel-good story of the century, so far at least. They are still working out how to manage that success, to keep it going and to improve on it. There are many regional and cross-continental concessions they will have to make, international business norms and rules they've never been party to before that they will have to adopt and participate in. If they want to keep the train rolling, anyway. And it's difficult for them, geographically speaking. They must keep Europe happy, North Africa, the Middle East. Not easy. OK. So, what is the plan. Who is going to Niamey?"

The question surprised him—this was supposed to be a simple data dump for Dittrich. They hadn't really compiled enough information to run an op yet. But there was only so much information he had access to, and they were running low on reporting that was helpful. "Well, as I said in my email, Thomas was unable to penetrate anything at the site in Niamey. Whatever they are working on there, it's off the grid—not connected to the internet. It would be a good idea to do some recon there. See what the security looks like, ID some of the employees as they come and go. Ask around in the area, see what the locals think is going on there. Then there is the Red Fig regional headquarters in Berlin. It wouldn't be too hard for Mike Collier's team to do a little digging."

Dittrich leaned back in his chair and went back to stroking his beard. Dolan could tell he was weighing things, positives and negatives, risk and reward. He leaned forward again. "Go for it. Do both. Can you do both at the same time? Let's see what we can see and if it's nothing, we can shut it down quickly. What I don't want to do is tiptoe through this in a linear fashion. Any little problem along the way and our efforts could be curtailed—we might not get another chance to have a look at everything. Believe me, I learned this the hard way. There are several ops I've been a part of in my career that were cut short because leadership kept a microscope on everything, then got scared when they saw something they didn't like. I don't want to be the reason that ten years from now we will be sitting here wondering if we made a critical mistake because we didn't run this one to ground. Additionally, if there is nothing there, we'll be in and out quickly. Less chance we'll piss someone off."

"Yes, we should be able to do both without any trouble," Dolan assured him. That was the extent of what Dolan was prepared to push for operationally. Still, Dittrich's apparent desire to get as much done as quickly as possible left the door open for him push the envelope. "There's also something else. We haven't discussed it yet, mainly because we're still gathering information and there's some risk involved that we're not used to dealing with."

Dittrich's brow furrowed, the hint of a smile on his lips. He was cautiously intrigued. "Tell me."

"One of our officers at Ankara submitted a report last year that included high tech proprietary data from Red Fig. Thomas is looking at it. So far it appears to be pretty sophisticated, algorithms that can manipulate social media to target specific groups of people based on certain demographics and user behavior. That, in and of itself, isn't even interesting; Facebook and Twitter, Instagram...they've all been doing this for years, and there's nothing illegal about it. The source contends, however, that the company was using the algorithms in an attempt to sway the Turkish presidential election for Avci, and that it worked spectacularly. *That* is *very* interesting."

Dittrich was listening intently. "But how do you intend..."

"Hold on, I haven't gotten to the best part. This source also claimed to have dirt on Avci's wife, something significant. He gave up some of the algorithms to prove he had access and credibility, then dropped that on our officer. But he wouldn't say what it was without a visa and safe passage to the U.S. Ankara Station looked into cutting a deal, but it was shot down, almost immediately."

"Because we didn't want dirt on Avci's wife," stated Dittrich.

"Yes. It wasn't information that was useful to us at the time. But here's the thing. He had inside access to Red Fig. There is quite a bit more he might be able to tell us. But this other information, whatever it is, indicates he may have had or might still have access to Avci's inner circle. Maybe to Solak himself."

Dittrich leaned back in his chair again and looked off to the side. On the wall hung a framed painting of an iconic John F. Kennedy photo taken by White House photographer Jacques Lowe as the President stood and listened to his advisors, arms crossed and head bowed. Apropos enough to hang there in the office of the Deputy Director of the CIA for Operations.

"So, what then?" asked Dittrich. "For one, we're not going to ask anyone at Ankara Station to investigate it. There would be too many questions. Is the source even active? We'd have to know who he or she is and approach them ourselves."

"Agreed," Dolan responded. "That's exactly what I'm proposing we do. We know who he is. The deal he tried to broker for the dirt on Avci's wife went just far enough. They looked into getting the guy a visa. Between the report and information we were able to get from the immigration office, we put two and two together. Yes, he is still listed as an active source, and that's why it could be tricky. We'll have to be very discreet. But I want to approach this guy and find out what he knows. And I'd like you to give me the authority to cut a deal if that's what it takes."

Dittrich smiled broadly. "I like it. We shouldn't leave any stone unturned but you're right, this one could be tricky. Does Andino speak Turkish?"

"Yes, he does. I want to send him to Ankara. I'll send Welker and Omar Haddad, the new guy from Amman, to Niamey. Collier and Stan Bolden can work with Thomas and probably won't even need to leave the Berlin embassy to do what they need to do with the Red Fig servers there."

"Sounds like a plan. And you'll sit tight, run things from Clarendon, right?"

Dolan regarded Dittrich carefully. This whole plan had come together quickly, right there in Dittrich's office. Sure, he had it figured out before he walked in the front door and it was all what he was planning to do anyway, but he'd been unsure if Dittrich was going to support everything, until now. Andino was an excellent counterintelligence officer, but Dolan didn't want to send him in alone. If there truly was anything nefarious going on, Solak could very well be pulling the strings. This source could already be marked. Solak or Avci could be keeping tabs on him. Any association with him could put Andy in their crosshairs. He needed backup.

"I'll be going to Ankara with Andy. Thomas doesn't need me around to do what he does; I don't understand much of it anyway. I'll remain in contact with him, Welker, and Collier. To be honest, sir, I'm not too worried about the other two ops, I believe they are low threat. What I don't want is for Andy to get into hot water because there was no one there to cover him. It's possible the source there is full of shit and just wanted a free ticket to the promised land. But there is more potential for fallout in Ankara, I think, if something goes wrong. If we're going to run three ops in parallel, I want to make sure they will all succeed and that no one on my team is put in a difficult spot. Not when it's avoidable."

Dittrich sat and thought for a moment. "What about your day job? Will it appear out of the ordinary if you leave so suddenly? That's not an insignificant consideration. Listen, if I were you, I'd send Fitzy with Howard to Niamey. Fitzy has experience in that region and he's fluent French. Isn't that what they speak there? And I'd send Omar with Andy. Neither of them would stand out. You, Michael Dolan, *you* would stand out."

Dolan shifted uncomfortably in his chair. Despite all his talk about hating micromanagers, Dittrich could be quite good at it himself. It was one of the reasons Lauren was always so frustrated with him. "Omar also speaks French. Not as well, but it's serviceable enough and he is the only one on the team who speaks Arabic, which could come in handy. It's not a primary language but they do speak it there. In any case, most people there speak either Hausa or Zarma, and none of us knows either of those languages. As for Fitzy, he's too high in the food chain to send into the field, outside west Europe anyway. And Paris Station needs him. Same situation with Collier in Berlin. They are more useful to me just staying where they are, frankly. Listen, I've already played this out every which way, and this is the best scenario. If we are going to run all three ops, I must be in the field, and I have to go to Turkey."

Dolan smiled then. "As for my job at American, that's what I have assistant professors for. They can cover for me. In any case, there isn't a whole lot going on right now. Midterms are graded. I'll be gone a week at the most. I'll just tell them I'm doing research. No one will miss me."

Dittrich tapped the desk with his fingertips rapidly, contemplating. "OK then, draw up the plans for all three ops and send them over to me. Assuming you turn up nothing at all, we can close the book on this within a couple of weeks, I think. I have a few other things I want REVENANT to investigate afterwards. If it turns out there's something there, well, then we can circle our wagons and decide how to proceed."

Getting up from his chair, Dolan reached over the desk and shook Dittrich's hand. "Sure thing. I'll have it all to you by close of business tomorrow. But there's something I want to do first. I would just do it but I'm letting you know first. I'm going to swing by the safehouse in Annapolis."

Dittrich said nothing. He squinted at Dolan for a moment, then slowly nodded his head in approval, as if it wasn't something he would have recommended, but that he understood Dolan's reasoning for wanting to do it.

On his way down the hall Dolan realized he was walking faster than normal and then he felt it, a trickle of adrenaline. Not enough to make him nervous, but sufficient to quicken his heart rate and generate a modest level of excitement. Finding and eliminating Lefebvre was all his team had been working on since he took over. But after their ops in Germany and Syria, all their work had been in a support capacity. On the periphery—nothing direct, nothing truly operational. This was the very first time he would direct a real-world, overseas clandestine mission. Three simultaneously, at that. He reduced his pace and shut down the adrenaline, sensing his heartbeat slow. Everything must be done precisely, perfectly. Nothing could be allowed to go wrong.

As he reached his car, he found himself whispering the French Creole line *An rien peut arrêter moi konin la.* It was from the Nine Inch Nails song 'La Mer.' To be unstoppable had never been a goal of his, per se—it wasn't something he *strove* for. It was more like a status quo state of mind, a *condition of mental existence* he expected to maintain, one that enabled him to realize his other goals. After the Berlin and Offenbach ops, he stopped using the song as a daily morning alarm. At the time it was as if the closure he experienced from capturing Sharif gave him permission to ease off. To relax. To be normal. After that, the mantra had come to feel Pollyannish. Ultimately, Dolan dismissed it as one small, repetitive piece of the elaborate self-defense mechanism he'd constructed to hide from his past. He hadn't listened to the song or even thought about it since. But he thought about it now.

As he turned the key, the Bronco's carefully tuned engine roared to life throatily. He knew that always wanting to win, *always needing to*, wasn't an idealistic or blindly optimistic expectation. Not for him. Dolan knew he wasn't psychologically 'normal,' which was fine. If he were, it was likely Dittrich wouldn't have chosen him to lead REVENANT. Directing such a team required someone with a very specific skillset. Someone without problematic, divergent, or linear thought processes. Emotional singularities that could, out of nowhere, negatively affect a mission. But what if a leader *did* have anomalous ways of thinking and operating, and whatever those incongruities were, they somehow had the *opposite* effect? Made the team stronger, more capable, more successful? Among other things, this is what Dolan believed he brought to REVENANT. He drove out the gate at Langley and gunned the engine, quickly accelerating beyond the speed limit, then easing off just a bit. For him, not being normal was a strength. An rien peut arrêter moi konin la. *Nothing can stop me now.*

CHAPTER SEVEN

The attendant on duty recognized him immediately. Dolan displayed his credentials anyway. Security protocols. She handed him a swipe card and he signed the guest log, annotating the date, time, and his reason for being there. Then he walked down the warm wood-floored hall of the otherwise normal-looking house. On certain Saturday afternoons in the fall, the roar of 34,000 fans could just be heard from the front porch as the Midshipmen faced their foes at Navy-Marine Corps Memorial Stadium, just over two miles away. With a long and winding gated driveway and situated near the middle of a heavily wooded, twenty-acre lot, the CIA safehouse was well-hidden from prying eyes. To call it a safehouse was a stretch, to be sure. It was never used as such and would never be. The truth was, SCALPEL, and now REVENANT, needed a facility to imprison and interrogate prisoners renditioned from overseas while keeping them off the books at Langley. Off the books everywhere. The true reason for saying it was a safehouse was that it was the only way to legally justify the funding that kept it operational.

At the end of the hall, he stopped in front of a nondescript wooden door and looked back at the attendant, nodding. A soft buzz was followed by a click and the door moved ever so slightly as the magnetic locks deactivated. Dolan turned the knob and pushed inward.

He was met with a rush of air as the hermetic seal was broken. The overpressure system mitigated any possibility extremely high-value inmates might be assassinated via a chemical, biological, or even a radiological attack. A large wooden panel glued to a heavy steel vault door effectively disguised access to the blast-proof and impregnable, reinforced concrete underground bunker. Once it was closed behind him, he listened for the click again, then stepped down into the basement. With a hiss the air pump quickly restored the overpressure, causing his ears to pop. At the bottom he used the swipe card to gain entry to a forty-foot-long passage with multiple cell doors on either side. Only three or four were usually occupied at any given time. Just over two years ago, Rolf Haussmann was here for several days undergoing enhanced interrogation before being transported to Harvey Point and ultimately, back to Germany where he was convicted and sentenced to life in prison for his part in the attempted terrorist attacks on the Paris Métro and U.S. Embassy in Berlin. The prisoner Dolan would visit today had been here a while now and barring any unforeseen circumstances, would die here.

"Hello Sharif."

He was sitting on a small cot and looked up but did not move as Dolan entered. He was bearded and gaunt, wearing a drab gray jumpsuit. His features were pallid and hollowed. Hands and feet chained together. He was a ghost of the man Dolan once knew.

Sharif's voice was a cautious, raspy whisper. As if he wasn't sure it would work. It was the first time in a long while he'd had the opportunity to speak. "Michael, is that you?"

"Yes. It is me. How are you being treated?" Dolan knew it was a stupid question as he sat on the floor with his back against the wall. He wanted to see Sharif eye-to-eye.

Sharif looked away. "It's OK. The food is fine. I know the direction of Mecca, so I can pray. I would like to see the sun again."

"I know it's difficult Sharif. But this is your penance. Serve it well and Allah will reward you."

At that, Sharif looked at him with anger, but it faded quickly. "Maybe you are right. I brought this on myself."

"Listen, Sharif, there is an important reason for me being here. Two reasons, actually. First, I wanted to let you know in person that your father has passed. We found him hiding out in Niger. He is dead." Dolan thought about telling Sharif he was sorry, but quickly dismissed the idea. It would be disingenuous. He wasn't sorry and he never would be. Lefebvre deserved what he got, and more.

Looking back at him he squinted, trying in vain to determine if Dolan was lying to him. He gave up quickly. It had to be true. "I am surprised it took this long. He was always a fighter, a survivor. Operational and communications security were everything to him. It bought him time."

"Are you sad?"

At that, Sharif hung his head. After a moment, he responded. "Yes and no. I am sad because he was my father and all the family I had left. Now I have no one. No reason to live. But at the same time, I am *not* sad. My father was not a good man. I've been wondering about this for a long time. I used to think he was following the will of Allah. This is what he always told me, and I believed him. And it is why I followed him and did what I did. Then, for a while, I didn't believe it anymore, that it was Allah's will. How could it be? And I was having trouble coming to terms with that, you see, because I know and understand that everything that happens in this world, happens in accordance with Allah's will. Regardless of the outcome. We, as humans, have free will to do the things we do, but Allah is the One who creates it for us. So, it *was*

Allah's will, but just because it was His will, it doesn't mean that the things my father did were *right*. The same applies to me and the things I did. I think that there were times when, as I was, he was greatly conflicted. You know, it was a war for him, and it was personal. Our family was attacked. He was answering to a higher power, to a cause that was larger than himself. Just because he was wrong doesn't mean *he knew* he was wrong. So, I am glad for him now. He needed to go. His conflict has ended. He has found peace, I believe."

Dolan leaned forward. "Have you found peace, Sharif? With yourself? Have you accepted what has happened to you?"

With his head still hung, Sharif began to laugh softly, almost maniacally. The laughing turned quickly to sobbing. He looked up once more, his pale face streaked. This time he locked in on Dolan's eyes. "That's the funny thing about it, Michael. I don't have a choice. I must accept it. I must because I cannot choose to die as my father did, for my convictions. I cannot even kill myself; they have seen to that. I have concluded, by necessity, that if I pray enough for peace, if I say it enough and think it enough, then that might actually *be* enough. It might just happen." With that, he wiped his face with his jumpsuit sleeve and composed himself as best he could.

"I understand." Dolan did his best to sound and appear sincere. After all, the real reason he was there had yet to be revealed. Telling him of his father's demise was an icebreaker, an exercise in trust-building. The sharing of an emotional event. So he could get what he needed. "Listen, Sharif, there is something else. Something I need help with. I know you've been interrogated for many months, and you've done well in giving us everything we've asked for, but I'm not sure we've asked all the right questions. And no, this isn't another interrogation. It's a discussion between you and me, and perhaps, another step towards redemption."

"What is it?" Sharif asked. He seemed genuinely inquisitive, willing to help. Or maybe he would do anything at that point, say anything to prolong any form of human contact, whether it benefited him or not.

"It's about how we found out where your father was hiding in Niger. Really, it was about who we heard it from, not how. Did your father ever mention anything about Red Fig Corporation, or Yusuf Solak? Yusuf Solak is the CEO of Red Fig. If not, what about any important Turkish contacts he might have had?"

Sharif thought for a moment. "Red Fig. No. It doesn't ring a bell. And I don't recognize this name, Solak. But you must know, my father's empire was vast—he dealt with people from many countries, including Turkey. Many of them would be considered important. Remember, at one time my father was also considered very important. I don't know that anyone my father worked with could have been tied somehow to his final hiding place, however."

Now it was time for Dolan to hang his head. He had to try. It had been a waste of time to come here, to be sure, but he couldn't move forward with three operations simultaneously unless he'd overturned every rock, followed every lead available to him. He had to prepare his team as best he possibly could. "OK Sharif, I believe you. Thank you for trying."

Sharif smiled then, wanly. "You're welcome, Michael."

Dolan got up and regarded his onetime friend and subsequent enemy. Now, after all that had transpired, he was neither. Dolan had expended considerable time over many months on self-examination in his own quest for peace. He was satisfied he'd done a good job. He felt it. He was content and, more or less, in a state of harmony with people and his environment in general. But in that moment, he realized there was one last thing he knew he must do. Something that would make today's trip worthwhile, even though he was walking away empty-handed.

"Sharif?"

His face was still red from the sobbing. "Yes?"

Suddenly, Dolan struggled. It was so difficult, more difficult than he thought it would be. The dark image of Sharif pushing Claire from the hotel balcony in Paris flooded his mind. Her twisted corpse on the cobblestones below, the growing halo of blood around her head. But he was stronger than this now. Tragic memories and regret, hatred and revenge—these things no longer drove him, held sway over him the way they once did.

"I... I forgive you Sharif." Dolan grabbed the door handle. "Goodbye."

Sharif began to cry once more but choked it back. "*Thank you,* Michael."

As Dolan stepped out of the cell, Sharif stopped him. "Michael, *wait.*"

He turned and looked through the half-closed door, not willing to go back in. "What is it."

"There was one company, Turkish, that my father worked with years ago. Several real estate deals, if I remember correctly. It probably won't help at all—it wasn't Red Fig, but there was also a color in the name. Black, black something. No, not black." He paused momentarily, looking at the floor in thought, then back up at Dolan. "I remember now—it was called *Blue Olive.*"

CHAPTER EIGHT

Roughly forty percent of Niger's population was destitute, a fact lost on the casual tourists in the plethora of good restaurants and open-air markets of Niamey. With nearly one million inhabitants, it was large, lively, and relatively modern by most standards. As one drove outward from the middle of the city, however, evidence of extreme poverty became more and more apparent. With poverty came the potential for crime. Fortunately, both their target and their hotel were in a safer part of town.

Though by now they'd worked together for almost six months and spent countless hours meeting with the rest of the team via secure video teleconference, Niamey was the first opportunity for Welker and Haddad to operate together in person. With a thick black beard and Middle Eastern features, Haddad could pass for a local. He was dressed in clothes bought from a local department store the day prior. He bunched up the shirt and pants and put them under his mattress for the night to put some wrinkles in them, then he patted them down with dust from the street in the morning. He looked as if he'd been wearing them for days. Having been stationed in Jordan, Morocco, and Egypt, the environment was not entirely strange to him.

Welker was another story. He was too white, too western. He was posing as a tourist in drab clothing, appearing as uninteresting as possible. For all his operational experience, this part of the world was new to him. His decades of field work were limited to Europe and a few operations in the Balkans, Colombia, and Chile. It didn't much matter to him, however. The *way* counterintelligence was done, the methods, never changed. Only the details were different. They drew up a surveillance plan well in advance of their arrival in Niger and refined it at their hotel the day prior after executing a walkthrough of the area.

The property was situated just east of city center. The large warehouse was directly behind and adjoining the two-story office building, accessible via an alley on the south side. A small metal sign over the front door read simply 'Red Fig Corporation' in dull amber letters. Two large, frosted plate glass windows on either side of the entrance rounded out the otherwise featureless cream-colored stucco facade. Welker was seated across the street at a café enjoying a beignet with a cup of tea. Haddad sat on a bus stop bench immediately in front of the office building. Though nothing could be seen through the obscured windows, a faint yellow glow penetrated from the interior. The lights were on.

Welker glanced at his watch. They'd been in place for a short time and rush hour traffic was beginning to ease. Eight a.m. on Monday, October 30th. The plan was simple—collect on whoever entered or left the building and analyze the data later. So far, no one had approached the door. Welker's video camera was well-hidden. The tiny, ultrahigh definition wide-angle lens blended into the stitching of his distressed brown leather briefcase. He had it trained on the front entrance, and it covered fifty feet in either direction.

"Three o'clock, two men in suits, walking together, black beards," Welker whispered, his lips barely moving as he brought the beignet to his mouth.

Haddad moved his head slightly to catch them in his peripheral vision, then adjusted his burlap backpack on the bench to get a good angle on the men walking toward him from his right. He pressed a small button on the side of the bag, triggering a cloning apparatus hidden inside. If they were carrying cell phones or tablets, the device could capture every bit of data on them if given enough time. The brief period as they walked by wasn't nearly sufficient for that, but what little was captured could give them an idea about their identity, who they've called recently, and perhaps some of their texts.

"Shit," said Welker, not bothering to cover his mouth. The two men walked by Haddad and kept on down the sidewalk, never turning towards the building. For the twentieth time that morning, Welker wrote the time in his small notebook along with a big 'X,' a reminder not to waste any effort on whatever Haddad's device might have captured from the two men. The vast majority of time on stakeouts was spent this way. Hours upon hours of multiple false alarms and nothing to show for it at the end of the day. The routine often paid off, however, with patience.

They repeated the exercise one hundred and twenty-seven times over the course of the next four hours. Noting a potential approaching employee, capturing video, initiating the cloning sequence. All dead ends. No one entered, and no one came out of the building. It was time for lunch, and Haddad had already long overstayed his 'waiting for the bus' cover; someone may have already noticed the oddity of someone sitting there for so long without moving.

"Let's break off and eat something," Welker whispered.

"Sounds good," responded Haddad as he stood up and readied to cross the street.

"Hold on," cautioned Welker. "Nine o'clock, young boy, looks local, coming out of the alley and turning your way."

Haddad remained standing, looking both ways as if watching for traffic. The kid looked about fifteen years old, wearing dirty jeans and a worn, oversized jacket. He was skinny and had his hands in his pockets. He passed within a few feet of Haddad, moving with a purpose.

"Let's tail him," Welker suggested.

"Copy. Think I should I clone him?" Haddad turned, following the boy at a distance.

"Yes," Welker replied. "He could have a cell." He left a few bills on the table, got up from his chair casually, and began walking in the same direction on the opposite side of the street with his briefcase cam pointed towards their young target.

The boy seemed disinterested in the pedestrians he passed, or in anything else. As if it were a normal but important routine. He certainly did not appear to worry that someone might be watching him. A block farther he turned right down a side street and ducked into a restaurant. Welker crossed the street and remained at the intersection while Haddad walked past the restaurant and stopped in front of a local shop, pretending to be interested in some of the handmade trinkets set out in front on a table. After five minutes the boy emerged carrying four plastic bags, two in each hand. The boy moved off again at a good pace, retracing his route. Haddad followed closer this time so he could initiate the cloning procedure. They tailed him as far as the alley. Haddad continued down the street while Welker lingered to watch him enter through a side door after knocking and glancing up at a security camera aimed down from above.

Back at the hotel, they ordered room service and began to review what they gathered. It wasn't much. Haddad connected the nondescript-looking black cloning device to a laptop to download the data while

Welker connected his video camera to his own computer with a USB cable.

As he downloaded the video, Welker started the conversation. "So, we know there are people inside. The kid is an errand boy. Probably local. It should be relatively easy to get information from him if we do it right and don't scare him off."

"I agree, though I think it's too early for that. He might go right back to his handlers and tell them about two foreigners asking weird questions." Haddad tapped a few keys on the laptop and scrolled through a simple comma separated value report downloaded from the device. At the end, he noted the time stamp and grinned. "The kid had a cell phone on him. Looks like we got most of it. Let's see what we can see."

"Shit yeah," Welker responded. He scrolled through the video, pausing at the point the boy appeared from the alley. "Anything interesting?"

"Well, quite a few calls, looks like local numbers. A bunch of texts too, all in French. Looks like there was enough time for the cloning to complete—we have a working soft phone copy. If anyone calls or texts him, we'll be able to hear, see, and record everything."

"Great," replied Welker."

Haddad tapped a few more keys. "Yep, he's an errand boy. The texts are all pretty mundane, menial tasks and such. The majority are from one phone number. There are no saved contacts, no names associated with any of them. A lot of calls received, not many outgoing. Most of the outgoing ones are also to that one number. I'll pass it on to Thomas. The last text was for the food order he was picking up."

Welker was frowning. "OK. Listen Omar, we'll have to stake the place out continuously. They went in to work very early, obviously. We were there at seven, and they were already there. They may be working odd hours." He sampled the rice and beans from his plate and chewed thoughtfully. "They have some security. A camera over the side door and controlled entry. I'll head back there in a bit; you can spell me at six. After that we'll decide if it makes sense to try to get inside tonight. Once we have more to go on. The area will be empty at night, so we'll have to make ourselves small. I don't like the idea of staying on the street with no café to sit at and no bus to catch."

"OK," Haddad replied. "Maybe they are going in and out from the back, from the warehouse? Do you think we could have missed that?"

"I doubt it. They'd still have to come out through the same alley the boy came out of, where the loading dock is. There's no other way unless there's a tunnel or something. The warehouse shares a common back wall with the businesses and stores on the parallel street. My bet is they're just working odd hours. Heck, we might be missing them right now. Hopefully it's not a twenty-four-seven operation; I'd like to be able to get inside. Another possibility is that they don't ever leave—they work and sleep inside. They live there." He stood up. "OK, I'm leaving my computer here. Are you done downloading? I'll take the cloner." He tapped his laptop with two fingers. "And study the video. Not just the boy, all of it. There could be something there we didn't see. I'm heading back now."

Welker quickly shoveled the rest of his food in his mouth, then detached the camera and reinstalled it in his briefcase. Haddad handed him the cloning device.

"See you at six," said Haddad.

"See you then," Welker replied with a wink. "And let me know right away if anything interesting comes across on the soft phone." He walked out of the room and closed the door.

CHAPTER NINE

Dolan had never been to Turkey. Several C-130 pilot buddies from his Air Force days had flown into Incirlik Air Base near Adana, each of them returning with one or more Persian rugs for their wives and the obligatory tins of Turkish delight for everyone else. Over the course of his eleven-year career with the CIA, Andino had been to Ankara twice. On one of those visits he took a recreational side trip to Istanbul. His Turkish was decent, but not great. Good enough for the field work they needed to do. The situation was not ideal, but this was primarily a fact-finding mission. Low threat.

"There he is," Dolan whispered. He passed the binoculars to Andino who squinted, then acquired the middle-aged man, now seated and conversing with someone else in the room. Then he began eating. His face was just visible between half-drawn curtains through the small window on right side of the modestly sized duplex. It wasn't an affluent neighborhood, but it was nice, on the outskirts of Ankara. Most of the homes were multi-family. No yards to speak of, with one and a half to two meters separating each building.

Their vehicle was a loaner from Ankara Station with local, non-diplomatic plates. It was older and dirty. There were dents here and there and the paint was faded. Its poor cosmetic condition was intentional, so it would blend in almost anywhere. It was well-maintained however, and the engine had far more horsepower than a car like that ever should. There were three secret compartments containing almost everything a field operative might need. One was underneath the dash, another under the back seat, and a larger one in the truck beneath the spare tire.

"Should we listen in?" asked Andino. He was holding a handgun-looking device with a wired earbud attached. It beamed an invisible laser capable of reading the minute vibrations in the plate glass of a window up to fifty meters away, enabling them to listen in on whatever was said inside.

"I don't see the point. He's probably just having breakfast with his wife. We know he's there now, though. The sun will be up soon, and he'll be on his way to work. Today we'll just follow and observe, see if anyone else has eyes on him. If not, it should be simple to decide where, when, and how to approach him. That thing might come in handy later, though."

"OK." He wrapped the earbud wire around the device and put it in his jacket pocket.

Thirty-five minutes later, the front door opened and Murat Demir appeared, a small tuckerbox in his hand, probably containing his lunch. He walked out to the street and turned left down the side of the dirt road. The sun was now peaking over the rooftops, catching the dust kicked up by his feet as he shuffled. Dolan watched him recede in the rearview mirror and started the engine. After waiting for oncoming traffic to pass, he made a slow U-turn and followed. Two minutes later Demir stopped among a group of people waiting at a bus stop. Dolan pulled to the side forty meters away.

A gray minibus pulled up three minutes later and picked him up with eight or ten others. Eleven stops later, Dolan was cursing under his breath; he wasn't used to this kind of chaos in the streets. There were motorcycles and mopeds everywhere, weaving in and out of traffic. Road signs were few and far between, and wherever there were lines on the road, staying between them seemed to be more a suggestion than a rule. He almost lost the bus twice.

"You're trying to apply your western driving norms. Don't," an exasperated Andino finally told him. "I've spent years driving in places like this. Think of it like a school of fish. Everyone is just maintaining safe minimum distance from each other, on all sides. Go with the flow. Which is a good point—why am I not driving?"

"School of fish…" Dolan muttered. "Andy, I'm driving because as you've already pointed out, it's something I don't have enough experience with yet. I have a good teacher next to me advising on how to do it better. So, thanks." Andino's suggestion made sense to him and after that, he found driving to be much easier.

The minibus dropped Demir off ten kilometers later near the center of Ankara. He walked the final two blocks to a small computer repair shop and went inside. Dolan parked with a line of sight on the store and left Andino to take up a position at a streetside café directly across. He ordered juice and a pastry, then settled as comfortably as possible into a white plastic chair. Over the course of the next nine hours Demir emerged twice, each time visiting a streetside tea vendor. Dolan and Andino switched positions at the halfway point. He returned home on another minibus at the end of the day. Tuesday was more or less a repeat of Monday. They captured video of his movements and reviewed it at night. Aside from a stop for groceries just down the street before catching his bus home on Tuesday, Demir's activity patterns remained unchanged. Two days was not a good sample size, but they did not have a lot of time. At no point was there any evidence he was being followed or watched, nor did he appear nervous or do anything out of the ordinary. It was time to approach him.

On Wednesday morning at ten a.m., he emerged from his shop and walked to the tea vendor. Andino, who was seated nearby on a bench, stood up and arrived at the vendor first. Demir walked in behind him in line as he gave his order, received his glass, and paid. He thanked the vendor and turned, intentionally bumping Demir and spilling his tea.

"Pardon me, so sorry!" said Demir, in Turkish.

"Oh, excuse me!" Andino replied. "That was my fault." He made a show of trying to wipe the tea off the front of his slacks.

"No, no, please let me buy you another."

"That's kind of you, thank you."

Dolan watched from the café as Andino handed his glass back to the vendor. A few moments later Demir handed him a new glass while sipping from his own and smiling.

"Thank you," Andino said, making direct eye contact. "That was very kind of you." He motioned for Demir to move away from the cart.

Demir was hesitant but followed a few steps, just out of earshot of the line of patrons. "It was my fault; it was the least I could do." He nodded politely in an attempt to end the conversation.

Before he could turn away, Andino put his hand on Demir's shoulder. "Mr. Demir, please. I would like to offer a kindness in return. Something I believe you've wanted for some time. Let's sit down for a moment. I only have good intentions. Please."

Demir's smile faded, and his face took on an ashen hue. "I do not know you. You do not know what I want."

"Forgive me for approaching you this way, but it is important that we talk. I know a little about you, and I really do have something you would be interested in." Andino maintained a jovial countenance as he spoke in his best, but somewhat broken Turkish.

For anyone who might be watching them, the entire sequence of events looked natural, Dolan thought. Andino was good at this.

"I don't want any trouble. Please, just let me go back to work."

"There is no trouble, Mr. Demir. Believe me, I only want what's best for you. The government of the United States wants what's best for you. For you and your family."

That caught Demir's attention. "What do you mean? Who are you?"

"I work for the United States, Mr. Demir. You can call me Sam. I know that a few years ago you expressed an interest to come to my country with your wife and daughter. Unfortunately, that never came to pass. I want to make that happen for you now. I would like to meet in a quiet place, tomorrow perhaps? There is information you have we think could be valuable to us. Would you be willing to talk to me?"

Demir's eyes were wide as he began to process what Andino just told him. Anyone surveilling Demir at this point might suspect something. *Wrap it up Andy*, Dolan pleaded silently.

Demir said nothing and nodded slowly.

"Good." Andino handed him a card wrapped in a ten-lira banknote. "You will meet me at this address tomorrow morning at seven thirty a.m., before you go to work. If you are honest and the information is verifiable, this will be very easy and will happen very quickly. You will come alone. You will buy something at a shop nearby, purchase some food, find a quiet place at this address, and begin eating your meal. While you are doing all of this you will act normal. Do not look around, do not look for me. Tell no one about me or this meeting, especially not your handler at the U.S. Embassy—he does not know about this and will disrupt the process if he knows. Do not even tell your wife. Am I clear?"

Demir shot him a look when Andino mentioned his handler, put the note in his pocket without looking at it, and again nodded. "Yes, Mr. Sam."

"Good." Andino smiled big and patted Demir on the back. "Until tomorrow then."

CHAPTER TEN

Back at their hotel, Dolan and Andino finalized their plan. They would meet with Demir in Kurtuluş Park. Dittrich gave Dolan limited authority by to pursue visas and political asylum for Demir and his wife and daughter. Whatever information he had must be valuable and vetted, however. Which means they would need, at the least, to have a good understanding of what he was bringing to the table before making any promises.

Dolan checked his Breitling Aviator. "Time to check in with Berlin and Niamey."

Andino nodded, reached into his duffel bag, and handed him a secure cell. Dolan dialed Welker first, then conferenced Collier in. He turned on the speaker and placed the phone between them on the coffee table.

"Hi guys, I have Andy here with me," said Dolan. Are Stan and Omar with us?"

"I'm here," replied Bolden, "Thomas is also dialed in at our end."

"Omar is here as well," said Welker.

"OK, we have a quorum. I'll give you a brief update on our progress in Ankara, then I'd like to hear what's going on in Niamey. Mike, you can fill us in on the Red Fig servers at the end." He then gave the team a synopsis of their surveillance on Demir and the plan to approach him tomorrow.

"I'm pretty interested to see what comes out of that," said Welker. "Could be nothing of course but based on what we've encountered down here in Niger, there is *something* going on."

Dolan exchanged glances with Andino. "Don't keep us in suspense, Howard. What did you turn up?"

"Well, we sat on the property all day Monday. All the windows are frosted over, so no opportunity to peek in. There was about an hour and a half we missed, around lunchtime. That's when we decided to switch to shift work and case the place twenty-four seven. That morning, no one entered the building. At first, we thought there might be nothing going on there, even though we could tell there were lights on inside. But one person did come out, a young local kid who appeared to be a courier. He goes out and gets food at least twice a day and runs other errands, bringing things back to the building. We cloned his phone. There wasn't a whole lot on it, just food orders and the like. But on day two, the texts and calls stopped coming in on the clone. Turns out it was a burner and he's using a different one each day. Michael, no one else has gone in or come out of the building except for that kid. Whoever else is inside, I think they are living in there, including the boy. We have no idea who he is; there are no contacts in the phone and none of the texts include any names. This morning I tried to walk in the front door, posing as a curious cloud service rep here on other business, but it was locked, and no one answered when I knocked. If the building is not tapped into the internet in any way, which is what Thomas told us, then we are going to have to go in ourselves. A third option is to confront and question the boy, which I am willing to do but I'm not sure it's worth the risk. It would have to be done delicately, and Omar doesn't like the idea."

"Let's not do anything drastic just yet," Dolan cautioned. "For now, I agree with Omar, risking exposure by cornering some kid who could very well be prepared by his handlers for that scenario seems desperate this early. They will have surveillance tech at the embassy you can check out. We got our hands on a car here from Ankara Station with some pretty useful toys stashed inside."

"Um, well we didn't check in with the embassy, Michael," replied Welker. "We rolled into this quickly and we don't have much time. Tipping anyone off at the embassy here that we have an active, off-books mission, even from the Agency, is a non-starter in my opinion."

"Howard, I get it but who said anything about tipping anyone off?" Dolan replied. "I asked the Chief of Station here for some help, told him we'd be gone in five days and if he wanted details on what we were doing he could call Dittrich. I'm not sure if he did or didn't, but we got what we needed."

"Don't get your panties in a bunch, boss." Welker was irritated. "I've been doing this a long time and one thing I've learned is that these small, backwoods stations don't have jack shit for tech compared to what they might have in an embassy the size of Ankara's. Another thing to consider is, the station here is all of four guys that nobody's ever heard of because no one cares about Niger, outside of our Reaper operations. They'll get very curious very quickly and they won't let it go, trust me. It's more trouble than it's worth, even if you get on the horn with Dittrich to grease the rails."

Dolan nodded. "I understand. OK. What's the feasibility of getting inside and looking around?"

There was a moment of silence on the line as Welker pondered the option. Clearly, he wasn't prepared for Dolan to suggest it. Finally, he spoke. "Well, we don't have blueprints. We know there are people inside, but we don't know how many. If the kid was getting food for everyone each time he went out, I would guess it's around seven to ten, which matches what Thomas found out about the visas. Unless there is some hidden tunnel they go in and out of, we know they never leave, at least not very often. The place has one visible security camera over the side door in the alley, but I suspect there may be more we can't see. If there is an alarm, I doubt they would keep it armed with people inside twenty-four seven. If we are going in, I'd use the front door and I'd do it at three a.m. or so. There is no reason to suspect they are working at night. Our cameras are night vis-capable, and we have NVGs. If we run into trouble, I have the dart guns."

The two injection handguns used compressed gas to shoot a 20-cc dart containing a fast-acting paralytic powerful enough to drop an adult man within five seconds. They were accurate to twenty meters. Welker ordered them online, along with ten darts, from a safari supply store in Kenya and had them shipped overnight to the hotel ahead of their arrival.

"Go ahead and do it. Have a foolproof escape plan in place if things go wrong, though. Text me when you are going in and let me know when you are out." Dolan was nodding to himself as he talked, a curious mannerism for someone who was otherwise very difficult to read. He only did it when speaking on the phone, and only when the conversation required some form of cerebral gymnastics. Putting various ideas through mental tests and checks and evaluating potential outcomes as he spoke. Weighing the probability and impact of failure against the value of reward that might accompany success. If they had more time, he would take a different approach. However, Dittrich capped all three ops at two weeks, which included whatever time it would take to fly everyone home and submit his final report.

"Roger that," replied Welker.

"Alright. Mike, what did you find in Berlin?"

"You guys are doing some interesting stuff," replied Collier. "Makes me want to get the hell out of Berlin and go have some fun too, to be honest. The majority of everything we do here is so layered with bureaucracy. It's rare that we'll have a traditional, old-school op here these days and whenever we do, I'm stuck here at the embassy, watching remotely. In any case, Stan and I called in a favor to get Thomas the Red Fig server access he needed without raising any eyebrows. By all appearances, the company runs a tight ship. Their international business in Europe appears to be on the up and up, and to be honest, most of the work done here isn't even associated with their IT cloud or mobile applications businesses. They do some marketing out of the regional office here, mostly for their profitable apps like eL8. There seems to be quite a bit of remote blockchain work being done on the servers, all of it concerning Hypotherion, their humanitarian crypto exchange. It looks like the actual coding, the primary software platform development, might have been done here in Berlin and not in Turkey. The exchange itself is openly advertised as being in Istanbul. Their headquarters building is there. A bank, essentially. But the servers are where the magic happens, the actual cryptocurrency blocks. There are five other server locations. The others are essentially copies of each other. They are used to distribute the ledger. I'll let Thomas explain that part. Anyway, we couldn't find anything related to Niamey or the work going on there, nothing about elections in Turkey. But we did uncover something interesting about Hypotherion. I'll let Thomas take it from here."

"Thanks Mike. Hello everyone, hope you are all staying safe," Freeman replied. "This is basic stuff, but it is technical, so stay with me. If you have any questions, go ahead and interrupt. The concept that Hypotherion was built upon was new at the time and remains the only example worldwide of a private crypto exchange where the coins are not considered currency. They do have the bank in Istanbul, but the bank deals in traditional currencies.

"Hypotherion is patterned after Bitcoin; the coding is nearly identical. There is a total of twenty-one million minable coins, and 6.25 coins per block. Over the last year there have been an average of two hundred and fifty coins mined daily. By comparison, the number of Bitcoins mined was around nine hundred a day. The value of a Bitcoin has been north of sixty thousand dollars. The crypto market is not stable, however. In 2022 it dropped to below twenty thousand and has been up and down since. The current value of a Hypotherion coin is much less, and as I mentioned, it's not a currency. First off, the miner never actually owns the coins that they find—one cannot transfer a Hypotherion coin into a cryptocurrency wallet to store and use it. All coins remain with the exchange in Turkey. The exchange uses the coins as its basis for outside investors to fund loans to foreign governments, mostly third world. Instead of being given, they are *attributed* to the miner. What the miner does get, however, are what they call non-transferrable Altruism Credits, a newer type of NFT."

"NFT?" questioned Welker.

"Non-fungible token," Freeman replied. "Something of value that does not physically exist. It exists only in code and cannot be copied or deleted. Anyway, when a needy country is approved for a Hypotherion loan and a miner's coin or coins are used to back the loan, the miner's name and whatever personal or professional information they want made public is published along with the amount of their 'donation,' which is set at the market value of the coins at the time the loan is disbursed. The name of the country and the nature of humanitarian relief provided through the loan are also recorded and attributed to the miner. Because it is considered a charitable donation, in many countries people can deduct the value of the Hypotherion coins used in a loan on their income taxes, minus the value of the carbon credits they receive."

"Wait, what? Carbon credits?" Dolan interrupted again.

"Yeah, right? I didn't know much about Hypotherion before embarking on this little op but trust me when I say the whole thing is incredibly unique. Credits for altruism wouldn't be enough to get a sufficient number of people to mine Hypotherion. Some professional crypto miners do it on the side specifically to offset the tax implications of mining Bitcoin, Litecoin, Ethereum, etcetera. But those are the power miners. The little guys operating out of garages can't afford to waste resources on it—it takes an incredible amount of computing power to mine cryptocurrencies in the first place. So, the question is, how do you convince small mining operators, other than making them feel good about helping the world, to participate? You give them *even more* good feelings about helping the world, and at the same time you give them something of real value.

"I'm almost done, and the context is important, so bear with me," Thomas assured them. "Every low-interest loan from the exchange comes with a contractual agreement that requires the borrowing government to do one of three things—to plant a number of trees or durable vegetation that correlates directly to the value of the loan, to federally protect a correlated number of hectares of previously unprotected land, or to do some combination of the two. That process generates carbon credits that are officially documented by the exchange and transferred to the miner, who can then sell them internationally via the exchange to companies, local and state governments, or individuals. Or they can be traded, just like any other non-fungible token. Except of course for the altruism credits—as I mentioned, those are non-transferrable. The trading aspects are complicated and not worth getting into, but the bottom line is, the carbon credits are worth real money, and the amount is not insignificant. A Hypotherion coin is worth about four thousand dollars right now, and the value of the carbon credit generated by mining one coin is nearly half that amount."

"OK, I can see why people might want to mine it then," Welker interjected, "but if this exchange in Turkey, if no one ever actually gets their coins, if the Hypotherion Exchange gets them all and maintains possession, what's to prevent them from suddenly telling every investor that the price is now zero, and keeping all the investor's money? It is not a currency—Hypotherion cannot be used to buy anything, the coins can't be traded for anything else. There is no true market. It sounds like a scam."

"Good point," Thomas replied. "I was about to get to that. And this is where it really is ingenious. You are right, there is no traditional market, and yes, Hypotherion, with oversight provided by the Turkish government, controls every coin. But this is where Red Fig deviated from the Bitcoin source code. The value of a Hypotherion coin is coded *right into the blockchain itself.* There is zero volatility—the price is determined specifically by an algorithm where the sole variable is the total number of Hypotherion coins currently mined, and the increase in value is more or less geometric. Because it is coded into the blockchain, and because blockchain is essentially unhackable due to its nonce architecture and distributed ledger, the value of a coin is always known, estimable, and immutable. To show good faith and to reassure investors, five percent of all monies held by the exchange is kept not in the Hypotherion bank in Istanbul, but at a bank in Geneva. The balance of that account is published on the internet and updated in real time via an agreement with the Swiss government. The whole thing, since it's taken off, has become an investor's dream and is better than gold when the markets are down. The very first coin was worth one dollar. By the time the final coin is mined, the value will be just north of two hundred seventy thousand. It was originally estimated that wouldn't happen for another hundred years or so. But Hypotherion mining is accelerating at an unusual pace recently. If that keeps up, mining could be complete in thirty to forty years. Or even less. There are other variables that affect this as well, like technological advancements that enable faster hashrates. A hashrate is basically the speed of a miner's performance."

Dolan was patient, but Freeman had a propensity to wax poetic on the intricacies of anything technological. "Thomas, I appreciate all the details but let's get to the point. What did you find, and how is it important to what we are doing. Please."

There was a short pause on the line as Freeman shifted gears. "Right, sorry. But all of this, it helps to understand where I'm going. Anyway, there was a spike in Hypotherion coin mining three weeks ago with a corresponding jump in the Hypotherion account balance in Geneva. On one day about a year and a half ago, there were one thousand one hundred and ninety-seven coins found. Remember that I said the average is around two hundred and fifty. It could be that someone, or more likely a coordinated group of miners with a shit ton of computing power redirected it all toward mining Hypotherion for twenty-four hours. In and of itself, that's not an incredibly unusual occurrence. But the number does stand out. It's a high number. Remember as well that the names and other info about the miners is made public if the miners allow. Well, of the total only one hundred thirty-two made their names public, and of those, only fourteen allowed other information about themselves, such as their home country, to be made public. Given that most people want at least their names to be publicly associated with their altruism, the number is astonishingly low. So now we have two data points that are multiple standards of deviation outside the norm. And the more I look at it, the more I think this was fraud—an inside job—or some kind of test."

"A test?" asked Dolan. "What do you mean, a test?"

"Well, it's two things. One is the timing. Though we can't determine where the miners are physically located, we do know by looking at the real-time change in Hypotherion's value that day that a little over one thousand coins were mined within twenty minutes of each other. That's the third anomalous data point. The probability of something like that happening during the normal course of mining is approximately one in three hundred million. Another important thing to remember is that coins are not mined all at once. Pieces are mined until a whole coin is uncovered. It is done by degrees. In this case, over one thousand *whole* coins were mined. When you factor that in, the probability that this event happened naturally is, statistically, zero. If this were fraud, it would have to be perpetrated by someone within Red Fig, probably a high-level coder, someone who's been with the project since the beginning and knows all the ins and outs and has power user access to everything. But if it's just a test, then we could be barking up the wrong tree. It would definitely be a weird test to do, as it implies that Red Fig is mining their own coins and the evidence is permanently coded into the blockchain. That kind of test itself would be considered fraudulent. But even if someone suspected fraud, the investors wouldn't even care, because they made a lot of money off it.

"Complicating matters, Hypotherion Bank publishes their coin information monthly, but only for coins associated with publicly released names. The ideal is, for those who are truly altruistic, there is no need to put their names out there, to say *hey, look at me, I'm a giver*. It's perfect cover for hiding something like this. No one will ever know anything about those thousand coins, except to the extent that they made the value of Hypotherion pop a bit within a short period of time. My guess is, if this was some sort of operational test, they were measuring the

97

entire system's capability to react to surge mining. But as I said, there is a counterintuitive risk involved.

"In any case, I would say they were trying to make sure their infrastructure and production environments can handle the forecasted uptick. The other reason it makes sense is, though it is a distributed ledger, it is distributed in a very limited way—there are only seven locations where servers exist, one in Berlin and the rest in Turkey. It is a private ledger, viewable only by the exchange and participating miners. And what miners are allowed to see is limited as well, which is not necessarily the case with traditional cryptos.

"There are quite a few power miners out there who go after Hypotherion who invest in it at the same time. It makes sense, because due to the valuation algorithm, they make money on the coins they own with each new coin they find, and the volatility is zero. They will never lose money on it. That trend is growing and as the value goes up, we should expect to see it happen more."

"If mining cryptocurrency takes so much computing power," Welker cut in, "how does a test like that even make sense? Red Fig would need to have some incredible setup with technology no one else in the world has to mine that many that quick. And why would they keep the ledger hidden from the public? From what little I know about blockchain, the records from new blocks are timestamped and contain the transaction data from the previous blocks, right? And new blocks cannot be altered without altering the parallel blocks across the ledger, which is part of the reason it is considered unhackable, right? So, to keep it hidden implies they want to be able to make changes to it without anyone noticing."

Thomas was ready for both questions. "To your first question, not necessarily. Remember that Red Fig coded the blockchain, and though it is very similar to Bitcoin, there are differences. And the most important difference is that the ledger is private. With Bitcoin the ledger is, well, everywhere. There is, potentially, a nearly infinite number of copies of it. That is the real reason it so unhackable. Because Hypotherion's ledger exists on only a handful of servers, it wouldn't be too difficult for them to hide changes to the ledger without anyone knowing. Especially because miners, who must be approved in advance with a verified digital signature, have limited access. All they would need is to have coded a backdoor, one that allows them to bypass the algorithmic problem solving and simply make the coins appear using fake accounts with fabricated signatures. As soon as they do that, it distributes. Nothing looks anomalous. I wish I knew more about Python, the language they used to code the blockchain. Even if I knew more, I wouldn't have had enough time to find what I was looking for, I think. The window we had was very tight—we had to get in and out quickly to prevent detection.

"To your second question, if I am right about what's going on with a backdoor, they would absolutely want to keep that secret. Any kind of back door makes the entire blockchain hackable if you can get access to the code. *Which I did...*" Thomas waited for someone on the call to acknowledge his accomplishment. No one bit, so he continued. "Of course, you also need to know where the backdoor is and how to access it. And its existence would totally negate any possibility of ever truly monetizing Hypotherion, which Red Fig has already said will never happen. So, they've covered their bases there.

"With traditional cryptos. it is important to have the ledger distributed, with many copies of every transaction so they can prove to the world that there is nothing untoward going on. If there were, the evidence of it would be in many different places, not just one or two or three. It would be impossible to cover your tracks. In this respect, Hypotherion is quite different. In addition to Berlin, there is a server in

Izmir, one in Bergama, another in Akhisar, one near Alaşehir, one is in Salihli, and another in Denizli. All cities in west Turkey."

Dolan sighed. "OK, thanks Thomas. So, at this point either there is fraud, or it could be a test, which would also be fraud. But neither means anything to us at all, as far as I can tell. I don't think this is enough information to be useful right now, but maybe it will prove helpful down the line." Then he stopped in thought. "But...what if we could find out where the miners of those one thousand plus coins were from, or maybe if we got their digital signatures? Would that information be helpful in helping us decide if this was a test, or if it's something more sinister?"

"Well, yes, that data would help," replied Thomas, appearing irritated "but like I said, the personal information for almost all of them was unpublished. And digital signatures aren't something that are directly associated with the coins themselves. And it wasn't something I was looking for when I went in. I would have to perform another hack. If I did, I might be able to see the IDs, but I wouldn't be able to tie them back to a person, or a location, or any other data at all for the reasons I've already explained. I would need to find the backdoor."

"Go back in," Dolan responded. "As you say, it's not something you were looking for. You never know, even if you can't find a backdoor, you might find something else. Let's not leave any stone unturned."

"Sure boss," said Thomas with a sigh. "I'll get with Mike and set it up."

"Thanks," Dolan replied. "Last thing I want to cover. I paid a visit to Sharif Lefebvre in Annapolis before we left. I told him about his father's death and asked him if he knew anything about his father's dealings with Turkey. He didn't know much but did tell me he had dealings with Blue Olive. Given that and where we found Lefebvre, I would say that gives us reason to believe there's a chance Solak or someone within Red Fig knew he was there, or even helped hide him there. So there's that.

"OK team, I'll compile everything from this meeting and report back to Dittrich. In the meantime, tomorrow is critical, I need to be kept in the loop on how things go in Niamey. Keep your eyes open for any connection with the AMA. Howard, I know you don't want to interact with the station there, but it might be a good idea to connect with one of the guys as part of your backup plan, to help if things go sideways. Let me know what you decide."

Welker paused for effect. "I understand your position. I don't agree with that course of action, let me think on it. Omar and I will talk it through."

"Right. That's all for now then. I'll backbrief Fitzy later and see if he has anything new out of Paris. Be smart and be safe." Dolan pressed End on the phone and looked up at Andino. "What does your gut say so far? Are we onto something here, or are we wasting our time?"

Andino smiled. "Too early to tell. In this business I've learned that incontrovertible proof of anything is very difficult to find, and that if you spend enough time specifically looking for evidence that supports a theory, you are always going to find it. And I'm not even sure we have a theory right now. I would say, as we follow up on any leads, we also need to keep our eyes open for anything that might indicate those leads are in fact *false*."

Dolan laughed. "Null hypothesis. Sounds like something Dittrich would say. But yeah, I agree, although my gut says there's something there. We were told to be careful, and yours is the right approach. Before we jump to conclusions, let's see what they uncover in Niamey. And until after we hear whatever Demir has to say. I have a feeling he's going to be a can of worms."

"I do too," Andino replied. "I do too…

CHAPTER ELEVEN

"So, we are going in with no backup." It was more of a statement than a question, and Welker could tell by his tone that Haddad was not OK with it.

"Listen, you may not like it, but you're going to have to trust me on this. The second we involve the station here, we risk losing control of the op. Those four officers are young and eager. They don't know how to let things go, to look the other way when they're told. While an internal exposure of REVENANT is not a death knell, it creates all kinds of problems I'm sure Michael and Dittrich don't want to have to deal with, and certainly not amid three ongoing missions. You need to accept it. We have a good plan and despite what you think, the risk is low."

Haddad frowned but accepted defeat. It went against his better judgement, but he trusted him. Welker's old-school aura of invincibility dimmed somewhat after being shot and rescued by Dolan during the last mission in Germany. But that kind of reputational damage had a way of healing with time. Eventually, it might even add to and strengthen his legacy. The problem was, if things went badly in Niamey there was no backup, no cleanup team, no medic if one of them was injured. It was just them.

It was two-forty-five a.m. Their outfits were dark and nondescript. The only thing that might call attention to them was the fact they were out at such an hour. They each carried a dart gun with reloads in an oversized pocket sewn into the left inside breast of their jackets and the rest of their gear in small black duffel bags. After checking their earpieces one last time, Haddad left the hotel room followed three minutes later by Welker.

Haddad turned the corner and finished the half-mile trek to the Red Fig building. He slowed as he approached, then stopped to light a cigarette while visually sweeping the area. As he had hoped, there was no one in sight. The storefronts and most of the business signs were dark. Traffic lamps at wide intervals along the curb cast eerie yellowish patches on the empty street. He positioned himself in a dark space between two of them and noted the lights inside the building were off.

"The place is dead. I'm heading to the door," Haddad whispered as he pulled the ski mask over his head and put on his gloves.

"Copy," replied Welker into his earpiece.

At the north corner of the building, Haddad pried open a grey utility box affixed to the stucco exterior and used a knife to cut the phone lines. He folded the knife, pocketed it, and moved to the front door. By the time he finished picking the lock he saw Welker emerge from the shadows and stop, thirty meters away to the north with a clear view of the building and road in both directions.

"Clear," said Welker.

After donning his NVGs, Haddad opened the door an inch and waited five seconds, listening. With no internet connection and the phone lines cut, the authorities would not be responding to a tripped alarm, but a siren could still go off inside. Hearing nothing, he opened it enough to scan the edges and the inside of the doorframe. No sensors, as far as he could tell.

"Door is clear."

"Copy."

Welker walked deliberately to Haddad, masked up with a camera in one hand and his duffel in the other. Just then, they both froze as a vehicle engine roared to life, muffled and echoing from the alley on the side of the building.

"Shit," said Welker. "Close the door, let's back off."

Haddad shut it quickly and they sprinted away from the building. There was no good place to hide.

"There," Welker pointed. They stopped in front of the adjacent building, a row of shuttered stores. One of them left display carts on the sidewalk, battened down and chained together. Crouching behind one of them, they watched and waited.

After thirty seconds they heard a second vehicle engine.

"You didn't think to check the alley first?" Welker looked at him.

"No. Sorry. I didn't think it was necessary, given the time of night."

"*Amazing,*" Welker replied sardonically.

The engine noise grew louder. A white box truck emerged from the alley, riding low. It turned south on the road, followed by a white minivan. Welker and Haddad had their cameras out by then, zooming and capturing as much video as they could. It was impossible to know who or how many were inside with so little light. The minivan followed the truck south and out of sight.

"What do you think that was?" asked Haddad.

"It could be that whatever was going on inside was just packed up and driven off for good, along with everyone who was doing it. They might have seen us casing the place. At least we have the license plates."

Leaving their cover, Welker and Haddad trotted across the front of the Red Fig building to the corner and peered down the alley. No activity, no more vehicles. Then they returned to the front, went inside, and closed the door behind them. Wearing NVGs again, they began a systematic search of the place, filming everything. The foyer and entry area were spartan with two lounge chairs, a small table, and a matching couch. A Turkish flag hung on the wall over a 1960's-era gray metal desk in the far corner. Welker went through the desk quickly. Only a few pencils and condiment packets from a nearby restaurant. Each room they searched was as empty as the first, on both floors. Even the storage rooms and closets were bare.

After they were done upstairs, the went back to the first floor and down the hall to a door that adjoined the warehouse. Haddad quickly defeated the keypad cipher box next to the doorknob and opened the door slowly. It was pitch dark inside, and empty. A typical warehouse, wide open with a very high ceiling, double-stacked rows of industrial-sized steel shelving across the back wall. There were two forklifts parked off to the left, and an exit to the right that opened up to the alley. There was also a huge aluminum roll door that provided access to the delivery dock.

"Let's turn on the lights. There's nobody here," suggested Welker.

"Really?"

"Why not. It'll make things go quicker."

Welker located the switches. They turned off and stowed their NVGs, and the warehouse was flooded with bright white light. Some of the storage shelves against the back wall had been turned into makeshift sleeping cubicles with mattresses, blankets, and pillows. In the center of the expansive floor were several brown foldup tables positioned end-to-end, with power cables and other wiring haphazardly strewn across. A pile of old, empty burlap bags occupied the far-right corner, vestiges of Solak's legacy import-export empire. Welker walked over and grabbed one, reading the faded stenciling out loud, "Blue Olive Sorghum." He stuffed it in his duffel. Other than that, the warehouse was nearly empty. Whatever they were working on here had been packed up and moved out, most likely in the box truck that left just fifteen minutes earlier.

"Look, ethernet," said Haddad. He was holding the end of a cable that was plugged into a router on one of the tables. A wire from the router was zip-tied to a bundle of others. Duct tape affixed the bundle along the floor to an ethernet port, electrical outlets, and other connections on the wall near the docking bay.

Welker walked over, looking perplexed. "Huh, Thomas is never wrong about these things. It looks like there is a connection, the lights are blinking green. We can ask him to take a second look at it."

"Just because the light is blinking green doesn't mean there is an internet connection," Haddad replied as he unzipped a small black bag. Inside was an aerosol can containing a highly specialized formulation of cyanoacrylate. Polymerization of fingerprint ridgelines using cyanoacrylate required sequestering items in a chamber under high heat—useless in the field when timing was critical. The formula in Haddad's can greatly simplified the effort—spray the surface, wait for the grayish fingerprints to appear, tape them, and bag them. They could also be photographed, unless the surface was also gray.

As Haddad worked on the tables and other surfaces, Welker scoured the rest of the warehouse for anything enlightening. Whoever had been there did a pretty good job covering their tracks. He found very little—some cleaning supplies, trash, some leftover food. IT hardware odds and ends, and a bunch of empty boxes stacked up near the door. No hard drives, no surveillance video for the camera in the alley. They took everything with them in the box truck. He did find several papers, however, at the bottom of a trash can.

"We might have something here," Welker exclaimed enthusiastically. "Looks like technical design drawings, you know, computer stuff. And this looks like software code, with notes off to the side."

He handed one of the papers to Haddad, who glanced at it and looked back up at Welker with a serious look. "Howard, the notes are in Russian."

"Let me see that." Welker grabbed the paper back and looked. "Holy shit Omar, you're right. I wasn't really paying attention, I just assumed it was Turkish at first."

"Why would Red Fig be working with Russians? Do you think this could be some sort of defense contract? Turkey never sided with the West over the Ukraine invasion; they are too invested with Russia. Or maybe they stole some Russian tech, and they're reverse-engineering it down here in Niger, out of sight?"

"None of this feels like a defense contract, or even stolen tech. There's no reason Red Fig would be working on something like that here, under these conditions. They are a multi-billion-dollar company. This warehouse looks more like something an underfunded IT startup might occupy. And the security was substandard, just one camera. And they didn't even have an alarm. Too much security draws attention—this was something they didn't want to stand out. It's why they made everyone live in the warehouse until the work was finished. It also looks like an operation that was done on the cheap so it wouldn't show up on the books, and so far away that no one would ever think to look here. And those Sorghum bags...are you thinking what I'm thinking?"

"Hmm, I think it's a stretch to connect this building to the plantation where we found Lefebvre. Sorghum is a common crop here in Niger. But it's not out of the question. We know Lefebvre had a business connection with Blue Olive."

"Right," Welker replied emphatically. "It certainly isn't out of the question. *It is* the question. Are you done?"

"I think so. I got eleven good prints and a few partials."

"OK. I think we have everything. Let's get out of here."

"Roger."

Welker shut off the lights and they walked quickly but stealthily on their black gum rubber soles into the office building and down the hall to the front entrance.

A barely audible shuffling noise made them stop in unison, listening. In a flash, a dark figure bolted out through the door to the stairwell just in front of them and sprinted for the exit. Before he got halfway there Welker dropped his duffle bag, reached inside his jacket, aimed, and shot the man in the middle of the back. His momentum propelled him forward and he collided into the door with a thud, then collapsed to the off-white ceramic tile floor.

"Make sure there isn't anyone else up there," Welker pointed.

"Got it."

He reloaded his dart gun and approached the inert form, face down. It was a paralytic—the man wouldn't be able to move, but he would be aware. He could still see and hear. Welker pulled the dart out of his back and recognized instantly who it was as he grabbed and easily rolled the small, thin frame over.

"The upstairs is clear," said Haddad as he rejoined Welker in the foyer. "Holy cow, it's the kid."

"Yeah, it's the kid. Tricky little shit—I don't know how we missed him during our sweep." Welker looked at Haddad, then back at the boy. "Let's take him back to the hotel."

"That's great. Just great..." was all Haddad could say.

CHAPTER TWELVE

"Are you positive you left nothing behind that could implicate us?" Solak asked sternly. "I don't want to find out later that everything I've accomplished is unravelling because my simple orders weren't followed."

"Relax," came the voice over Solak's phone. "We cleaned the place up before we left. There were some odds and ends lying around, but no drives, no servers. Everything that we coded on, we brought with us. And we sanitized the building, wiped everything down."

Solak hung his head in thought. "OK. The new tenant arrives next week, so even if you did screw something up, it will very likely be mitigated by their moving in. Now we will move to the next phase. When will it be ready to launch?"

"It's ready to launch now. All we need is the go-ahead from you, and I press the button. When do you want it done?"

"Not yet," replied Solak. "But the time is approaching. Be ready. And remember, if this doesn't go as planned, if anyone on your team screws up, you get nothing. And of course, I disavow any knowledge of you or the operation. We've covered our tracks well and have contingencies in place to erase all connections instantly and permanently between us and you. Do you understand, Mikhail?"

"Yes, I understand, Mr. Solak. As I said, relax. We have this covered. Just say when."

Solak ended the call.

For maybe the first time in his life, he was nervous. Everything he had worked for, all he had sacrificed up to now, was riding on Mikhail and his team's next steps. He didn't like the idea of relying on outsiders, but they possessed very unique and critical computing abilities and architecture he required, but lacked. He could finish it himself, perhaps not as cleanly, but using Mikhail's team was a far better option for multiple reasons. In its entirety, Solak's plan was so complex that he had come to marvel at his own creation. The fact that it remained invisible to the world was nothing short of a miracle. And it would remain invisible, at least until public knowledge of its existence didn't matter anymore. And that time was close at hand.

The second thing causing him anxiety was how to shape it for Adem, so that he will accept it and participate. He couldn't be an unwitting participant. *I must begin with that now*, he thought as he opened the doors to the library.

Avci was seated already and looked up with a smile as he entered.

"I don't have much time today; my plate is full. And I have the meeting with our Minister of the Interior at three. Have a seat, Sidika has already made our coffee."

Solak grabbed the chairback and looked sideways at Sidika, who slipped quietly out through the door. Then he sat.

"I'll get straight to the point then, Adem. The discussion you cut short yesterday, about me helping you..."

Avci stopped stirring his drink and looked at him intently.

"We both know that everything I've done to-date has been more than just helpful to you. My efforts have enabled elevation of our country on the world stage. We are now included in political, economic, and diplomatic circles formerly controlled exclusively by the West, China, and Russia. We are now a recognized and valued participant in spheres of influence that make Turkey a world player. You didn't make that happen; *we* did. Together."

"That is not in dispute, my friend," Avci acknowledged warmly.

"I know," Solak replied. "What I'm getting at is this. I tried to bring this up yesterday—my efforts in this area have not stopped. We are at a point where if I did, we could backslide. Our economic recovery, our new trade deals, none of these are guaranteed to continue. A seminal event like Covid-19 or the AMA attacks in Jordan and Germany—things like these hurt our economy disproportionately in comparison to larger nations. Turkey could quickly be relegated back to its former stratum, a second-tier power that very few take seriously. That cannot happen. I am taking steps to ensure that it won't."

"Yusuf, what do you mean? Is there something you are doing with Red Fig that I don't know about? Or with Hypotherion? Covid and terrorist attacks are events that no one person, no single company, no matter how large, can control." Avci knew by now to never underestimate his longtime friend. The man was smarter than anyone he had ever known. But this was something different.

Solak inhaled carefully. "Yes. I am doing something with Red Fig. And with Hypotherion. It's something I've been working on for years now. In fact, Hypotherion itself was established in part with this outcome in mind—that it would be used to strengthen Turkey's position globally. And it has. But as you know, if the work economy were to fail, for whatever reason, our investors could back out. Or, they could move into it. Yes, Hypotherion's value would be unaffected, but the flow of investments and interest we've accumulated from our loans to other countries needs to remain sufficient to back the total value of the coins that are mined. My idea was that, if the world economy did tank,

Hypotherion might become a haven for investors because of its non-volatility. But that non-volatility is just code. The true value is based upon the amount of money we have in the bank combined with the value of the loans and interest that are outstanding. Right now, those two values are roughly equivalent. If there is a rapid economic downturn, that could change—one way or the other. I have a plan that would ensure the financial integrity of Hypotherion. When that downturn occurs, with my plan, countries that are affected the most will be much more likely to reach out to Hypotherion for loans, which will demonstrate the strength and durability of the bank and exchange. Current investors will stay with us, and new investors will see Hypotherion as the safest bet available. More importantly," Solak paused, crossing his legs and taking a sip of coffee, "any effect by a negative global economy on Turkey can be instantly mitigated. The bank will support Turkey first and foremost. Hypotherion gives our country a critical edge in that respect."

Avci looked at him, stunned. "Yusuf, how much money does Hypotherion have right now? You do realize the amount needed to do such a thing, to bail out our own economy with others as well in such a situation—it is astronomical. Not even the United States has such ability."

"I'm aware," replied Yusuf. "I've had it modeled. We are talking about hundreds of trillions of Lira. And no, we have nothing that approaches that much right now. But we have a solid foundation, and my plan will ensure that if the time comes, we will have the necessary funding. Hypotherion is a huge success. What I am doing will accelerate that success. Greatly."

Avci was still unconvinced. How could he not be? Yusuf was talking about one bank in Turkey controlling more money than any other in the entire world. He was well aware of Hypotherion's success and had touted it across the world. It was one of his main talking points. They'd helped so many nations, and in such a short period of time. But he had no insight into its inner workings. He'd allowed Yusuf and Red Fig to operate with relative autonomy. And why wouldn't he? He trusted Yusuf with his life.

"Yusuf, if you are asking my permission, you will have it. I know what you are capable of. But this...this is difficult to believe, that you have a credible and executable plan for this. I first need to know how you plan to do it."

Solak nodded. This was the moment of truth. His friendship and ministerial position hung in the balance. "Adem, what I am about to tell you is going to sound controversial. It is a step forward from what we did during your campaign. What I will need from you is steadfast support as I execute my plan. There may be times when I require certain latitudes I and Red Fig wouldn't normally be afforded. Federal financial oversight of Hypotherion will have to be curtailed. We can explain that by saying the world would lose confidence in Hypotherion if the exchange were under a single government's control. I will also announce that I am steeping down from the board at Hypotherion. It needs to look like I've recused myself because of a conflict of interest. There have been calls for this as you know, mostly outside Turkey, due to my ministerial job. That move will strengthen our position. But I must be clear here—even though I'm no longer on the board, I will still be controlling the decisions of the board. It must be this way, because without me, they will flounder. Hypotherion is mine, no one knows it like I do. I must keep my finger on the pulse."

Avci was growing visibly impatient. "Yusuf, you are right, this is controversial. What you are proposing is extremely dangerous. I wouldn't agree to such a thing unless there were significant circumstances that compelled me, and right now I'm not aware of any. I cannot grant anything, I wouldn't, until I know why it needs to be done, and how. Tell me. I only have a few minutes left."

Avci would end up making a call to reschedule his meeting with the Minister of the Interior. What Solak had to say seemed too important. Although he was amazed at the scope, breadth, and potential rewards of the plan, there were aspects of it that caused him great concern. As Solak laid it all out for him, however, he began to understand. If it didn't go like clockwork, or if the wrong person or organization or government were to become aware, it would be difficult to pass off as wholly legitimate. But his friend's plan seemed to have great merit. By the time Solak was finished explaining, Avci was cautiously on board. The outcomes were too advantageous, and Solak seemed to have every angle, every potential risk covered.

Of course, Solak didn't tell him *everything*. Avci wouldn't know everything until it was well past the point of no return.

CHAPTER THIRTEEN

"He's *dead?*" Dolan asked incredulously.

"I darted him, that was it. He didn't seem sick when he was running for the front door in the building, that's for sure. He was a quick little shit," Welker assured him.

"Holy cow, Howard. How do you know it wasn't the paralytic that killed him? I mean, you ordered it from Kenya. It's not what we're supposed to use in the field. Maybe the dose was too high?"

Welker shifted his cell phone, pinning it between his shoulder and cheek as he continued to pack his bag. "No. I've used it before. The dose wasn't too high. It was the only way to get what I needed without going to Niamey Station. We waited two hours for him to recover before grilling him. He was fine by then. He spoke French, so Omar talked to him. We gave him a Coke, some food and money, and he was happy. I think at that point he was glad it had happened to him. But his eyes were getting glassy right at the end, and he started breathing fast. I was a little worried, so I tailed him out of the hotel, after we let him go. He got maybe fifty yards down the sidewalk and collapsed. I think the men he was working for poisoned him right before they left. Covering their tracks."

"What?" Dolan exclaimed. "That's horrible. You left him there?"

"Of course. Didn't want to risk being seen with a dead kid on the street. I'm sure you understand."

"Right. If he was poisoned, I think it's safe to say that whatever Red Fig was doing there was either illegal or at the least, very controversial. What did he tell you?"

"Well, murdering a child is definitely illegal. Anyway, there were seven men there, and they all worked and slept in the warehouse. They were coding something, impossible to tell what. But here's the kicker— five of them were from Russia."

"Russia? Thomas told us there were seven employees with visas, but that they were all Turkish."

"I believe the kid," Welker responded. "Their cleanup job was good, but not great. We found printouts of diagrams and coding in a trash can that had notes in the margin, written in Russian. I already sent the fingerprints we found and the license plate numbers to Thomas. Omar and I have looked through all the video several times and haven't noticed anything else that might be useful. But the kid, the errand boy, they used him to clean the place, too. Apparently, it was he who accidentally threw the printouts in the trash, along with the leftovers from their last meal. He gave us a little information about each of the men, but not much of it was valuable. He gave us the same common Turkish names that were on the visas Thomas dug up."

"Is there any chance the kid can be tied back to you and Omar? Did anyone see him with you?"

"I doubt it. Omar left to get the car so we could bring him to the hotel without being noticed. We took him through the back door. It was around four a.m. at the time. And I don't think anyone saw him leave. There's no one at the hotel's front desk after midnight."

"OK. We shouldn't assume anything. I want you to pack up and leave Niger as soon as possible. Get yourself checked out at the embassy clinic before you leave. Hopefully, whatever he died from wasn't contagious. Take precautions. Andy and I could use you here—so get on a flight to Turkey."

"Sure. But there's one other thing we found in the warehouse. A pile of old burlap bags. The label on each read *Blue Olive Sorghum*. Lefebvre was hiding out on a Sorghum plantation only a few hours' drive from Niamey, and we know he had business with Blue Olive at some point. I don't think that's a coincidence. I'll write it all up after we arrive in Ankara."

"OK. Thanks Howard. Safe travels." Dolan pressed end on the cell phone and looked gravely at Andino. "There is something very sinister going on here. I'm beginning to like the theory that Solak was hiding him, but what would he have gotten from that? Lefebvre had to be giving him something in return. Something big—there's no way he would have taken on the extreme risk of protecting the most wanted man in the world without major compensation. Whatever that compensation was, maybe Lefebvre stopped giving and Solak decided to pull the plug. Or maybe Lefebvre had just become too big of a liability, especially now that his good buddy was the President. Any liability for Solak is a liability for Avci."

"Who knows," Andino shrugged. "I agree, there is much more to this than meets the eye. But we must get going if we're going to be on time to meet with Demir."

Dolan checked his Breitling and grabbed a brown rucksack off the hotel bed. "Right. Let's go."

Kurtuluş Park was near the center of Ankara and within walking distance of Demir's shop. They tailed him from his home as they had the past two days. He followed the same pattern, taking the same bus but getting off one stop earlier. Dolan and Andino watched as he went into a hardware store, emerging with a small plastic bag. He purchased some food as instructed from a street vendor near the park and walked in. Dolan let Andino out of the car nearby, who followed at a distance. Demir selected a secluded spot under a tree near the middle of the park and began to eat while Dolan parked the car within line of site of his location. Two minutes later, Andino approached and sat down beside him. Demir looked up at him cautiously.

"This is the visa paperwork for you and your family." Andino handed his phone to a confused Demir. "Look at the screen. Scroll down."

He held the phone in his palm and dragged his index finger vertically, reviewing each page. "But I haven't signed anything," he questioned.

Andino took his phone back. "That's all that's left. All I have to do is print this out, get signatures from you and your wife, and send it in. I can have your visas ready and have the three of you safely on a flight to the United States the next day. But first, I need to know if the information you have is worthwhile. So, help me out Murat. Help your family. What is it that you know?"

Wind noise was making their conversation difficult to hear. Dolan repositioned his earpiece while scanning the park. No one else in sight.

"Mr. Sam," Demir began, "as you know I can't tell you everything until I am in the United States with my family. Those pages on your phone, they are nothing. You could be showing me that just to get the information, and then you'll disappear."

Andino looked at him seriously. "You have my word, although I understand why you feel you cannot trust me. I wouldn't either if I were in your position. But you must give me something if there's even a chance that I will do something for you in return."

Demir took a bite of his food and chewed thoughtfully. "I've already given as much of the targeting algorithm and election interference information as I am willing to give at this point. But I will tell you this." He looked Andino dead in the eye. "Avci's wife was murdered. And it wasn't because of that crazy story about some other man being the father of her unborn child. Avci had nothing to do with it. She was killed because of one thing, and one thing alone."

Dolan was straining to hear, realizing they might be on the verge of some breakthrough intelligence. Andino looked at him questioningly, impatiently.

Not breaking eye contact, Demir continued. "President Avci's wife was murdered because the algorithms weren't working as well as Yusuf Solak thought they would. I was on the team that developed them. They were giving Avci a boost, yes, but not enough. You see, we did a lot of modeling. The models would predict the outcome of using various algorithms in social media, and other IT processes designed to either boost or restrict certain types of communications. For instance, Red Fig's email application was designed to send political emails from organizations tied to the opposition party to a spam folder while ensuring emails from organizations favorable to Avci's party always went to the inbox. But I digress. None of it was enough. He was going to lose; the models were all wrong. So were the polls.

"One day when I was working, I found a new folder on our development server that was password protected. It seemed strange to me, since I should have had access. So, I hacked into it. Within the folder I found another model that appeared to be a new version of one I'd created months before. But significant changes had been made. It took some time to figure out, since the notations within the coding were vague, and referred in many places to an 'event.' I studied it for three weeks before I realized what the event was. Individually, the notes and coding related to the event were not illuminating. But by studying all the changes stochastically, it became obvious to me that the model's main variable was public sympathy, and the potential event that would trigger that sympathy was the death of his wife. Unlike the other models, I felt this one was very accurate. If his wife remained alive, it showed Avci losing the presidential election by a thin margin. If she were to die close, but not too close to the election, he would win in a landslide. And as we both know; she did die, and he did win convincingly."

Andino did his best to maintain composure. If what he was saying was true, it meant that Solak single handedly stole the election for Avci and was willing to murder his wife to make it happen. If news of this were to get out, it would rock the world. "Can you prove any of this, Murat? Do you have a copy of the model?"

"Yes. I do. When I realized what it was, I was going to take it to the authorities. But then the President appointed Solak as the Minister of Industry and Technology. Solak had become too powerful, and I knew I'd be putting me and my family in danger. I even began to wonder if Avci might be in on it. Ultimately, I decided he probably was not— how could he be? Then, shortly after I discovered what the model really was, I and my whole team were laid off. At the time, I wondered if it was because someone noticed my hack. But then I realized if that were true, they would have come after me; imprisoned or killed me. It was too big a conspiracy for them not to. My director said Red Fig didn't need us working on the algorithms anymore. It seemed strange, to be honest, because we'd been continuing to use them to boost Avci's image and popularity. It was almost as if the company decided none of it was necessary anymore, that his popularity was skyrocketing, and his success was on autopilot at that point. So, yes, I have the model in a safe place. Once me and my family are safe in the U.S., I will give…"

Dolan was listening intently—what he appeared to be offering was nothing short of earth-shattering. He couldn't believe that Demir's handler had decided to turn down this kind of information…but incredibly, such is politics. Then, as Demir was about to finish speaking, he slumped forward, face down in his lap. Andino put his hand on the back of Demir's head, then look side to side, frantically.

"Andy, what the fuck just happened?"

Andino stood up and began to walk brusquely away. "Someone just took him out. I didn't hear the shot. Must have been suppressed. We were being watched."

Dolan started the car. Tires screeching, he accelerated towards Andino, who was about eighty meters away. He held the steering wheel with his left hand and his weapon with his right. "I'm coming to you."

Andino launched into a sprint towards the speeding car. Dolan hit the brakes as he got close, only to watch Andino's head snap back suddenly, eyes wide and mouth agape. He fell forward to the ground and tumbled into a heap. Dolan stopped just beside him, opened the door, and quickly surveyed the park, his weapon trained as he swept left and right. Seeing no on, he lifted Andino in. He'd been shot once in the back. Tires screeching again, he gripped the steering wheel with two bloodied hands and sped towards the exit. He heard and felt the *pop pop pop* as three rounds hit the car, one ricocheting off the bulletproof rear window. His heart was racing. As he drove, he watched the mirrors and searched for movement, any clue as to who it could be. Nothing.

As he turned down the side street, he glanced back at Andino, yelling desperately. "Stay with me, Andy!"

He was laying across back seat, gurgling and spitting up blood. After one last sputtering breath, his eyes rolled back in his head and he went limp.

CHAPTER FOURTEEN

"Thomas," Bolden prodded. "I don't see how we're going to get what we need without going in. We need physical access."

"Patience, grasshopper," Freeman whispered as he typed furiously on his keyboard. They were looking at the same screen, Bolden from Berlin, and Freeman in Clarendon.

Bolden sighed, not understanding what was scrolling in front of him. *This isn't what I thought it would be,* he lamented to himself.

"Thomas, can you at least tell me what you are doing? I can't make sense of this."

"Yeah, just a minute…" He tapped a few more times. "And, execute!" Freeman said with a flourish. "OK, I've just uploaded a self-deleting worm into the Red Fig server. It will replicate itself on the other servers in Turkey and search for disparities in the blockchain code of each. Basically, I'm trying to determine whether it is a true distributed ledger, or if it is just made to look like one."

"And this will help us, how?" asked Bolden.

"Well, the code should be identical on each server. If it's not, the worm will tell us what the difference is. And if it is different, we know that the Hypotherion exchange is up to something. It'll also do a few other things that might be helpful. We'll have to wait."

"How long?"

"Well, that depends. The worm is designed to attach itself to an outgoing server update, or to an automated response to an incoming one. Though the Berlin server is not actually part of the ledger, as I said before there is work done on it that pushes to the ledger. My guess is that it will happen quickly due to the constant activity on the crypto blockchain. Miners are in there twenty-four seven. It's a super-dynamic and ever-growing software ecosystem, of sorts. Lots of updates." Freeman smiled with pride at his flowery description.

"Won't there be some kind of antivirus on the servers that constantly looks for things like this worm?"

"Yes of course. But I know what they are using, and the worm disguises itself as a...well, let's just say the antivirus, penetration detection, and other defenses can't see it because it's designed to look like something that is supposed to be there anyway."

"Aha," replied Bolden. "Thanks for dumbing it down for me."

"My pleasure."

"So, what's next? Do you need me for anything else?"

Freeman paused to think. "Not really. When I'm done, I'll need you to shut down the DNS recursor there at the embassy. We'll need to turn it back on, probably tomorrow, to go back in and see if any data gets returned from the worm."

"OK, well what's left to do then?"

"I've got one more thing I want to try. The backdoor. I told you guys before, I don't know where it is, and I'm afraid to search for it because that's something that might get us noticed. But sometimes things like this are much easier to find than you think." He was tapping like a madman again, the keyclicks sounding like a barrage of gunfire.

"Nope," Freeman said matter-of-factly. More typing. "What, holy shit!"

Bolden leaned forward, trying to deduce from the screen what Freeman was excited about. "What? What is it?"

"I'm in, holy shit holy shit. It's not on the Berlin server, it's on another one. I was able to connect to it. Am I good or what? I can't believe…and look, the worm is already returning data. Holy shit!"

"OK, slow down Thomas, great work. Let's makes sure we…"

"Wait," Thomas interrupted. "We must get out. NOW! Shut the system down Stan. They can see us. There must have been a tripwire at the backdoor, something I missed. Shut it down!"

"OK, OK! I'm shutting it down." Bolden used his mouse to toggle the DNS Recursor to 'OFF' and slumped back in his chair. "What do you mean when you say that they could see us?"

All the excitement was gone from Freeman's voice. "It means that somewhere, maybe in Turkey, maybe here in Berlin, maybe both, there are alarm bells going off. They will see that someone hacked into their network and accessed the backdoor. They won't know who or where we are, but they'll react to it, they'll install safeguards. It is highly likely that we won't be able to get back in. I commanded the worm to erase itself before we backed out. Whatever data we got, that's all we're going to get."

Bolden was nodding in thought. "Good. They don't know who we are or where we are, and we got some data that could be useful. Sounds like a win. Let me know what the data tells you. I'm going to go brief Mike."

"Sure thing, thanks Stan. But hell, I was in! So close…"

"Don't worry about it, Thomas. It's a win."

"I suppose. I'm going to look at the data we got. At first glance, there's not much there but a couple things…"

"What?" Bolden pressed.

"Well, I didn't have time to download any of it, but there was a database behind the backdoor. It looked like a huge repository of PI. Personal information. Could be nothing more than a backup of coin and carbon credit owner data, but it looked like more than that. It was huge. Could be Hypotherion investor details I suppose. Also, the exchange states publicly that there are six servers in the distributed ledger. It looks like there might be more than that."

CHAPTER FIFTEEN

Dolan waited impatiently as the secure VTC booted. He sat alone in the wood paneled Top Secret SCIF at U.S. Embassy, Ankara. After a few seconds, Dittrich appeared on the screen. "Sir, I…"

"What the actual fuck, Michael?" The Deputy Director didn't explode as Dolan thought he would. He said it softly. This was a Dittrich he hadn't seen before; he was gravely disappointed. Disappointed in him.

Dolan was in pain. Had he become careless? Did he go too far? Andy was dead, and it was his fault. "We watched Demir for two days. We never noticed anyone observing him, no counterintel. Whoever it was, they must have seen Andy with him at the first meet. They must've heard the conversation—it was a sniper shot, a high-powered rifle. They were set up and waiting for the meet. We never saw the shooter, and believe me, I was looking. There was no one else in the park, as far as I could see."

"Damn it." Dittrich shook his head slowly in disgust. "We agreed, Michael. You would take every precaution. Kid gloves. This was a fact-finding mission…"

"I know. I agree, we moved too fast. We should have watched him a few more days before approaching him. The second meet should have been in a wide-open area. I made some bad choices, and I take responsibility. I…"

Dittrich cut him off again. "Enough. Pack everyone up and come back. You can finish your reporting here, just bring the whole team to Langley for debriefing. I've already sent an Agency aircraft your way, should get there in a few hours. Bring Andy's body with you, and don't do anything else. The entire operation is shut down, as of right now. We need to determine what the fallout from this might be."

He could feel his blood pressure rise; his temples were throbbing. "Sir, the whole team?"

Dittrich paused in thought. "Not Fitzy. And Mike and Stan can stay in Berlin. If I need something from them, I can call them. But you, Welker, and Haddad, you need to come home."

"Sir, before we pull the plug, there's a lot you don't know yet. Obviously, there is something going on here, what happened to Andy and Demir is just part of it. Based on what we've found, I think Yusuf Solak, Adem Avci's Minister of Industry and Technology, was working with Russia in Niamey. Whatever they were working on was sensitive enough that they would murder someone to keep it hidden. They were using a local kid at the Red Fig site to run errands each day, and we think they poisoned him as they packed out. Eliminating loose ends. We were able to talk to him before he died."

Dittrich couldn't believe what he was hearing. "You mean to tell me that we already have *three* casualties associated with this op?"

"The kid would have died whether we were there or not. We were lucky to get what we could from him before he passed. He verified there were five Russians working at the site. We found some documents there with notations in Russian as well. Anyway, there is a lot we still don't know, but I can say with some confidence it's *possible* it was Solak who set Lefebvre up in Niger. I think he might have been hiding him, but then gave him up when things got too hot. We know Lefebvre had dealings with Solak in the past when he was running Blue Olive. One of Blue Olive's main exports in Niger was Sorghum…"

As Dolan spoke, Dittrich's visage morphed slowly from disappointment to incredulity.

"The plantation. When we were planning the raid, if I remember correctly, the documented landowner had been dead several years, and before that it was state-owned. Can we trace it back to Solak somehow?"

"We're looking into it. I do believe Sorghum from that plantation might have been exported via the Blue Olive Niamey warehouse."

"Really?"

"Yeah," Dolan acknowledged.

"OK." Dittrich interlocked his fingers on the desk in front of him. "Let's do this—finish your reporting on everything that's happened to-date. Send them directly to me. Put Andy on the bird I'm sending and arrange for one of the Marines there to escort him back. I'll notify Athens Station. Sit tight for now; don't do anything else until I get back with you. Is there any chance that whoever killed Andy also identified you?

"Hard to tell. Only Andy made contact, I was sitting back both times, watching for counterintel. It depends on whether they simply noticed Andy at the first meeting, or if they saw us following him in the car. Whoever it was, they took shots at me when I went in to grab Andy. In that situation, though, they wouldn't have gotten a good look. It all happened very fast, and they must have been some distance away—I never saw them."

"They saw your vehicle," Dittrich stated.

"Yes. I've already turned it back in. They'll repaint it and change the plates. It's not traceable to me or the Agency. Not an issue."

"Any trouble from the Station? They must have questioned you."

Dolan nodded. "The Station Chief grilled me. It didn't last long, I just kept telling him to contact you. I'm surprised he hasn't already called."

"Understood. I'll calm him down. Mitch is one of the good guys," responded Dittrich.

"Thanks. Depending on how things pan out, I may need their help again at some point."

"Don't get the cart ahead of the horse Michael. I said sit tight for now. I need to review everything and assess. I don't know where we are going from here yet."

"Yes sir," acknowledged Dolan.

"Right. Now, what are Howard and Omar doing? Are they still in Niamey?"

"They're on their way here, should be landing soon. I didn't want them in any hot water, if someone was able to tie them to the kid."

"OK, good. That's it for now, hunker down and wait for my call."

"Yes sir."

The screen went black. Dolan eased back in his chair and gathered his thoughts. He had to be far more careful. Andy had a wife and three children… And this mission felt much bigger than a threat to national security. There were global implications. Through Solak, Red Fig, and Hypotherion, Avci was leveraging power that Turkey had never had, historically. The more he thought about it, the more convinced he was that the Avci regime had the entire world hoodwinked. There was an evil atmosphere surrounding the whole thing, and there was no separating Avci from Solak. The President of Turkey was involved.

CHAPTER SIXTEEN

"Mr. President, can I speak to you for a moment?"

Avci glanced at Solak, then shook hands with the three men in front of him, each thanking him profusely and wishing him well. He turned to Solak. "Yusuf, it's a bad time, I'm about to speak."

They stood facing each other in the dark, just offstage. The Master of Ceremonies was introducing Avci.

"It must be now, Mr. President. They will wait for you." Solak pointed to the crowd, which was applauding loudly.

Avci was irritated. "Quickly then. What is it?"

One of my former employees has been murdered, here in Ankara. The MIT had him under surveillance, they think he might have been trying to sell state secrets, social media algorithms we used for your campaign."

Grabbing the edge of the curtain, Avci's countenance didn't change. "We can talk about this after I speak. Why the urgency? And why am I hearing this from you, instead of the National Intelligence Organization Director?"

"You're hearing it from me because Industry and Technology controls a branch within the MIT. I'd be the first to know of threats regarding such things—you approved the measure shortly after my appointment. Regardless—I need your approval again, to launch an investigation into those who perpetrated the act—operatives from within the U.S. Embassy. I don't have enough agents to do it. We believe the CIA is behind this, and time is of the essence. We cannot let these criminals escape the country."

Avci cocked his head questioningly. "The United States? Are you sure? We just gave them Lefebvre. There is no way they'd authorize such an operation on Turkish soil. They owe us, they owe me, in an extraordinary way. You must be mistaken."

"I am sure. We have video and audio evidence. Added to that, there was an attempted hack on our server in Berlin yesterday. It was noticed right away. As far as we can tell, they were caught before they could do anything or steal any data. We are still looking at it. We've upgraded the system and it shouldn't happen again, but the timing of it... It's the first time we've been hacked, and there's no way to tell who it was. What we do know is, it was very sophisticated. Adem, please just say the word so I can put this in motion now. I'll tell you everything I know when you are done here."

With a worried look, Avci conceded. Just as quickly, a broad smile came across his face as he turned and strode confidently toward center stage, waiving at the people. The noise from the crowd was deafening. Solak watched him take the podium, then walked to the backstage exit, already on the phone with his operations team embedded within the MIT.

♦

An embassy car brought Welker and Haddad straight to the safehouse. As soon as they arrived, Dolan initiated a conference call with Fitzhenry, Collier, and Freeman. When all were ready, he kicked off the meeting.

Welker and Haddad looked around the room curiously, noting Andino's absence.

"First things first. Andy and I met with the source you identified, Howard. Turns out he had some valuable intelligence to offer. He said that Avci's wife was murdered to generate sympathy among the Turkish people, to turn the election in Avci's favor. Our efforts were cut short, however. Demir was shot, and Andy was too. Neither of them made it. Andy's gone."

Silence on the phone. Welker's and Haddad's faces drained instantly. They exchanged nervous glances, then looked back to Dolan.

"Turns out Demir was being observed, unsure who it was. We tailed Demir for two days and never noticed him being surveilled. I spoke with Dittrich already, he sent a plane for Andy's body."

"My God, oh my God..." Fitzhenry came through the speaker. Welker hung his head. No one else spoke.

"Our orders are to finish our reports. I'll send them to Dittrich, and he'll let us know what to do. I think there is a good chance he's leaning towards canceling the mission. It all depends on our reporting. I think we can all agree at this point that we've begun to uncover something sinister here, and what you write needs to reflect that, in no uncertain terms. Don't leave anything out. The smallest, most insignificant detail could be the one thing that breaks this wide open—I can't say that enough, as you know. Before I send them to Dittrich, I want everyone to share their reports among the team. Read everything. Then review your own reports again and refine them before you give them to me. If I have anything to say about it, we are not leaving until we've finished here, and that includes finding and dealing with whoever killed Andy. You have until midnight tonight. Any questions?"

Still, no one spoke. Each of them understood the risks involved, but it was still a rare thing to have a colleague cut down in the field. Spies who were caught were almost always interrogated and returned to the U.S. *persona non-grata*. That's if they had diplomatic immunity. Less often, and if they were not approved diplomats, they'd be imprisoned. Sometimes, they'd be used later in quietly negotiated prisoner swaps. Very rarely were they executed; they were far too valuable. It could be that whoever killed Andino and Demir was not Turkish intelligence, a person or group not beholden to the traditional ways of doing these things. But that was unlikely.

Dolan went to a cabinet against the wall and returned with a bottle and four glasses. He poured a finger of whiskey in each, then motioned to Welker and Haddad to take one. "Fitzy, Mike, Thomas, please join us in a toast." He waited until they acknowledged they were ready. The three in the room raised their glasses toward the fourth, left resting in the middle of the coffee table.

"To Andy," Dolan said.

"To Andy," proclaimed the rest. After drinking, Dolan, Welker, and Haddad set their empty glasses next to Andy's. A moment of silence followed.

"OK team, let's get to work," Dolan ordered.

◆

"Fitzy, what's up?" Dolan asked.

"Well, to begin with, I want to offer my condolences. I know what it's like to lose someone in the field. To wonder if it was my fault. It's a difficult thing to shoulder. What's important is that you learn from the experience and honor his sacrifice. It seems to me that you did the best you could, under the circumstances."

"Thank you," Dolan responded. "I keep running through those two days in my head, trying to identify what we did wrong, to see what I might have missed. I can't nail it down. I don't know."

"You'll probably never know. Maybe you didn't do anything wrong. Sometimes it's just the way the ball bounces. Don't let it distract you, there is still work to be done. After reading everything, I do believe this is something we have to run to ground. In fact, I think you and I need to have a conversation."

"Sure, OK. What do you want to talk about?"

"No, not like this. In person. There are some ideas I want to share with you, and I certainly could tell you over a secure line, but I don't want to. I believe this is the kind of conversation that requires us to see each other, physically. There is so much that is lost over the phone or a VTC, you know? Body language, eye contact, all that. I guess you could also say that I need to control the environment, to control you in a way. There are aspects of this operation…Avci, Solak, Hypotherion… They're drawing way outside the lines. The whole thing is not even close to normal. You know, what we've been trained for. There could be things, important things, that we are not seeing because they're not part of our playbook. I'll need your undivided attention. It needs to be in person, and I think it should be sooner rather than later."

It was a curious request. What could it be that it couldn't be said on a phone call? Was he worried that someone might overhear on Dolan's end? "Fitzy, you know you have my respect and admiration. There isn't anyone on the team who thinks otherwise. But you should also know, right now isn't the best time to be pulling chocks. Dittrich told us to sit tight…"

"I think it's a perfect time, actually," Fitzhenry countered. "You're not going to be doing anything for the next day, maybe three. Who knows how long it'll take Stan to figure out what he wants to do.

You might as well use that time to hear me out. Have the station fly you up here. We can have our talk, and you'll be back in Ankara the same day. And don't worry about Dittrich. If he says anything, I'll talk to him."

"I don't know. It doesn't feel right. Why can't it wait?"

"You're going to have to trust me, Michael. Just come up here."

CHAPTER SEVENTEEN

The entire flight, Dolan's mind switched back and forth between the loss of Andino and Anne. He felt guilty even thinking about her. How could he when one of his team had just been gunned down, and on his watch? When he arrived at the Embassy in Paris, he'd be just a few kilometers from her. If she's in town. He didn't know; he hadn't spoken to her in weeks. Should he contact her? Would it be unethical? Immoral? Dittrich wouldn't approve, but Dolan also knew Dittrich wouldn't give him too much trouble over it as long it didn't delay his return.

As the plane touched down, he had still not decided. He would hear what Fitzhenry had to say, then think about what to do. Even if he saw her, it would have to be quick. For now, he partitioned the thought away and prepared himself mentally for his meeting. A vehicle met him at the aircraft. Forty-five minutes later he was going through embassy security.

Fitzhenry greeted him with a handshake. "Welcome to Paris, Michael."

"Thanks Fitzy, I wish it were under better circumstances."

"I know. Such a terrible thing. I'm truly sorry. How are the rest taking it?"

"In stride. Clara and the kids are flying back from Athens today. No details on the service yet. I talked to her, after Dittrich. God, that was difficult…"

They remained solemnly silent in the elevator, then walked the hall to the CIA's suite door. After locking away their cell phones in small cubbies, Fitzhenry swiped his badge, entered his code, and led Dolan to his corner office. He closed the door behind them.

"Make yourself comfortable. Can I offer you anything?" he asked Dolan.

"Maybe some water?"

"Sure. You see the minifridge there in the corner?" Fitzhenry asked. "Grab me one as well."

Dolan took two bottles from the fridge and handed one to Fitzhenry. They sat opposite each other on two identical, modest leather couches, a low wooden coffee table between them.

"Thanks," Fitzhenry said as he unscrewed the cap and took a swig.

Dolan got right to the point. "Now, what is so important that I had to get on a plane and fly all the way up here?"

Fitzhenry laughed, a slight grin on his face. "Yep, I reckon you are one part curious, one part peeved. And I'll be honest with you, this is going to go one of two ways. You're either going to leave here much less curious and even more pissed off than when you came in, or you'll decide that what I have to say has some level of merit. Regardless of the outcome, I felt it was important that I give you the opportunity to decide for yourself."

"OK…" Dolan responded hesitantly.

"Are you religious, Michael?" Fitzhenry asked pointedly.

Dolan regarded him questioningly. "I wouldn't say so. I'm Catholic, but not overly devout. I consider myself spiritual. Why?"

"Have you read much of the Bible?"

"Fitzy, what does this have to do…"

"Look," he cut Dolan off. "There is a pattern of events here, things that have happened before and along the timeline of this operation. From your perspective, from Dittrich's, it feels like something nefarious is going on. Something that could be harmful to the security of the United States. I sense that as well. But this pattern, the data points fit too comfortably…" He looked up at the ceiling, searching for the right words. "It's like Avci, Solak, and those around them are using an old playbook. Someone else's playbook."

"I have no idea what you mean, Fitzy. What playbook?"

Fitzhenry stood up and walked to his desk, picked something up and brought it over. He placed it on the coffee table in front of Dolan.

"The Bible? You think they are what, Christian sympathizers or something? Avci is a softcore Islamic fundamentalist."

"No," Fitzhenry shook his head. "The Bible is a book, but there are many books within it. I am talking about the very last book in the Bible. The book of *Revelation*."

Dolan's jaw dropped; for a moment he didn't know how to respond. He had great respect for Fitzhenry, he was a giant among men at the Agency. But this… "I'm going to assume there is a lot more to this, so I'll withhold judgement for now. But come on, Fitzy…"

Fitzhenry rolled his eyes and Dolan chuckled at his unintentional pun.

"Yes, there is more, of course. And don't get me wrong, I'm not saying that what is going on in Turkey has been foretold, or anything like that. But there are similarities between what is unfolding there and what is in the book. That's it. So, let's start with the name of the crypto they're using to back their bank, with all the altruism and carbon credits and such. Hypotherion." He opened the Bible to near the end, thumbed through a few pages, then turned it 180 degrees with his index finger just above a particular passage, Revelation 13:2.

And the beast which I saw was like unto a leopard, and his feet were as the feet of a bear, and his mouth as the mouth of a lion: and the dragon gave him his power, and his seat, and great authority.

He continued as Dolan read. "This is the King James version. In its original Greek, the third word of that passage, *beast*, is *therion*. The word therion appears thirty-eight times in the Bible, thirty of those are in Revelation. There are two beasts in Revelation, the first and the second. The first beast is said to 'come out of the sea' and is bestowed great authority and power by 'the dragon.' The second beast, who is a false prophet, comes 'out of the earth' and his purpose is to instruct the people of the world to worship the first beast. Both are aligned with 'the dragon,' in opposition to God, and they persecute 'the saints' and those who will not worship the first beast. Together, they influence nations across the Earth to prepare for and begin the battle of Armageddon."

He paused there to give Dolan a chance to complain about the conspiratorial inutility of what Fitzhenry was telling him. But he said nothing, listening and waiting for Fitzhenry to finish.

"So…we have a dragon, which you might call the devil. We have a first beast, who comes from the sea and who some might call the antichrist, and then we have a second beast, who is basically the antichrist's righthand man. This is where I ask you to humor me and wait until I'm done. I'm not saying Avci and Solak are these beasts, or that Avci is the Antichrist. That's not my point. It is worth noting, however, that Avci spent time in the Turkish Navy. At sea.

"The prefix 'hypo' has a few meanings, the most common of which is 'beneath' or 'under.' It can also mean to increase, or augment, or to stimulate. Taken the second way, Hypotherion means *to enable the beast*. So far, none of this has theoretical value. I get that. But there is more. And this is what got me thinking about Revelation in the first place. Thomas told us the Hypotherion ledger is distributed on servers located in Izmir, Bergama, Akhisar, Salihli, one near Alaşehir, and in Denizli."

"You're forgetting Berlin," Dolan interrupted.

"No, I am not," Fitzhenry replied. "I've read Thomas' reports. There is work done on the Berlin server for the exchange, and the original coding was done there, but no part of the ledger is in Berlin. If it were, Thomas would have been able to get us far more information than he did. The ledger is, in its entirety, within Turkey. But here's the interesting part. Each of those cities in Turkey are mentioned in the book of Revelation. They are the locations of the seven churches that the prophet John sends letters to, right at the beginning of the book. The city names have changed, but it's them."

"So, if I may poke a hole in this, that's only six cities. Again, unless you're including Berlin," Dolan quipped.

"I'm not including Berlin. As I said, the ledger doesn't reside on that server. There is a church mentioned in Revelation, Ephesus, the ruins of which are just to the south of Izmir, near Selçuk. During Thomas' last hack, he identified what he thinks is a seventh server there, one that is not advertised as being part of the distributed ledger."

Dolan nodded thoughtfully. "Yes, yes, I remember from his latest report."

"Yes. When I read that, that's when I decided to talk to you about all this. It sounds crazy, I know. Like a jigsaw puzzle when you first dump it on the table. But I found all the edge pieces, and I'm connecting them. A picture has started to form. Listen, the probability that Solak coincidentally chose to put seven servers in those specific cities is near zero."

"But not zero." Dolan hung his head. Coming here had been a waste of time. It certainly wasn't worth risking Dittrich's wrath. He'd probably found out by now that Dolan made the trip.

"Michael," Fitzhenry cautioned, "I don't think you understand me. Look, there are a few possibilities here. One, Solak and Avci have used parts of the book of Revelation to plan for and map out his rise to power. Maybe one or both think Avci is the second coming of Muhammad—believe me when I say that there is a growing number of people in the Middle East and elsewhere who believe that; I'm not kidding. Antithetically, there is another large and growing demographic that believes Avci is the antichrist, and they point to things like the fact he was born in and grew up in Bergama. According to the book of Revelation, Bergama is the very place where Satan's throne is to be erected. The book also hints that the antichrist will be born in lands that now reside within present-day Turkey. So, perhaps one or both of them think *that* might be true. That Avci really is the antichrist. It's the most unlikely scenario, but let's be honest, crazier things have happened throughout history. The third possibility is that it's part of a big ploy; they are trying to harness the power of mysticism. They *want* the world to wonder if one or the other possibility is true, knowing full well themselves that both are not, but also knowing that if enough people believe, their power can only grow. Then of course there is the last possibility, that it is all just coincidence. Though again, the probability of that is minute.

"There are other things, and I'm not going to bore you with all of them, but two of them are worth mentioning. In the book, the first and second beast work together to bring about Armageddon. War, death, famine, plague, earthquakes, etcetera. What do you think they were working on in Niger? Whatever it was, it's not good. I think we both know that. Three people have been murdered so far over it."

"You can't tie Demir and Andy to Niger," Dolan argued. "They were killed because Demir was being watched. They suspected he would try to sell sensitive information."

"Perhaps," Fitzhenry replied. "But I really do think it's all connected. The second thing—Revelation tells of the mark of the beast. That without it, people won't be able to work or buy things. This is the whole purpose of Hypotherion—to get disadvantaged countries back up on their feet with huge, low-interest loans after experiencing financial and natural cataclysms."

"Thanks Fitzy," Dolan offered politely, "but I'm not sure any of this is going to help. I know you are a religious man, and I respect that. And yes, there do seem to be quite a few coincidences here that make it easier to wonder if what you're saying might be true. But let's be honest, they are Islamic. They have the Quran. If there were a religious playbook they wanted to use, it wouldn't be the book of Revelation."

"Perhaps, perhaps not. Islam respects all prophets, Jewish and Christian alike. The three religions are much closer than you think. And Solak has western leanings. He is not considered to be a hardline Muslim."

"I believe you." Dolan stood up abruptly. "But I must head back to Ankara. I don't want to be here or enroute if and when Dittrich decides to put us back in play."

Fitzhenry stood up as well. "I understand. Just think about all of this with an open mind. Have a safe journey."

"Thanks Fitzy." Dolan turned to leave, then stopped. "Fitzy, I still don't understand why we couldn't have done this over the phone."

Fitzhenry nodded. "I've had a good career, Michael. I'm also true to my faith. I was able to reconcile both without much internal conflict because I made certain rules for myself. So the lines would never be blurred." He took a step forward, placing his hand on Dolan's shoulder.

It was a not a patronizing gesture, but a paternal one. "In this case, it's different. It's unlike anything I've ever been involved in. It's not too much of a problem, mind you, because I'm kind of on the sidelines here in Paris. I am part of the team, however, and I do bring things to the table. But with this…it's difficult for me to see some of the lines. As much as officers and leadership within the Agency say they like and respect me, there are those in powerful positions who would jump at the chance to kick me to the curb. I don't want to giftwrap that reason for them. But also…"

He walked back to the couch and sat again. To Dolan, he seemed tired. "I couldn't talk to anyone else about any of this. I couldn't chance having anyone overhear. And I knew this would sound fantastical, even to you. I might be the only person in the Agency who would give any credence to it at all. I'm probably the only one who'd have seen it. Connected the dots. It's not a theory, I can't say that enough. It's…an unlikely number of correlative events and facts, is what it is. Michael, you are very intelligent, logical, and fair. All I ask is that you to keep this in the back of your mind. If any of what I've shared with you begins to look less like coincidence and more like coherence, do the math and reevaluate. Over time, you may begin to think there's something there."

Fitzhenry leaned back and took another drink from his water bottle. He looked satisfied, as if he was happy with how he was answering Dolan's question. "You can't hang up on me here in my office. I knew the chance you'd take any of this seriously would be diminished greatly if we discussed it over the phone. It's just too easy to dismiss. The psychological effect of being able to hang up on something you disagree with, something you deem nonsensical, is too strong. If any of it turns out to be true in some way, I want us to have considered all the angles." He placed his hand on the old leather-bound Bible. "Because if any of it *is* true, well, we have their playbook."

CHAPTER EIGHTEEN

The Luxor Obelisk caught his eye as they moved along the eastern flank of Place de la Concorde. Over 3,000 years old, the twenty-three-meter monolith was moved to Paris in the 1830s and was one of two nearly identical artifacts originally erected on either side of the portal to the Luxor Temple in Egypt. Its slightly taller twin remained there. This one was out of place. There was nothing Parisian or French about it. Spoils of conquest. The pair belonged together, in Egypt.

"To the airport, sir?" asked the driver.

Dolan didn't answer right away. Anne was unaware he was in Paris. It could stay that way. He didn't have much time. In any case, she may not even be able to see him. He glanced back again at the obelisk.

"Not yet. I have another stop to make." He gave the driver her work address.

He felt it coming, the end. A swirl of emotions engulfed him. This close, her pull was simply too strong. It easily overcame a hesitant sense of shame, that to see her would be self-centered. A short-term gratification that might somehow lessen the eventual impact of a great loss—the end of their long-term and somewhat dysfunctional, though powerfully deep relationship. Perhaps his subconscious was nudging him to use this opportunity to end it, here and now.

It was a straight, fifteen-minute shot in traffic along the Seine River to City Hall. The grand Hôtel de Ville had been the headquarters for the municipality of Paris since 1357, and for the mayor's office since 1977.

"Just stay at the curb, I won't be long," Dolan told him as he got out of the vehicle.

The last time he visited her here, he had just decided to embark on a very dangerous, unsanctioned mission. One that would lead to him being severely wounded. Along the way, he killed people. Bad people, terrorists. But he killed them, nonetheless. Up close and personal. The entire experience fundamentally changed him. Some of those changes were good… Ultimately, he came to understand himself better and by consequence, found a serenity he never knew was possible. Anne had been a big part of it. She was the catalyst. Maybe more than that; she was the *reason*.

He gave his name to the receptionist and was told she was there and to have a seat while they called her. He surprised himself with how good his French sounded. It rolled off his tongue as if he'd never left Paris. As if he decided back then to just stay here with Anne, for good. To forego Berlin and all that might have followed. A few minutes later, the door behind the receptionist opened halfway and Anne popped her head out at an angle, smiling broadly, her long auburn hair covering part of her face. She stuck out a hand, motioning with her finger for him to come. He got up abruptly and went to the door, opened it fully and followed her into the hallway. The door closed on its own and she launched herself at him, engulfing Dolan in a hug. She was crying.

"Listen, you," she whispered, in-between sobs.

They held each other. People walked by, regarding them curiously, but they ignored the interruption. Or they didn't notice. Eventually Dolan pulled away so he could look at her.

"Hello, beautiful."

Anne wiped the tears from her face. "I think this is the part where I say, *why are you here, mon canard, is everything alright?*"

They laughed, both remembering every detail, every moment of the last time they'd spoken in that very spot in the hallway.

"Everything is fine, Anne. I had a meeting at the embassy. It was last-minute. I didn't want to tell you ahead of time, in case I had no time to see you. As it is, I only have a few minutes."

She shot him a feigned look of disapproval. "Pas assez bon!"

Anne was right, a few minutes wasn't good enough. Maybe he shouldn't have come? "I know. But it's all I have. How have you been?"

"Like this, like that, you know. It's OK. What about you? We haven't spoken for so long...I know you needed space, so I gave it to you. Yet, here you are, *à partir de rien*. You just show up out of thin air." She folded her arms across her chest and cocked her head questioningly. "What I don't know is, is this a good thing, or not? You know, it would be better if I knew what is going on with us." She unfolded her arms, took his hand, and begged him with her eyes for an answer.

"I am so sorry Anne. I've been very busy, but that's not an excuse. I know I've been...difficult."

"Oui," she responded flatly.

"I...We need to talk. Not now, there just isn't enough time. But soon. Listen, I've been travelling a lot and it's going to be like that for the next couple weeks. But afterwards, I'll be there for you. For us. We can talk then, about the future." He took her other hand in his.

"Hmm. That is so Michael Dolan—to wait for the future, to talk about the future. It hurts, you know. But I forgive you..." She was sad, but hopeful.

"I won't hurt you again, I promise."

As soon as he said it, he regretted it. It could end up being nothing but a terrible lie. His mind was racing. He didn't know what else to say.

"I love you." Nothing was truer than that.

She looked into his eyes and beamed. *"You are everything to me."*

He smiled back, remembering those words from their last meeting here. Only it was he who had said it to her back then. At the time, it was the best that he could do; he wasn't sure he truly understood what love was. It was Anne's love for him that had broken that barrier down. He understood it now. And she was the *reason* he understood. He knew as well that if he didn't demonstrate that to her very soon, he would lose her forever.

CHAPTER NINETEEN

"I knew you were going," Dittrich said bluntly. "Fitzy gave me a heads-up. I would have expected to hear about it from you, however. Things are dynamic right now. I'm getting pressure from the Director. This little jaunt of ours has landed us in hot water."

Dolan stifled a sigh of relief. "I'm doing what I think is best for the team and the mission, sir. And with respect, you've always given me the latitude I need to do what I believe is necessary. If you want me to check in with you every time, that's only going to slow things down." He held his breath and waited.

"I get it," Dittrich replied, "and yes, you have latitude, but I made it clear that this mission was to be handled in a different way due to the sensitivities involved. Just keep me in the loop, OK?"

"Yes sir. Understood."

"Good. Where are you now?"

"Just taxiing in at the airport. I'll be back at the safehouse with Howard and Omar in an hour and a half."

"OK. So, what was your meeting with Fitzy about?" Dittrich asked "He was elusive about it on the phone."

"Yeah. He asked me to go up there, said it was sensitive. Wouldn't talk to me about it on the phone either. I was skeptical about flying all the way up there without knowing what it was for, but in retrospect, I understand." Dolan paused, making sure he could tell Dittrich what he *should* tell him without betraying Fitzhenry's trust. "He has ideas about the possible motivations behind what we've uncovered here, and in Niger. I would categorize it as a somewhat radical...no, progressive? theory. Let's just say, it's not ready for mainstream consumption. And given that we were under surveillance in Ankara without knowing, and that it led to the death of one of our team, he wanted to make sure it was very close hold."

"Right. Well, that's not much of an answer, but I'll trust your instincts. I've read all the reports. When I first told you to investigate this, I had a gut feeling something was off. Now it's more than that, there's something happening there. What I don't know right now, though, is if I want to keep REVENANT on it. You guys are too tactical for this, I think. This looks and feels like a long-game play. Maybe we should give it to Ankara Station."

Dittrich was testing him, Dolan could sense it. He wanted to know if he agreed with him. "You could be right. It's hard to tell right now, we just don't have enough information. But that's the key, right? Who is going to collect? If we hadn't gotten involved, right now Andy would still be alive, but we'd have nothing. I think our best course of action is to dig a little deeper and see if we can connect the dots. If it's bigger than what REVENANT can handle, we can give it to Ankara. At least by then we'll be handing off something actionable. Right now, all we have is a lot of unanswered questions."

"If I let you stay, you have to promise me something," Dittrich responded.

"What is it?"

"You don't do this for Andy. I've already got someone on that, to find out who killed him and Demir. If they find anything, I'll pass it on. You stay out of that, OK?"

Dolan exhaled cautiously. He wasn't going to lie to himself—doing exactly that was part of the reason he wanted REVENANT to stay on the mission. "I can promise you that revenge won't be part of the equation. But if we happen upon an opportunity to take care of that loose end, I'm not going to pass it up."

Dittrich remained silent for a moment, assessing Dolan's response. "Shit, Dolan. I'm getting a lot of half answers from people today and I've had just about enough. Moving forward, I need you to be completely transparent. This is a particularly difficult situation, I get that. You know you won't be able to request backup, right? And forget about tasking satellites. If the National Reconnaissance Office got wind of this... You're going to have to do everything old-school. That should make Welker happy. Another thing. If you're going to be there for a while, it would make sense to have a cover. Do you think you could set something up with a university there, maybe give a briefing on the Miltner-Dolan Model or something?"

Dolan was sure he heard a hint of sarcasm. "I don't know, let me think about it. Those things are usually arranged well in advance. I'll get back with you on it."

"Sure. Until then, exercise extreme caution. You have no explainable reason for being there right now. This has international incident written all over it. Stay on it, but keep me better informed."

"Yes sir."

Dittrich ended the call.

REVENANT had been given new life, a second chance at figuring out who killed Andino, how the Turkish government was able to locate Lefebvre in Niger, and who it was that located him. Dolan was close to convinced that the 'who' was Solak, but the reason for it was eluding him. Whatever the reason was, he knew Demir's and Andy's assassinations were indelibly linked to it somehow.

The captain was standing in the cockpit doorway, smiling. "End of the line," he said. "Need help with anything?"

Dolan unbuckled his seatbelt and grabbed his briefcase from the seat in front of him. "No, thank you. I appreciate the ride."

"No problem, have a good one," he responded, then turned back into the cockpit to button things up with his copilot.

A slick black BMW was waiting for him as he exited. The driver got out and greeted Dolan with a nod.

He stopped short of the BMW. "Hi, you from the embassy?" Dolan asked.

"Yes. Good flight?" the driver replied, opening the rear passenger side door.

"I think I'm going to find my own way back," Dolan told him.

He looked confused, then marginally irritated as he closed the door. "Are you sure?"

"Yes. I apologize for you coming all the way out here. It's a last-minute thing. Hey, since you're here, do you mind asking the pilots if they need a ride?"

He hesitated. "We're not supposed to…"

"I know, but since you don't have to drive me anywhere, you might as well. I would appreciate it greatly."

Still reluctant, the driver gave in. "OK, sure. I'll have to call it in though."

"Thanks a lot," Dolan responded.

The embassy car was too visible. Given all that had transpired, the probability he'd be tailed was high. He couldn't risk exposure of their safehouse. Dolan stood a much better chance getting there unnoticed on his own. Especially if the driver left with the pilots, instead of him, in the back seat. There was no flight manifest, and the BMW windows were tinted. It could throw off the MIT, or anyone else who might try to track his movements.

Dolan caught the attention of a baggage handler who walked him to a door between two of the gates. His heartrate elevated slightly as he navigated the concourse crowd of Esenboğa International Airport. His senses were on high alert, though he had no reason to suspect the MIT had been successful in identifying him at the park. At the baggage claim he exited and flagged a taxi.

The ride was uneventful, but that didn't keep him from watching carefully for stalkers. The sun had set. In some ways, identifying a tail at night was easier, at least for him. There was less distraction in his peripheral vision, and abnormal driving was easier to spot. He'd spent enough time on the streets of Ankara by now to recognize that abnormal driving might actually mean someone who was driving too carefully. By American standards, most drivers here were aggressive. Headlight movement and turn signal usage were easy-to-see, dependable indicators.

Though he remained vigilant, his thoughts were a whirlwind of activity. It was times like this he was truly grateful for his photographic memory. It allowed him to analyze information, test hypotheses, and make objective conclusions without referring to notes or worrying that he'd remembered something inaccurately, or not at all. One thing he kept coming back to was the presence of Russians at the warehouse in Niamey. Since their invasion of Ukraine, nearly every operation having anything to do with Russia had to be approved by the Director himself. There was a lot going on obviously, particularly in Ukraine, but it was all very tightly controlled and briefed to the President on a regular basis, and the President needed plausible deniability for anything REVENANT was involved with. As a result, his team had essentially been carved out of the entire mess. What he didn't want was to have to hand off what could be lynchpin intelligence to another team. He needed more information on what they were doing in Niger.

The taxi dropped him at Dürümzade, a popular Turkish fast-food restaurant three blocks from his destination. Dolan went in and ordered an adana lamb and beef kebab, which he ate casually at a table near the front window. Finished with his meal and satisfied no one was watching him, he walked a backstreet to the safehouse and entered through the rear door. Welker and Haddad looked up as he entered, both lounging in the living room watching a soccer match on a small, antiquated television.

Dolan set his briefcase on the floor, turned the TV volume all the way down, and plopped on the couch next to Haddad. "Hi guys, anything new?"

"Radio silence," Haddad answered. "Bored out of our minds here."

Welker looked at him expectantly. "Enlighten us, great leader. What was Paris all about?"

"First things first. I had a call with Dittrich. We've been given authorization to continue, with the understanding that we must be that much more careful. I'll be the first to say that I don't see what we could have done better, given the timeline we were working with and the resources and intel on hand. But we must assume the MIT or others could be watching us at any time. Howard, can you get Thomas on the phone?"

"Sure. Good news about the mission. But Paris. You're being cagey, boss."

Dolan sighed. "I'll tell you what I told Dittrich. Fitzy has some ideas about what we've found, a theory of sorts, but it is not ready for primetime. I don't even want to get into it at this point. If any part of it begins to pan out, I'll ask him to lay it out for the team. But until then, it's not worth getting into."

"And you flew to Paris and back just for that?" Welker asked incredulously. Then his tone changed. "Is it possible there was a second reason for going up there?"

Dolan shot him a stern look. "No. Get Thomas on the phone."

Welker grabbed his secure cell from a side table and after three rings, connected with Freeman. "Hey Thomas, Howard here. I'm going to put you on speaker."

"Hi guys, how can I help?" Freeman asked.

"Hello Thomas. Listen, I know you haven't had a lot of time yet to work on it, but I'd like to know what you think about those printouts from Niamey. Have you begun looking into those?"

"Ah, yes," Freeman replied. "I started, but I haven't finished yet. I was going to send you an email later today about it, because so far, it's more than a little interesting."

"How so?" asked Dolan.

"Well, initially the notes in the margins didn't have much intelligence value, as far as I could tell. I ran the code through our databases and didn't get a hit, which means it wasn't anything we could recognize as a threat. You know, a virus or something. Our software looks not only at the code, but how it's written—some hacker organizations leave signatures, you know, they write certain types, or lines and blocks of code in the same or similar ways, repeatedly and in a unique manner. It also analyzes any notes typed within the code, though there are none on the pages we have.

"So, after I didn't get any hits, I went back to the handwritten notes. They seemed to be directions, instructions for the coder, to make significant changes to the code. That got me looking at the code a little closer, to see if I could figure out what the changes were. I had to make some assumptions, but the more I looked at it, the more it looked like it could have come from HIVE."

"Shit, are you serious?" Welker blurted.

"Yes."

"Help me out, Thomas," Dolan said. "I'm not familiar."

"You know about Vaults Seven and Eight, right?" asked Freeman.

"Yes," Dolan replied. "It's the trove of Agency tools that Joshua Schulte gave to Wikileaks in 2017."

"Sort of," replied Freeman. "Vault seven was documentation that described ninety-plus hacking, malware, and other exploitation capabilities the Agency has developed and collected from other sources. A lot of what we took from other sources had been updated and improved so we could turn around and use it against the bad guys. To date, all that's been published in Vault Eight is the source code and development logs for HIVE. Unlike much of the rest, HIVE was developed by our Embedded Development Branch from scratch. It's a multiplatform malware suite. We built and maintained the backend infrastructure and gave it a public-facing interface that could transfer pretty much whatever data we wanted from target desktop computers and mobile devices. It could also execute specific tasks while hiding behind public domains through a masking interface called Switchblade."

"So, what you're telling me is, you think Red Fig took HIVE source code and is adapting it for their own purposes?"

"In a word, yes. But like I said, I still have some checking to do. What's genius about it is that they changed it enough that our software was unable to match it to HIVE, at least not with the sample we have, which is very small. If the code had been identical or even close, it would have been flagged right away. I believe the updates they made have three specific purposes. First and foremost, to make it work. This is old and known malware—it has been largely defensed for years at government, corporate, and even consumer levels. They needed to make changes to avoid those defenses. Second, they needed to avoid detection, which they did effectively, as I explained. Third, they are able to defense against counterattack, mainly because we don't know what those changes were. Finally, anyone in the world can download the HIVE source code, but it would take a very sophisticated hacker to do what it looks like they're doing with it, and I'm not talking about Red Fig. If Red Fig could do it, they wouldn't have brought in outside help. Though our system didn't flag any signatures or notations, I can say with a high degree of confidence that this is not the work of a government cyber organization or legitimate IT corporation. The changes I see on those printouts are reminiscent of a few of the more notorious Russian hacking groups. If I had to put money on it, Nobelium is number one on the list. They perpetrated the SolarWinds hack in 2020 that compromised over 100 U.S. companies and federal agencies, and they have ties to the SVR. The Sandworm Team is another we should investigate, though I would say they are a distant second. Sandworm has several aliases, including Black Energy, ELECTRUM, and Iron Viking. They've been around since about 2009 and specialize in targeting foreign government leaders, institutions, and critical infrastructure systems. Particularly in Ukraine, the United States, and Europe. I wouldn't put it past them."

"If what you're postulating is true," said Dolan, "that would explain all the secrecy. Unfortunately, they are very likely back in Russia by now. Any luck with the fingerprints and license plates from the box truck and the minivan?"

"Yes and no," Freeman responded. "Both vehicles were rentals, and both were returned the morning after Howard and Omar encountered them to separate, local rental companies. The driver licenses used have local addresses that didn't pan out, and the names on them don't match any of the names on the seven visas. Same story with the credit cards. It looks like they were fake identities created specifically to lead to a dead end. I couldn't determine whether either place had security cameras onsite, so they probably don't, or they are not networked. If Howard and Omar were still there, we could learn more. No hits on the fingerprints."

"OK. After the death of the local kid, I don't think going back is an option," remarked Dolan. "If we did, it would have to be me. Or Stan. And I'm not sure either of us should break away right now. My guess is, our window of opportunity to review any footage is short—offline systems tend to overwrite themselves after a few days, especially the older ones."

"Correct," Freeman agreed.

"Let's keep that in our back pocket for a day or two," Dolan replied. Do you have any conclusions as to what Red Fig might try to do with an altered version of HIVE?"

"I really have no idea. My kneejerk reaction is that they might use it as a business intelligence tool. To spy on their competitors, gain significant advantage in the IT space. That's what makes the most sense. Illegal, of course, but hardly something REVENANT would be involved with unless it was clear they planned to use it on U.S. companies."

"While that might be its intended capability, I can't shake the feeling there's something else, something bigger going on here." Dolan replied.

Everyone was quiet, waiting for Dolan to give them guidance. He was deep in thought, weighing risk and reward of a particular strategy, one he knew would be interpreted as extremely controversial. By Dittrich, and by his team as well. It was so controversial, in fact, that if he were to go down that road, he might have to keep it to himself. It could backfire in ways he was ill equipped to understand, and he knew that. But if it worked, it might just break the case wide open and allow REVENANT to stay on the mission much longer. At least until they could hand off something actionable to Ankara Station, and hopefully, exact some form of revenge for Andy's death.

Dolan broke the silence. "Dittrich wants me to have a cover here. I am inclined to agree, though there is a risk Andy's shooter might be able to recognize me. I believe it's one we should take, however. It will give me a freedom of movement that would help us considerably. And if we do it well enough, it could put me in the places we want or need to be without the additional logistics. I think I could justify a cover for one of you as well." He pointed to Welker and Haddad. "You'd have to be my aid, or assistant or something. That wouldn't appear unusual, I don't think."

"Assistant?" quipped Welker. "That's for you, Omar. I'll stay in the shadows."

Everyone laughed. "That's fine, Howard," Dolan replied. "You're too old for that role, anyway. And Omar will fit in better, given his appearance and his Arabic, which is a minority language here. It will make things easier. The problem we have is timing. I'm going to need some help—we need to reverse-engineer this, so that it looks like it was planned earlier. Thomas, I need you to come up with some recommendations. It can't be anything where I have a formal role; that won't work. It needs to be a conference, or a facility tour or something. The targets must be high value; Hypotherion, Red Fig, people tied closely to Solak within his ministry. Come up with a draft agenda for me. Once it's official I'll let American know that's what I'm doing. Right now, they don't have a clue. I just told them I had to take some time to do research. Luckily, I have enough sway with the Dean and faculty to do as I please, though I don't want to push it. Something here in Ankara, and something in Istanbul, maybe. That would give us an opportunity to case the Hypotherion Exchange. And all of it needs to be relevant of course, something to do with the courses I teach, or something related to disease proliferation and control."

"The Miltner-Dolan Model," Welker added sarcastically.

Dolan stared him down. "Yes, the Miltner-Dolan Model. Thomas, keep it to a week, starting tomorrow. If we must extend, we can, or we can go dark at that point if we have to. You should add other activities, cultural excursions or whatever to fill it out. But not too remote, and not too much. Put a lot of slack in the schedule."

"Understood," Freeman replied. "I'm pretty bogged down here, though."

"I know," Dolan acknowledged. "I appreciate all your work Thomas. Prioritize this for today, then get back on the HIVE code."

"Sure thing."

"OK, thanks Thomas, that's it for now. Take care."

"Stay safe guys," Freeman replied, then hung up.

Dolan glanced at the muted television as a forward from the home team scored the winning goal in spectacular fashion, just as time expired. The camera focused in on the team's celebration, then on the crowd. Dolan smiled, wondering if that was how the mission was going to go. If there was any time in his life when he felt out of his depth, however, this was it. But he had faith in his team and in himself. Even if they were forced to cede operational authority to Ankara at some point, they'd be part of the win in the end. And they *would* win, one way or another.

In that moment he decided to move forward with his controversial plan. He would need to buy a local burner phone and email an address that was forever burned in his memory. One that was given to him by an unlikely savior back in Berlin, Germany. At the Ritz Carlton. It was a resource he'd tapped before, with very favorable results.

Since then, however, global geopolitical shifts had significantly changed how the clandestine world operated in certain regions. For him, right now, this would be unknown territory. Nevertheless, his gut told him it was the right move. If it turns out that he was wrong, Dolan could be putting his entire team in great danger.

CHAPTER TWENTY

"It was a diplomatic flight. They arrived at Esenboğa from Paris," Dogan told him.

Solak was concerned. "Who was it?"

The man looked down at his shoes. "I'm not sure. We had an officer on the tarmac to tell us when the vehicle left through the gate, then we followed it to a house in Baglabarsi. One of two men got out of the car and went in the house. Then the car dropped off the second man at a house a few kilometers away and returned to the embassy. The two men…they are both contract pilots. We checked them out."

"Pilots?" Solak asked, confused. "Is that a normal thing, for the U.S. Embassy to send a driver for the pilot? Was there a second vehicle?"

"No. I mean, I don't think so. Our man on the tarmac would have noticed a second vehicle."

Solak put his hands in his pockets. Immediately he began fidgeting with his Kirmizi-beyaz stone, then pulled it out and looked at it thoughtfully. "The plane came from Paris, yes?"

"Yes."

"Empty."

"It appears so. Perhaps they brought it in to preposition it? To pick someone up later," Dogan offered.

"Perhaps," Solak said softly. Then he flipped the stone in the air, caught it, and opened his hand. *Black.* "Keep eyes on the plane. I want to know who gets on it, and where they go. Watch the pilots, see where they go, who they talk to. Bug both houses. And put more men on the U.S. Embassy. I want dossiers on everyone coming and going who could be the man we are looking for."

"Yes sir. That will be a lot of work I think, the description we have is vague. Two meters tall, black hair, slender. It's not much to go on."

"It's a start," Solak said pointedly. "Now go. I have things to do."

"Yes sir," Dogan replied, backing courteously out of the room and closing the door behind him.

Solak often wondered if the MIT had given him second-tier officers. Enough bodies to placate him, but of such a quality that losing them wouldn't hurt the MIT in any significant way. Dogan was by far the best of the bunch. He would have a talk with Director of National Intelligence about it. Yes, it was strange enough that the Ministry of Industry and Technology would have control at all over MIT personnel. But Solak was doing critically important and sensitive work that overlapped between Red Fig, the Hypotherion Exchange, and his ministry. Work that must remain hidden from prying eyes and defended at all costs. Solak made the pitch, the President agreed, and it was made so.

In the meantime, things were coming together. He could sleep better at night now that his collaboration with the Russians was essentially complete. The warehouse in Niamey was vacated and sanitized, loose ends had been eliminated. They still had to complete the target sets, which his team was working on now. After that, all that was left was quite literally the push of a button.

The green phone on his desk rang suddenly, waking him from his reverie. He picked up the receiver quickly. "Yes, Mister President?"

"Are you alone?" Avci asked.

"Yes."

"Give me an update on Individual One." Avci sounded stressed.

"I don't have much to tell you at this point," Solak replied, "other than we are doing everything we can to find out who he is. I've increased surveillance on the U.S. Embassy, and we are tracking all their diplomatic flights in and out of Turkey. There was one aircraft that arrived yesterday from Paris. Their Embassy sent a car to pick up the passengers, but only the pilots were picked up."

A pause on the line told Solak Avci was thinking. "You...you need to be careful here, Yusuf. This Demir guy is one thing, but we are treading in dangerous waters with U.S. spies. I am considering having the MIT Director handle this. Your team is small, and you don't do this for a living. I don't want this to come back on you, or me."

Solak gritted his teeth. "Adem, I have it in hand. I believe that if we don't do this ourselves, we'll be at risk of exposure. Individual One did not meet with Demir. Demir told him nothing, and the other man who was killed had no time to tell him anything, either. I think we are fine."

"The second man," Avci asked, "were you able to identify him?"

"Yes," Solak responded. "He was an economic minister from the U.S. Embassy in Athens. I think he was CIA. It's the only logical conclusion. He had no reason for being in Turkey. Remember, we suspected Demir had been meeting, or was trying to meet with someone from the U.S. Embassy here in Ankara. It is why we were watching him in the first place. But then he stopped. This was very likely a new continuation of that."

"Yusuf, as you might imagine the death of a CIA officer will not go unnoticed. We may not hear anything about it formally, because it is the type of thing that 'never happened.' But they will be on high alert now. It will cause them to do more digging. We don't need or want that kind of attention."

"I'm taking care of it, Adem. There will be an article run in the papers tomorrow about Demir's death. We fabricated a story. It will say Demir was killed by a drug gang after he owed them money and couldn't pay. It's a good article, very convincing. It will run in the Sabah, the Posta, and the Hürriyet. It will be everywhere online by tomorrow afternoon."

"OK, well that is a start. What about the CIA officer?"

"He's not mentioned," Solak responded. "There was no body, so it makes sense that the article doesn't mention him. There were no witnesses. It might just be convincing enough that the CIA backs off. Their guy got caught in the crossfire. Wrong place, wrong time. It's almost perfect."

"Almost," Avci countered, "is not perfect. Listen, you need to find Individual One, and fast. We need to know what he knows. If what he knows is nothing, Praise Allah. If it is something, we have a big problem because he's most likely already reported it. Either way, find out and then take care of him. If you can't do it quickly, I'll pull you off it. Understand? The clock is ticking."

The line went dead before Solak could answer. He detested when business got between him and his good friend. *Such is the way of a consequential life*, he thought. 'Take care of him.' Surely that wasn't a kill order? Solak would have the man eliminated in any case, but it was unlike Adem to be this way. To say such things. Adem had always preferred to let the shadowy parts of politics remain in the shadows, and Solak had always protected him from it. Though he needed Adem to play his part in Solak's plan, this was different. It was the type of line he could not let Adem begin to cross. These things were *his* responsibility.

CHAPTER TWENTY-ONE

"Hello Michael. It's been a long time. Ah, wait just one moment..." Yuri Kuznetsov thanked the waitress and took a sip from the cup she'd brought him. He was seated alone in Café Frauenhuber, Vienna's oldest and most renown bistro. "OK, I am back. Sorry for that, my coffee just arrived."

"No worries," Dolan responded. "Yes, it has been a long time, Yuri. Thank you for agreeing to this." He'd just been handed his order at Dürümzade.

"You are lucky I am in Poland; I wouldn't have been able to call from Russia. I have to say, I'm surprised to hear from you, given the circumstances." Kuznetsov smiled. He liked Dolan. In a parallel universe, he felt he would trust the man.

Just as Dolan was breaking protocol by contacting Kuznetsov without the Agency's knowledge, Kuznetsov was calling him without informing his leadership at the GRU. Dolan knew it was a small miracle he'd responded to Dolan's email. Informing Kuznetsov of rogue Russian scientist Ivan Vasnetsov's location in Algeria was still paying off, apparently. But the risks involved with contacting Kuznetsov now versus then were far higher.

"I need your help, Yuri," Dolan began. "And I'm not sure that I have much to offer in return." He set his glass of ayran, a traditional Turkish yogurt drink, next to his kebab plate at his usual window table. He sat with his back against the wall.

"I see. That is not a good way to begin this kind of conversation, Michael," Kuznetsov responded. "Particularly since our governments aren't that friendly right now."

"I understand. But I don't know what else to do. Let me explain what it is, and then we can decide whether it makes sense to go any further."

"Of course. I'm assuming this has little to do with your coursework at American University," Kuznetsov gibed.

"No," Dolan responded, "it doesn't." He almost felt flattered Kuznetsov was still keeping tabs on him. "It's a little more important than that. Let's just say there is a big tech company that has a very strong, direct relationship with a certain country's federal government, and that this company may also be collaborating with a Russian hacker group. At this point I'm not in a position to say *why* they are collaborating, but I can tell you, unequivocally, that it is not a good thing. People have been murdered to prevent information about it from getting out. What is the possibility you might be able to investigate from your end?"

"Hmmm. The big tech company. We are not talking about Twitter or Facebook or Google, are we?" Kuznetsov questioned.

"No. It is not American, and the government in question is not the United States."

"Hmmm," he said again. "It is not enough. You will have to tell me more, Michael. At first glance, unless the government is my own, this sounds more like something in the SVN's or Spetssvyaz's wheelhouse. Spetssvyaz is the FSB's Service of Special Communications and Information. But like I said, tell me more."

"It's not yours. And I know what Spetssvyaz is," Dolan assured him. "I have it on good authority that the hacker group is likely either Nobelium or the Sandworm Team. It appears they've been working with an IT company to rewrite the code of a CIA malware suite called HIVE, so that it can't be detected or defensed. If they are successful, it could allow this company to target any server, computer, or mobile device worldwide. Since the company has deep ties within its own government, this would in turn give that government the capability. What I need is validation from your end that it is one of these groups. More than that, I need names, addresses, the IP addresses of their servers, and anything else you can give me."

Dolan pulled the phone from his ear suddenly as Kuznetsov let loose a full-throated laugh.

"Michael Dolan, you don't ask for much, do you? With nothing to give in return, no less. Do you know why we let groups like Nobelium and Sandworm exist?"

"Because what they do often aligns with Russian national security directives," responded Dolan.

"Exactly. These guys are not stupid. I mean, to do what they do requires above-average intelligence, to be sure. Rewriting something like HIVE…this is the HIVE from Vault Eight, right? So, they are smart. And they know this as well—they are on a tight leash. The moment they decide to target a Russian company, or our government, or a Russian-friendly country, it is the moment they will be eradicated. They know this. As a result, they always color inside the lines. So to speak."

Dolan was losing him; he could feel it. He needed to lead on that he knew more than he did. "Yuri, in this case they are definitely coloring *outside* the lines. The country we are talking about is…let's just say that their strategic allegiances lie somewhere between the United States and Russia. A Russian hacker group enabling such a country with this type of offensive cyber capability would be indirectly responsible for any damage done to the people, companies, or governments of any number of nations allied with the Russian Federation. More importantly, we are already onto them. When we bring them down—and believe me, we will, with or without you—but when we do, the entire world is going to know Russia was involved. The question you must ask yourself is, do you want Russia's involvement to be with the intentional enablement of a global cyberattack, or with the prevention of it?"

Kuznetsov bristled. "You say 'us,' Michael. Do you mean the Central Intelligence Agency in general, or are you involved again in yet another shadowy black ops team? If so, I'll be honest, your guys did it right this time. I really did think you had left the CIA for good. Where are you now?"

Dolan withheld a sigh. "Yuri, forget about where I am. For all intents and purposes, *us* means you and me. Do yourself and your country a favor and dig into this. If you don't find anything, then you have nothing to tell me. But if you do find something, and I think you will, I believe you'll understand I'm right. That's all I'm asking—investigate it, get me the information, and I'll take it from there."

Kuznetsov took another sip of coffee. Dolan wasn't threatening him. He was making a case that it was in Russia's best interest to intervene. The only problem was, Dolan already said he didn't have much to offer. Was he lying? There was no need to decide just yet. One thing he couldn't do was report any of this. It would raise too many questions, not the least of which was, how did a CIA officer know how to make direct contact with a senior member of the GRU? It could lead to more questions and potentially reveal he'd kept Dolan as a secret source these past few years. No, either he and Dolan would never see or hear from each other again, or Dolan was telling him the truth and there was something to be gained.

"Michael, here's what you can expect. I'm going to think on this first. There are certain resources to which I have access. If one of these groups is involved in something like HIVE, I may be able to find out, after which you may receive an email from me. I can't tell you *when* that might happen. That email may or may not have some or all the information you are requesting. If you get this email from me...you need to pay attention now...if you get this email, you will need to transcribe what is says, or you can take a screenshot. You won't be able to respond to the email or forward it or copy any of the text in it. Once you close it, it won't be there anymore. It will have a self-destruct feature. Do you understand?"

Dolan didn't attempt to mask his sigh of relief. "Yes."

"Or," Kuznetsov continued, "you won't get anything from me at all. That's it."

Dolan's exuberance was immediately dampened. "I understand. But even if I don't hear from you, Yuri, thank you for looking into it. And I am grateful for any action you might take on your end to shut this down, even if we never know anything about it. But let me be clear—this situation is dire, and it is time sensitive. The more information I have, the quicker I can prevent it from going down. If you do reply, try to make it sooner rather than later."

"Noted," Kuznetsov replied flatly. "Before we sign off, though, the country in question. Is it Turkey?"

Dolan had been amazed with how much Kuznetsov knew about SCALPEL back in Berlin. This was yet another reminder that the Agency can never underestimate the capabilities of Russia's intelligence organizations. "I can't confirm or deny that."

"OK. That helps," Kuznetsov replied. Keep checking your email. It may or may not come. Until then, stay safe my friend. And remember, you still owe me."

Yes, Dolan thought. He owed Kuznetsov, big time. For saving his life, and Anne's. It was a debt he'd likely never be able to repay. "Understood, Yuri. Thank you. Stay safe as well."

With his index finger, Kuznetsov traced the thin scar line from his left ear to his Adam's apple, an unconscious habit when deep in thought. As Dolan responded, he realized what he was doing and stopped. The scar was given to him many years ago by a longtime source he'd found out was playing both sides. It was an enduring reminder that in this business, trust is not given, nor could it be earned. There was simply no such thing. He hung up and removed the battery and SIM. With both hands beneath the table, he broke the flip phone and placed the halves with the battery and card in his jacket pocket. Then he smiled and settled back in his chair to finish his coffee.

CHAPTER TWENTY-TWO

Haddad returned to the safehouse with thirty minutes to spare, a brown paper bag in one hand and a suit in the other. "It's not tailored, no time. They were able to hem the pants. But it fits OK."

"You don't have to look fantastic, Omar, only I do," Dolan quipped.

"I can't believe you brought a suit with you," Haddad countered. "It smacks of vanity. There's no way you could have known the mission would turn out this way."

"He's always been a pretty boy," Welker cut in.

"Always have a plan for the most logical outcome," Dolan retorted. "I brought two, by the way. Hurry up and get that thing put on. We must leave soon."

Freeman came through, and Dolan sent an email to the Dean at American with the sanitized details of his research activities. Dolan was to attend a one-day regional security workshop held by the Ankara Center for Crisis and Policy Studies on Monday. A Red Fig board director was listed as a member and would be in attendance. On Wednesday, they would travel to Istanbul for the last two days of a blockchain technology conference hosted by none other than Hypotherion. The conference was already full, apparently, but Freeman was able to sway them to add Dolan and his 'assistant.' He sprinkled in a few side trips to local attractions, such as a tour of the Ephesus ruins. That would give them reason to be in the vicinity of the Selçuk server, housed in a rather nondescript office building. At about a five-hour drive from Istanbul, it wasn't the closest of the seven. But given its curious off-the-books status, it was more likely than the others to contain useful data.

They stayed up late the night before, brainstorming how to uncover more about Red Fig's apparent ties to the MIT, where the upgraded version of HIVE might be located, and whether it made sense to try to hack directly into the Hypotherion exchange servers. After Freeman and Stan's latest intrusion was noticed, all further attempts to penetrate via Berlin had been blocked. The most unlikely op they discussed was an attempt to breach the Hypotherion Exchange itself in Istanbul. It would be little different, risk-wise, than attempting a bank robbery. Except they weren't interested in what might be in the vault, it was data they were after; where the money was coming from, and where it was going. And whatever they looked for or found, they were to keep their eyes peeled for Russian fingerprints, whether they led back to the IT workers in Niger, or anywhere else. The conference was being held less than a block from the exchange.

When the taxi arrived, Dolan grabbed his briefcase and joined Haddad in the back seat. Welker left twenty minutes later with another loaner from Ankara Station. It was a similar, though not the same vehicle. They weren't yet finished repainting the first one, and irritated enough by the damage to push back, at first, on loaning them another. Welker would spend the day just fifteen minutes away casing the Red Fig Corporate Headquarters complex.

They arrived fifteen minutes early, signed in and received their nametags. Haddad was visibly irked that Dolan's was pre-printed, while he was relegated to writing his name on a blank, rectangular sticker with a Sharpie.

"This thing is going to fall off thirty times today," Haddad lamented.

"You'll pull though buddy, stay strong," Dolan replied with a smirk.

They took seats near the middle of the modestly sized auditorium and waited as people filtered in. The Red Fig executive, Ahmet Aslan, was a panelist along with an IT CEO from China, a Japanese cybersecurity company CIO, and a famous social media influencer from Singapore. To the right side of the stage, a Chinese interpreter stood ready at a microphone. The rest of the participants would be speaking English. One of the prime architects of the European General Data Protection Regulation (GDPR), the Belgian mediator would guide discussion of the key topic, *International and Corporate Responsibilities with Protection of Personal Information.*

The event was three long hours of conversation, debate, and Q&A. There wasn't much to be gained from the roundtable itself, other than the opportunity to study and dissect Aslan's personality and the answers and opinions he provided over the course of the panel's discussions. What *was* worthwhile was the opportunity to speak with him during the networking social immediately afterwards. As soon as the event ended, Dolan handed his briefcase to Haddad, then casually got in line behind a few others to talk with him in the reception room next door.

"Good afternoon, Michael Dolan from American University in Washington, D.C." He shook his hand and smiled warmly.

"Ahmet Aslan, Red Fig Technology Chief. Nice to meet you Michael," he replied.

"I must say," Dolan went on, "that I'm more than impressed with how Red Fig has exploded on the scene these past few years. Five years ago, no one had heard of you. Now you're competing with the industry leaders. Impressive."

Aslan smiled. "Yes, we are a success story. We've been fortunate in accurately predicting IT networking and social media trends, and in shaping our products and services to match in real time. Michael Dolan…Do I know you? Your name is familiar." He pointed to Dolan's nametag. You are a professor at American?"

"I am," Dolan replied. "I teach Global Security and Foreign Policy."

Aslan nodded. "Well, I'm glad you were able to attend today. I must ask, how does IT protection of personal information relate to global security?"

"I think we can agree," Dolan answered, "that information technology touches everything, and protection of personal information, especially across international borders, is highly relevant. You may have heard of my work, the Miltner-Dolan Model. It is the current global standard in predicting pandemic spread and mitigation effectiveness."

Aslan held up his index finger, nodding. "Aaahh, yes. That is how I remember you. So, let me guess, you are doing research on how personal information can be masked when using such a model? Trying to prevent the need for such things as a digital vaccination passport?"

"Sort of. The model itself doesn't need PI. What I'd like to do is convince the powers that be, like the World Economic Forum, that they don't need it either.

"I see," said Aslan. "I wish you much luck with that, you might need it."

They both laughed. Dolan could tell Aslan was trying to wind up their conversation so he could get to the next person in line.

"Listen, I know your company does a plethora of algorithm work. Given Red Fig's growing prominence on the world stage, I'd like to influence you as well. Would you like a copy of my published thesis? You might find it illuminating, or you can use it to put yourself to sleep at night."

They both laughed again as Aslan responded. "Yes of course, do you have a copy with you?"

"I do. Just a moment." Dolan walked back to Haddad and held out his hand. Haddad gave him the briefcase. Dolan opened it quickly, retrieved a copy and walked it back to Aslan, who was already speaking with his next admirer. He handed it to him, smiled, and rejoined Haddad.

"How long will it last?" Haddad asked.

"About a week. Hopefully, that is enough, and we'll get something out of it."

Dolan then sent an encrypted text to Welker.

Aslan is live

Ten seconds later he replied.

Copy

"OK, what do you think, ready to get out of here?" Dolan asked Haddad.

"Yes, I'm hungry, and the food here is terrible."

CHAPTER TWENTY-THREE

Dolan and Haddad checked into separate rooms at the New Park Hotel, then walked to a nearby Mediterranean restaurant. The hotel was a short cab ride from the safehouse, where Welker would continue to stay. It was also situated directly across the street from Kurtuluş Park. It was the last place the MIT would suspect Andino's accomplice might be hiding out, in plain sight no less. Added to that, the New Park didn't require credit card payment. Less footprints.

They ordered their meals, then Dolan pulled out his cellphone and tapped the bottom right corner of the screen four times at one-second intervals. The screen changed, revealing a suite of CIA proprietary app tools. He tapped the 'ear' icon and selected Aslan's name. The top half of the screen then displayed a map of Ankara, with a red dot showing his position. He was back at Red Fig Headquarters. The bottom half showed a list of files, each a recording of whatever the bug in the spine of his thesis had picked up since activated back at the Center for Crisis and Policy Studies.

"I still think it was a big risk for you to have Freeman put that bug into your thesis," Haddad said pointedly. "It highlights you immediately if it's ever found."

"I know. But he'd have to tear the book apart to find it. And if there's a chance down the road to recover it, we will. Unfortunately, we lack access on this mission to many of the resources we usually have. Which means we must take risks we're not used to taking. Dittrich understands that. He himself said we have to do this the old school way."

Haddad ate his meal quietly while Dolan's thoughts took him back to his discussion with Fitzhenry. It bothered him that someone on his team put stock in what was arguably an extreme conspiratorial hypothesis. An apocalypse, end of world-type conspiracy. Two things tempered his concern, however. Fitzhenry's storied and spotless legacy, and the fact that there were too many touchpoints between what they'd uncovered to date and what Fitzhenry presented to Dolan in his office. On the surface, one could argue it was statistically impossible without being true somehow. The counter argument was that if you look hard enough for evidence to validate a theory you are invested in, you will always find it. And Fitzhenry was religious enough for that to happen in this situation.

In such a case, one must begin from a position that the hypothesis is wrong—a null hypothesis that must be rejected based on the data. It was a position that was easy for Dolan to take, as he didn't believe for a second that it was remotely possible. But the locations of the servers. Hypotherion's name. Even their team's codename, REVENANT, was strikingly similar. He shook his head at the thought. Dolan would need to try to prove statistically that what Solak has been up to has no meaningful relationship with the cryptic events that unfold within the Book of Revelation. Fitzhenry had offered alternative hypotheses that were far less unlikely, and they were also in play. He would keep all this in mind as his team uncovered more.

Dolan ate two forkfuls of rice and turned his attention back to his cellphone. Aslan's red dot hadn't moved. He sent a quick text to Welker.

Can you talk?

Three seconds later his phone buzzed.

"What's up boss," Welker asked.

"Just wanted to touch base. Anything interesting to report?"

"Actually, yes," Welker replied. "Have you listened to any of the recordings?"

"Not yet," said Dolan. "We checked in to the hotel and we're grabbing a late lunch."

"OK. Well, I've been listening live since Aslan walked into the building. The audio is pretty good; he must've put your thesis on his desk or in a bookcase nearby. He made what sounded like a few administrative-type phone calls, talked to his secretary, all in Turkish. We'll have to wait until Thomas can get someone to transcribe everything into English. Then he went quiet for a while. Sounded like he was working on his computer. Then, someone called him, about twenty minutes ago. Right away I knew something was up because his voice changed. He sounded cautious, quieter. And he was speaking English."

"Well, what did he say?" Dolan pressed.

"It was an argument, sounded like he felt that whoever he was talking to was breaking an agreement. What he said was, *'Under no circumstances will we launch it from here. The copy I have is just a backup, I'm not even sure we're even set up, security-wise, to pull everything off. As agreed, you will execute the launch, and I don't care from where, as long as it's done when you are told. Just do it.'* There was more, and none of it would've made sense to me, except that he mentioned Niamey."

"He mentioned Niamey? Shit, I think we just got lucky, Howard. You think he was talking to one of the Russians?"

"Dunno," Welker replied. "Whoever it was, I think it's safe to say they weren't Turkish."

Launch it. What could that be, thought Dolan. "What do software companies launch?"

"Computer programs. Software products. Apps?" Haddad offered.

Dolan shot him a look. "Thanks Einstein."

"I don't have a clue. Probably not missiles," Welker came back.

"Probably not," Dolan agreed. "Anything else, Howard?"

"Nope, that's it for now."

"OK, stay on it then. Are you good? Where are you positioned?"

"I'm good. Found the London Times and read that for a while at a bus stop across from the main gate. Getting a bite to eat myself now at a McDonalds nearby, if you can believe it. I'm barely within range, so I will get it to go and move a little closer. I haven't found a good place to hide the relay yet."

The relay would continue to receive the bug's transmissions after he left and upload the audio files to a secure server via cellular network.

"OK. Stay safe buddy," Dolan said. "We'll see you back at the house later." He ended the call.

They finished eating and walked back to the hotel. When he got to his room, Dolan took the burner phone from beneath the false bottom of his briefcase, inserted the battery and powered it up. He tapped the browser icon and logged into the email account he used to contact Yuri. Nothing. He sighed, turned it off and removed the battery. Then he put it back in its hiding place. *Wishful thinking,* he thought. *Yuri is unlikely to give me anything on this.*

Dolan booted up his laptop, enabled his VPN, and logged into the secure REVENANT server using a password, facial recognition via the screencam, and the fingerprint scanner on the keyboard. There was one email from Freeman. He'd finished his analysis of the printouts from Niamey and determined with certainty that the lines of code originated from HIVE. Of great interest was that the changes made were not just to evade malware detection; there appeared to be new functionality added. Several lines of new code, along with some of the handwritten notes, led him to believe that an additional instructional algorithm had been added. It was impossible to tell what it was for, given the small sample size. But it was definitely new and not part of the original HIVE. It could be, Freeman thought, that this part of the application would send commands to other applications or programs after running user input or information from a database through that new algorithm. It looked like an automated capability. One that could execute commands in microseconds that would take hours, days, or even months (depending on the volume of information) with human analysis and manual data entry.

Based on this, HIVE's original capabilities, some of the data from his hack on the Berlin server, and what the team already knew about Red Fig and Hypotherion, Freeman was wondering if Solak's intention could be to use *FrankenHIVE*, as he wittily named it, via a masked integration with one or more of the company's existing cloud or mobile applications. It was something he intended to dig into, though he warned it might be prohibitively time consuming to do so.

To Dolan, Freeman's findings weren't of much use. Not right now, at least. Too much speculation based on too little information, and nothing immediately actionable. Which meant they needed to double down on intel gathering. He decided that attempting to breach the Hypotherion Exchange would be too risky, but Freeman had been working on a wireless server penetration option. One that wouldn't require them to break in and gain physical access. All they would need to do is walk in during business hours with the device and get close enough to a wireless access point, then let Freeman do his magic remotely. The main problem with it was, that type of penetration was likely to be noticed quickly. Within minutes, security could lock down the building and they'd be trapped inside. He'd decide about that later, after talking more with Freeman about how it would work. Breaching the ledger server building in Selçuk, however, was a real option. The security would be much simpler to defeat. Additionally, Freeman postulated that the patch put in place in response to his Berlin penetration would do nothing to prevent a physical access hack.

A response from Yuri with intel about the involvement of Nobelium or the Sandworm Team was what he really needed. That would take the politically charged focus off President Avci and Turkey and put it on a foreign adversary. Which would give him the ammunition he needed to push for more resources and broad three-letter agency intelligence support.

CHAPTER TWENTY-FOUR

Dolan sat on the living room couch in the safehouse, his legs crossed on the coffee table. Freeman was on speakerphone. "I don't want any of us to fly anywhere. Too visible. If someone notices the breach in Selçuk, it wouldn't take too long for them to put two and two together. Howard, Omar and I will take a bus to Istanbul, and you'll drive the station loaner to Selçuk. I don't like the idea of sending you there without backup, but I don't see a better option."

"That's fine," Welker nodded. "I agree with that approach. That way we can tackle both in parallel."

Haddad looked first at Welker, then at Dolan. "Are you sure, Michael? What if Howard gets rolled up? I mean, the Ephesus ruins is already part of your itinerary. Why not just stick to it?"

"The cultural detours are optional," Dolan answered. "If things go sideways at Selçuk, you and I have an alibi and our cover is secure. If we all went, the MIT would find out soon enough about my itinerary and see I was in both places. As long as his cover isn't blown and he doesn't get caught, they won't be able to pin it on Howard. No one knows he's here. This way, we muddy the waters. There's another thing we can't forget—Demir. He said he had a copy of the algorithmic model implicating Solak in the death of Avci's wife. We need to get back to

Ankara as soon as possible to try and find it. There is no better leverage we could have than that. Besides, the intelligence value of it is priceless. Headquarters would have a field day with it. Or they would bury it. Who knows. But we must find it."

Welker grunted his approval, but Haddad looked unconvinced. "Alright. But I feel like we're taking unnecessary risks. We're all alone here. I'm beginning to think we're out of our depth."

Dolan frowned. "It's the job, Omar. If we do it well, we'll be fine. Yes, the risks are high. But I'm not asking any of us to do anything that's beyond our capacity to do. As soon as we have enough intel we'll push for more resources, or we'll package it up and pass it off. One or the other."

Freeman cut in on the speakerphone. "Guys, it's worth noting that the value of Hypotherion has gone up rapidly in the last twenty-four hours, and it's not slowing down. It's up fourteen percent and climbing. That would require a huge increase in mining activity. The international financial markets are all abuzz about it. It seems unnatural—something is going on; I just don't know what. Anyways, I'm good with handling both Istanbul and Selçuk, just make sure you stagger them. I'll need at least an hour in-between."

"Welker will run his op at three a.m. There won't be any overlap. And I'm still not inclined to hack the Hypotherion Exchange, Thomas," Dolan replied. "It will be very difficult to pull off. We don't even have your wireless device yet, and we're leaving in the morning."

"It'll be at the embassy today," Freeman replied. "It should already be there, in fact. Give the station a call. I can't impress upon you enough that where the money is coming from, where it is going—that is where we are going to hit paydirt, I believe. Hacking the ledger server might prove worthwhile, but I'm betting on the exchange."

"OK. Howard, can you swing by there and get it?" asked Dolan.

"Sure," he replied. "I'll give them a call."

"Thanks," said Dolan.

Welker got up, took his phone from his jeans pocket, and walked out of the living room to the kitchen.

Dolan settled back in the couch to think. A thousand wheels were spinning in his head, and he was irritated that he couldn't slow them down, mate one with another. The gears weren't matching. They still had too little information. Not that they'd had plenty of time to get it; rather, he was surprised how far they'd come in just a few days. But at such a cost. Was it worth it? That was something that remained to be seen.

CHAPTER TWENTY-FIVE

Welker arrived in Selçuk just before Dolan and Haddad made it to Istanbul. He found an older, locally run motel and paid for one night with cash. After grabbing a quick bite to eat at an open-air café nearby, he notified Dolan of his arrival and returned to his room. He was bushed from the drive. After washing his face and brushing his teeth, he set his phone alarm for two a.m. Then he removed his shoes and crawled into bed fully clothed.

At one fifty-eight, Welker opened his eyes and threw off the thin blanket. He downed a cup of water from the bathroom sink, silenced his alarm, laced up his shoes, and went out to the car. Fifteen minutes later he approached his objective. A drive-by revealed tight physical security. It was a single story, square, drab concrete structure with a flat roof set back from the main road and surrounded by a high chain link fence topped with concertina wire. No windows, just the entry door at the front. Standard call box and magnetic swipe entry at the gate. There were no guards, however. That would mean there was very good electronic surveillance in place. Either way, it made things much easier. Several pole-mounted floodlights with security cameras attached below just inside the fence perimeter gave 360-degree coverage of the building exterior, property grounds, and areas just beyond the fence line.

Welker drove a hundred meters beyond the edge of the lot and parked off the side of the road. His black nylon bag contained a night vision scope, a high-resolution zoom camera, and a compact device capable of identifying and pinpointing a multitude of energy wavelengths across visible, infrared, and radio transmission spectrums. A few other standard tools of the trade were thrown in as well. He walked back and stopped about thirty meters away.

It was a rural area. With a population of less than 30,000, Selçuk was more a town than a city. It was a very strange location to maintain a server as important as this one. A small warehouse adjoined the property on the left, an auto repair shop stood across the road. Neither appeared to have electronic surveillance in place. The lot on the right was undeveloped.

After turning into the empty lot, he took position behind a large rock with a good vantage and used his night vision scope to slowly pan the entire facility. He noted the cypher lock on the front door. Then he took photographs, about a hundred in all, of each section of fence, the cameras, grounds, and the building itself. Finished with that, Welker put the scope and camera back in the bag and pulled out the third device, holding the ocular to his eye. Again, he panned the fences, grounds, and building. He noted thankfully that the fence was not electrified. He could plainly see three laser tripwires along the inside of the fence on all sides, spaced from one foot above the ground to about four feet at the top. The sensors were mounted on the floodlight poles. A concealed motion sensor above the door rounded out the non-visible security measures.

Welker pocketed the device, made his way back to the car and retrieved a second bag and foldable aluminum ladder from the trunk. Then he returned to the vacant lot, moving towards the back of the property to view the rear of the building. No rear entrance or windows. He set the ladder on the ground and reached into the second bag, withdrawing a high-energy laser. He aimed the laser at each of the cameras covering the back side of the property and building and burned the optics of each in quick succession. Then he picked up the ladder and approached the fence. After cutting the chain links vertically to open a large enough hole, he climbed through and stopped just short of where he knew the laser tripwires to be. Welker unfolded the ladder to its full twelve-foot length, then folded it into an A-shaped stepladder. Next, he used the muti-spectrum sensor device to pinpoint the exact location of each laser and lifted the ladder above his head and over.

After climbing to the other side, he carefully removed the ladder, unfolded it again to its full length, and propped it against the back of the building. He climbed to the top with his two bags in hand. Then he made his way to the curved aluminum exhaust vent. It took him twenty minutes to remove the fixture and steel security bars within, and another five to cut through the ducting below before lowering himself inside with a Teflon rope. He turned on the overhead lights and initiated a video call with Freeman.

"I'm in. This is what I'm dealing with. Tell me what to do," said Welker.

He held his cellphone out, showing Freeman video of the six-foot high rack of blinking equipment.

"OK, hold it still," Freeman responded. "There, third from the top. Plug the USB drive into that one."

Welker did as he instructed.

"Good. Give me a minute."

Welker sat cross-legged on the floor as he listened to Freeman's rapid keystrokes so many thousands of miles away. Three minutes later, he appeared to have what he wanted.

"OK Howard, that'll do it. You can remove the USB. I'll take it from here. Stay safe."

"Copy. Out." Welker hung up the call, pulled the drive and turned out the lights. Fifteen minutes later he was in the car and headed back to his motel room.

CHAPTER TWENTY-SIX

The bus ride was egregiously long. Flying would have taken a little over an hour, driving a rental, roughly five and a half. Seven hours and forty minutes after they left the station in Ankara, Dolan and Haddad arrived at the Otogar Terminal in Istanbul. They retrieved their bags, found a taxi, and headed to their hotel. It was modest but comfortable, and within walking distance of the WOW Convention Center. With Freeman's wireless device tucked away safely in Dolan's briefcase, they checked in and had their things taken to their rooms while they grabbed a quick meal before retiring for the night. They were both exhausted from the trip. After showering, Dolan once again checked his burner phone for any message from Yuri. Nothing. He did get a text from Welker on his secure cell, who'd arrived in Selçuk without incident.

Dolan slept, but not well. Though he had nothing but confidence in Welker's abilities, Haddad was right, to an extent. Sending him there on his own was a great risk. And despite all evidence to the contrary, Welker wasn't infallible.

They met in a quiet corner of the hotel restaurant for an early breakfast of eggs, cheese, black olives, tomatoes, and tea. They spoke quietly, though they were the only patrons. It was seven a.m.

"First off," Dolan began, "Welker got in and out without incident. Freeman has access to the server."

"Whew," Haddad said under his breath. "Thank God."

"Yes. Also, there's been a change of plans. I stayed up late last night thinking about this. We are going to give the exchange hack a go, and you're going to do it. Today. I'll attend the conference alone. If anyone asks about your absence, I'll tell them you weren't feeling well."

Haddad inhaled carefully. "You…want me to do it, alone? That's not the way we briefed it, Michael. One of us needs to be on watch, for the authorities, police. To cause a distraction, if necessary."

"I know," Dolan agreed. "That's the way we planned it. Like I said, I thought a lot about this last night. I need to be at the conference to maintain my cover and get what I can from our targets. We just didn't have enough time to prepare for both operations, and we're short on manpower. Don't worry, you can do this."

Haddad nodded thoughtfully. "Right. So, now that we've changed the plan at the last second, which is almost always what turns out to be the first misstep in an error chain leading to failure, what advice do you have, so I have less of a chance of fucking up?"

Dolan laughed, then turned serious. "You're right to be questioning me on this, but not because I'm wrong. Yes, you won't have me as a lookout. You'll need to be more vigilant, of course. Think about your position inside the exchange with relation to the exit. Try to keep the lobby in full view, remain near a wall, but not a corner. As we drew it up, you'll enter and look around a bit, as if you've never been there before, which you haven't. Know where all the security guards are posted, where the security cams are. Look for an information kiosk, anything with papers and forms. Spend some time there, take a few items, walk around a bit until you lock on a signal. Once Thomas gives you the OK, settle down somewhere nearby. Try to position yourself between the guards and the exit and pretend you're filling out an application for a loan or something. No one is going to think anything of it. But keep one eye on all the guards. As soon as they realize there's an intrusion you will know right away. At least one of them will react quickly, and they will begin communicating with each other. At that moment you'll have maybe thirty seconds to get out before they contain the room."

"What if I don't get out, Michael?" Haddad asked directly.

Dolan sighed and sipped his tea. "If you don't make it out, you're going to have to swallow it. Your earpiece as well. It's not going to be comfortable, but there's no other way. And you can't let it get caught on camera. You'll have to be eating something already, maybe a candy bar."

Haddad looked at him exasperatingly. "Swallow it? Why not just pass it off to someone else? It has a self-destruct component. I don't want that thing inside me."

Dolan smiled. "I wouldn't either, believe me. Thomas won't hit that button if you have to eat it, believe me. And it should continue working even after you swallow it. Bottom line, they'll frisk you, ask you some questions, and let you go. If they find it on you, that's it. Thomas will make sure the device is remotely destroyed. They won't be able to get anything from it, but you'll be taken into custody, and it'll be very difficult to get you out."

"And *your* cover could begin to unravel," added Haddad.

"Yes, it could. If you don't do what you're supposed to do. But you will."

"Of course," Haddad acknowledged.

"In any case," said Dolan, "I have complete faith in your ability to pull this off. I've already updated Thomas about the change in plans, and he's ready to go. It needs to happen this morning."

Haddad stabbed an olive and chewed it slowly. "Understood. You're right, this is the best way. I'll be fine."

"I know you will, Omar. You will."

◆

The Hypotherion Exchange was an impressive building. Above the main floor, six additional stories made it the second highest building in the area after the WOW Convention Center. It was more than half a block wide, with seven mammoth white marble columns supporting a monolithic slab centered at the middle of the building and shielding the seven revolving doors. The entire façade was travertine and glass. It was artistically understated, yet undeniably an architectural masterpiece. Omar took it all in as he walked casually along, noting the position and type of each parked vehicle, the flow of pedestrians. Which shops across the street would be suitable to duck into, which ones would not. There were no marked police cars in the area.

He made his way to the entrance and followed a line of people inside. The recent surge in Hypotherion's value was attracting investors, to be sure. That was good for him today, as the bank was bordering on crowded. There were eight teller lines, all with long queues.

Haddad maneuvered to stay with the densest part of the throng, then reached into his jacket pocket and felt for the power button on the small, round device.

"It's on," he said, without moving his lips.

"Copy," Freeman replied via his earpiece. "Walk the room. I'll let you know when to stop."

There were five security agents that he could see. Two near the teller desks, two others near hallways leading to internal offices at opposite ends of the room, and one near the entrance. It was going to be difficult to keep them all in view, and impossible to stay between all of them and the entrance. As he meandered the crowd along a route that crossed the room, he noted the long table near the teller lines stocked with various forms and other papers.

"Anything yet?" he asked impatiently.

"Negative," Freeman replied. "Keep going."

Nervously, Haddad fished the chocolate bar from his breast pocket and opened it as he walked by the lines. He stopped at the table and selected a few items, then moved on toward the far end of the room. His heartrate jumped as the security guard at the west hallway entrance noticed him, then subsided as he looked away. He continued walking and sat on one of the long padded benches positioned against the wall, to the left of the guard. Taking a bite of the candy bar, he put it back in his pocket and began looking busy filling out an investor's application.

"It's working, sit tight."

Freeman's voice startled him, but he didn't let it show. He kept writing as his eyes probed the room, searching for any sign of commotion, any clue they might be on to him.

"OK, I'm in," Freeman came back. "I'm trying to get by a firewall. Remember, as soon as I get through, they're going to know very quickly. If they're paying attention, anyway."

Haddad said nothing back. He was beginning to sweat, and he casually wiped his forehead. He felt cornered. At the far end of the room and away from the entrance, he was not in a good position to make an escape. His eyes darted from one guard to the next, expecting them to draw their weapon at any moment.

"I'm through," said Freeman. "Don't move."

Haddad looked down at the form. There was nothing left to fill out. It was all nonsense anyway, and hardly legible. He folded it and put it in his breast pocket, then unfolded a pamphlet about the benefits of investing in Hypotherion. There was so much adrenaline in his system he could hardly think straight. He could sense the impending failure of the mission. They were going to notice the breach and converge on him immediately; he could feel it. He would be arrested, disavowed by his own country, and spend the rest of his life in a maximum-security Turkish prison. He would be tortured for years. And then he would die.

Freeman broke him from his hysteria. "OK I'm done. Turn it off and get out."

Haddad immediately reached into his pocket and pushed the device's power button. "Copy," he whispered back. Then he stood up and began the long walk back towards the front doors. His heart was pounding so hard he could feel it in his ears. He watched the guard at the entrance for any sign of trouble. Step by step. The ten seconds it took to reach the front of the room felt like an eternity. But nothing happened. Haddad made it to the exit and walked out. He turned right on the sidewalk and mingled right into the crowd as if nothing had happened.

◆

At two blocks wide and over 6,500 square meters of floor space, the WOW Convention facility was Istanbul's largest congress center. It was the type of venue Hypotherion commanded, given its unprecedented worldwide financial and technological success. There were other events going on here this week, to be sure. But the Blockchain Technology Conference was the main event. It was made very apparent; everywhere he looked, Dolan saw the red, white, and black Hypotherion and Red Fig banners and signage. He found the registration tables, waited in line, and received his and Haddad's badges and lanyards. Scanning faces for his two targets all the while.

Dolan walked among the crowd to the main amphitheater where the keynote address was to be given in a few minutes. Most of the seats were full, with some conference-goers still filtering in. He chose a seat near the back and sat down, quickly checking his cell phone for any messages from Haddad or Freeman. Nothing yet.

A man walked on stage and welcomed the crowd, then began introducing the speaker, the CEO of IBM. After nearly three minutes of listing off all IBM had done to back and improve the future of blockchain under his watch, the man then threw a curveball at the audience.

"But before he comes out to talk to us, I've just been told that we have a very special guest today who wants to say hello. Ladies and gentleman, Principal Owner and CEO of Red Fig, Turkey's own Minister of Industry and Technology and the mind behind the creation of Hypotherion, Yusuf Solak!"

Dolan strained his eyes, searching the stage. Solak was not supposed to be here… He needed to get closer. There were still a few open seats in the middle, but much closer to the front. He got up quickly and walked down the aisle, then made his way slowly to his new seat, apologizing several times as each person got up to let him by.

Seated again, he watched as Solak took the podium and held his arms out to the crowd.

"Good morning, future of technology!" he yelled into the microphone. The crowd was going nuts. *The IT world loves this guy.*

Solak waited until the applause died down, then continued. "Welcome to Istanbul, my friends. I am so delighted to be able to join you this morning, if only for a few minutes. I found myself here on business today and couldn't pass up the opportunity to participate in such an important event. As you all know, blockchain does things for technology that cannot be done in any other way. It facilitates the secure verification and traceability of multistep transactions. It lowers the cost of compliance; it accelerates data transfer processes. Blockchain aids in contract administration and product auditing. As our keynote speaker will tell you, blockchain significantly increases security, transparency, and makes our processes more efficient."

Solak paused there as the applause started again, then slowly bled off. "When I first conceptualized Hypotherion, I realized the sum value these attributes can bring, not to the world of finance, but to the *world*. Those in need. The *people*. As of today, the Hypotherion Exchange and Bank has provided just over two point seven trillion euros in low interest loans to governments of countries challenged by crisis and disaster across the globe. In doing so, we have also generated carbon offsets to the tune of over one hundred and seventy million hectares of protected land, more than any other single green environment endeavor in the history of the world. And it's not even close."

More applause. Dolan shook his head in wonder. *This guy is something else.*

"And I started it all using blockchain. Think about that for a moment." Solak took the microphone from its cradle and walked from the podium to the middle of the stage. "We're talking about a technology that was created before its time. When it first emerged, it was more of a curiosity than anything else. A peer-to-peer network with no central authority sitting on top of the internet, developed by someone with the pseudonym Satoshi Nakamoto. We don't even know who Nakamoto really is. That was in 2008. Then came Bitcoin. And the rest is history, right?"

Many in the crowd yelled "yes!" while others clapped and hooted.

"*NO!*" Solak yelled firmly, his left hand in a fist. The amphitheater went still.

"With respect to blockchain, and what it can do for the world, history has only just begun. Hypotherion is just the start. But it's an important beginning. So, no matter why you are here this week, whether you work in banking, or logistics, or auditing, remember that there is no real ceiling on what we can do by embracing the benefits of such a technology. And I'll boast a little here, because though Bitcoin may capture more of the international press, Hypotherion has been far more beneficial to the people of the world in very tangible and measurable ways. Its creation was an event horizon. A revolution against the mainstream idea of cryptocurrency. To be more precise, *Hypotherion is a revelation...*"

Dolan was shocked for the second time in less than five minutes. *Did he really just say that?* Solak continued as the thousand wheels in Dolan's head instantly shifted all at once in a multitude of directions, taking new positions and changing speeds. New connections made. Gears mating gears. His null hypothesis just became more difficult to prove, however slightly. *Stop. It means nothing,* he cautioned himself. *Stay focused.*

Solak left among a roar of applause. The announcer could hardly be heard as IBM's CEO walked the stage, no doubt fuming at being marginalized in such a way, and that no matter how good his performance was going to be, he'd just been preemptively upstaged.

Dolan glanced at his phone again. No messages. He tapped one out quickly to Freeman.

Status?

A few seconds later, Freeman responded.

He hasn't left the hotel yet. ETA onsite about an hour.

OK, he thought. *Less than two hours from now, we'll either be another step ahead, or Omar will be in jail...*

Dolan continued searching among the sea of people for his two marks. One was a former colleague of Demir's who still worked at Red Fig. The other was a Hypotherion executive and Board Director, who should have a seat at or near the front row. Freeman ran the names of all those registered for the convention through Agency and other databases to pinpoint a handful of individuals who could be targeted for intel. It seemed an impossible task to find these two though, without being able to see their faces. There were so many people here. He would have to wait until the keynote address was over.

Forty-five minutes later IBM's CEO was finishing his presentation to moderate applause. Fifteen minutes of Q&A followed, and the audience was released. Dolan stood but didn't move down the row to the aisle, electing instead to use his vantage to continue searching. Sure enough, he recognized the Hypotherion exec, Deniz Duman, as he stood up to leave from the front row. Dolan began a slow shuffle to the aisle to arrive just as Duman walked by.

He timed it perfectly and climbed the stairs close behind him. He reached into his left breast pocket and activated Welker's cell phone cloning device. It worked best when there was only one phone in the vicinity but could be set to clone multiple devices at once if necessary, which ensured the correct one was captured. It was an easy thing to figure out which was which after the fact.

They continued slowly up until they reached the exit. Duman turned left and Dolan followed. *Ten more seconds.* He counted down. *Five, four...*

"Doctor Dolan?"

He took another step, not wanting to curtail the cloning procedure, then stopped and turned. A tall, well-appointed man in his late fifties with a long graying beard stood facing him.

"Hello, yes," Dolan said, without missing a beat. He smiled at the man. "I am Doctor Dolan. How can I help you?"

"Minister Yusuf Solak wishes the presence of your company. Would you be able to join him for a moment?"

Dolan was on guard instantly. How could Solak know he was here? Why would he want to see him? How could they have found him so quickly in such a throng? The hair on the back of his neck stood on end. "Minister Solak wishes to see *me*? May I ask what it is about?"

The man remained stone-faced. "The Minister wishes to meet you. Please come this way."

He turned to walk to the right, placing his palm on Dolan's shoulder. His instinct was to pull away, but he resisted. The chances of this situation occurring for anything other than a bad reason were very, very low. Everything he'd been taught and experienced thus far with the Agency was screaming at him not to accept the offer. But he went with the man anyway.

As he was led towards a staircase nearby, Dolan's phone vibrated. He resisted the urge at first, but then gave in. He maneuvered slightly behind his escort and looked at the message, from Freeman.

Success.

He sent a quick reply.

Copy. Comms out for now.

Dolan felt a wave of relief as he followed the man up the stairs, which helped him focus more on the task at hand—level setting his head before coming face to face with the man who may have ordered the murder of his friend and colleague.

The tall, bearded man exited the stairwell at the third floor and led him down a long, empty hallway. He stopped in front of an unmarked door and knocked.

"Sir, Doctor Dolan."

The door opened. An even taller, much broader man stood in the way. He looked Dolan up and down, then motioned him inside. Dolan thanked his escort and walked in, immediately suspicious. There was no one else in the room. "Sir, I was told…"

"Please spread your arms and legs," he interrupted. "I have to frisk you first."

Dolan did as he asked, praying the man wouldn't notice the cloning device. It was disguised to look like a cell phone, but anything beyond a cursory examination would show that it wasn't.

The man patted him down, pausing as he palmed both Dolan's cell phone and the device.

"Please remove your jacket," he told him. "You will get it back after meeting the Minister."

"Sure, no problem," Dolan replied. He took it off and handed it to the swarthy man, who took it to a closet and hung it up inside. Then he motioned Dolan to a door at the back of the room and opened it, motioning him inside.

"Doctor Michael Dolan, welcome." Yusuf Solak was grinning broadly, holding out his hand. "I'm sorry for the security. It's protocol. Please, make yourself comfortable." He sat on one of two plush velour chairs. "I'm sure you are wondering why you've been pulled away from the convention." He was still smiling.

Solak looked and acted the part. Impeccably groomed facial hair, perfect skin. He was wearing a shimmering, superfine navy wool suit. His cufflinks and tie bar were gold. His English was smooth and effortless with just a hint of an accent.

"Good morning, Minister Solak," Dolan offered politely as he took his seat. "I greatly enjoyed your opening remarks. Thank you for the invitation to meet with you. And yes, I am curious as to your motivations."

"I'm glad you enjoyed it. There was a great response from the crowd, I think. It's important to represent the organization whenever I can. I believe very strongly in the vision and mission of Hypotherion. Added to that, showing my face instills confidence in our investors."

He reached behind his chair and placed a crystal decanter and two glasses on the table. "Drink?"

"Yes, thank you," Dolan replied.

"Scotch whiskey. Aged twenty years," he offered as he poured two fingers in each.

They raised their glasses and Solak offered a toast. "To the future."

"To the future."

They tapped glasses and drank.

"Two days ago, you met my Chief of Technology, Ahmet Aslan. It was at the Center for Crisis and Policy Studies."

"Yes," Dolan acknowledged. "Fascinating man."

Solak looked away and laughed. "I don't know about fascinating. But he is good at his job. He told me of your discussion, and of your gift to him."

Dolan bristled internally. This could be nothing more than an elaborate setup. *They found the bug...* "Yes, I sometimes carry them with me. It seemed appropriate."

"But not today."

"No, not today, unfortunately," replied Dolan. "I can send you one, of course."

"Only if it's autographed," Solak responded with a wink.

"Of course."

Solak poured them another drink. "So, I don't have much time, I have matters to attend to back in Ankara. So, to the point. I am very familiar with your thesis. I've read it. Brilliant work." He pointed at Dolan.

"Thank you, Minister."

"I've also studied the Miltner-Dolan model. An amazing application of your work, and if I may say so, quite ingenious. I've used mathematical elements of it as inspiration for improving some of the algorithms Red Fig uses in a few of our software products. So, we are connected by what we do. As soon as I realized you were in Turkey, I tried to find out where you were staying but was unable. So, I had my staff contact American University. When they told me you would be here in Istanbul today, on the very day I was planning to be here on business, I instructed the registration desk to tell me when you checked in. The moment you did, I sent Kartal to bring you up after the keynote. And here you are."

"Here I am," Dolan repeated cordially. "I am flattered by your comments, particularly coming from a man as accomplished as yourself. Thank you."

"Not at all," Solak waved his hand. "We are of the same ilk, you and I. It is a rare opportunity. When great minds cross paths and share ideas, the synergistic result is a whole new breed of innovation. Your work with Miltner is a prime example of that. For me, that's the stuff of life." He paused to pour them both another drink, downing his in one gulp. Dolan followed suit. "I'm afraid I've run out of time, Michael. Before you go, however, I'd like to invite you to Red Fig Headquarters. When will you be back in Ankara? Would Saturday at noon work for you? I can give you the VIP tour, and we can have lunch there. I feel we have much more to discuss."

It was all Dolan could do to contain himself. They were *not* the same. Solak was a murderer, and probably worse. His blood was beginning to boil. On the outside, he remained serene and unencumbered. "Thank you very much, Minister, I accept. I'd originally planned to attend two days of the conference, but just yesterday I decided to return to Ankara tomorrow. I look forward to it."

"Michael, please, call me Yusuf. It's settled then." Solak stood up and held out his hand, smiling again from ear to ear.

Dolan agreed, shook his hand, and left the room. He nodded at Goliath as he retrieved his jacket from the closet. After checking that both his phone and the cloning device were still there and unmolested, he put it on and stepped out through the door with the full impact of what had just happened finally hitting him.

CHAPTER TWENTY-SEVEN

By four p.m. on Friday, Dolan, Haddad, and Welker were all back at the safehouse. Dolan initiated a call with Freeman. Despite how exhausted they were, there was little time to rest.

"First of all, what a coup," Dolan began. "Honestly, I don't see how either op could have gone any better. I never made contact with my second target, but incomprehensibly, I gained an audience with Solak himself along with an invitation to visit RED Fig Headquarters tomorrow."

Welker was shaking his head incredulously. "Amazing. You're a fucking unicorn, Michael Dolan."

Dolan laughed. "And get this. Solak told me he used mathematical elements of my model as inspiration for some of the algorithms they've incorporated in some of Red Fig's applications. He's a fan. OK, enough about that, what have you got for me Thomas?"

"A lot," Freeman came through. "Though I'll be honest guys, there's so much to look at I don't have near enough bandwidth for it. I asked Dittrich for some help and…"

"You did *what?*" questioned Dolan. "Why did you do that without asking me first?"

"Um… Well, because it's too much. I need help, Michael. Anyway, Dittrich seemed surprised at our activities. I told him what I know. Sorry, I thought you'd been updating him. He wants you to call him."

"Now you know why I don't want you going over my head," Dolan admonished. "I was waiting until we had some hard-hitting, verifiable intel and a good idea about what we're up against. Until then, we're here on borrowed time. Anything we do or say that makes it look like we can't do this ourselves means a quick trip home. Do you all understand?"

"Yes sir," Freeman acknowledged sheepishly.

Haddad nodded. Welker rolled his eyes.

"What did you find, Thomas?" asked Dolan.

"Bottom line, the server in Selçuk was a direct hit. Remember the backdoor I found via the Berlin server? I was able to get in, but only got a glimpse of what was inside. Well, it turns out this server IS what's inside. Not only is it a part of the ledger, but it also stores a vast database of personal and financial information. What is strange and scary, however, is how big it is. IP addresses, demographic details, banking information, usernames, passwords and more…for over six-hundred million people. And it's constantly updating and growing."

"Holy shit. Is that number correct?" Howard blurted.

"Yes," Freeman confirmed. "And I double-checked. Over six-hundred million unique individuals. Not accounts, individuals."

Dolan was overcome immediately by an extreme sense of urgency. His gut was telling him that if action wasn't taken soon, something terrible was going to happen. And only REVENANT was positioned to do it. But they needed more.

"You still have access Thomas?" Dolan asked.

"Yes. Unless someone notices the breach, either at the server site or the malware I installed, I should have it indefinitely."

"They're going to notice," Howard interjected flatly. "I burned out six of the security cameras. Whoever monitors them is probably already there investigating. Plus, there's other damage to the fence and roof. My guess is, you'll be offline within the day."

"Oh." Freeman sounded crestfallen. "Well, that's unfortunate. I've been imaging everything I can but like I said, it's continually growing. And there's constant communication between that server and three others somewhere else, although I can't determine where those three are. Whoever is running them knows what they're doing."

"Thanks Thomas, good work. What about the Duman clone?"

I haven't touched it yet. I'm just now looking at what we got from the Hypotherion Exchange. At first glance, it doesn't seem very helpful. Standard, run-of-the-mill transactions. I'm going to run it all through an algorithm to sort it out, there are over seventy million. I'll be looking for pattern breakers, exorbitantly large investments, etcetera. I'll get back with you on it, probably tomorrow."

"Punt the clone over to Berlin," Dolan recommended. "Put Stan on it."

"I don't know," cautioned Freeman. "You know he's not so technically inclined…"

"He can figure it out," Dolan replied. "He's got a whole team of nerds over there who can help him."

Welker chuckled. "Michael's right. We need to spread the work around."

"Last thing," Dolan said. "Aslan. Anything new there? I spent a lot of time on the bus going through the recordings but other than the one where we think he's talking to the Russians, they're all in Turkish."

"I've run them all through a machine interpreter," responded Freeman. Most of them are short but there's an awful lot of them, and AI interpreting is not the best as you know. So, some of it comes out as gobbledygook. So far, it doesn't look promising."

"Kick those over to Stan, too, Thomas. I want you focused on the server and everything in that database. I know he has a couple Turkish linguists up there."

"Sure, OK," agreed Freeman.

Dolan stood up from the couch. "That's it for now then. Again, excellent work, everyone. Thank you."

♦

Dolan was careful not to let the high he was riding after the previous day's successes get in the way of their current task—finding Demir's algorithmic model. He mentally reviewed their plan as Welker drove the embassy loaner eastward.

It was four a.m. as they left the car about a block away. Aside from the quarter moon peeking through a partially obscured sky, a lone underpowered streetlamp by the bus stop provided the only light. They passed beneath it and onwards. In the distance, a dog's barking echoed mysteriously through the still streets.

Welker picked the lock, and they entered the duplex silently through the front door. Aided by night vision monoculars, they walked past the dining room and kitchen, then split up in the hallway. They each stopped by one of the two bedroom doors. Dolan's was partially open. He peered inside, seeing Demir's daughter sleeping soundly in her bed. Welker gave him a three-two-one finger countdown and they entered simultaneously.

Dolan approached the young girl, just twelve years old. He took a square cotton napkin and small aerosol can from his pocket. For a moment, he observed her. How horribly sad she must be now, with her father gone. The terrible lies told about him in the nation's newspapers. All because Demir tried to do the right thing. It made him hate Solak even more. Suddenly, he realized he hadn't felt that way about anyone since Sharif Lefebvre. But he'd worked through that. It took a long time, but he did it. It made him wonder if he was slipping. He couldn't let his emotions get in the way. *Stay focused.* He draped the cloth over her face and sprayed the aerosol on it. Three quick bursts. She moaned slightly and was still. He pocketed the cloth and can.

"Aren't you done yet?" Welker asked from behind, startling him.

"Yeah, I'm done. I feel bad having to do that to her. No dog?"

"No dog. And mommy is out like a light. Don't worry, they'll just be sleeping in a little longer than usual." Welker slapped Dolan on the back.

"Good. Let's get started then."

Over the next two hours, Dolan and Welker went through the entire house and everything in it. They found two laptops, four portable hard drives, seven thumb drives, and a handful of SD cards. They copied all of it onto a 10-terabyte solid state drive.

As they were packing up and making sure nothing looked disturbed, Dolan turned to Welker. "I don't think we have it. He wouldn't leave it lying around the house. To do a proper search, we'd need five men and a week. We'd have to tear the house apart."

"I know," Welker acknowledged. "But we don't have five men, and we don't have a week. Heck, I doubt it was ever in the house. He probably uploaded it online somewhere. But we do what we can do."

"True. All true," Dolan replied.

Satisfied they'd done their best, they left the house. Welker locked the door with his pick tools, and they headed back to the vehicle.

CHAPTER TWENTY-EIGHT

Dolan arrived via taxi at ten minutes to noon. The gate guard checked his driver's license against a list on his clipboard, then waved him in. The driver dropped him at the front door of the main building.

Once inside, he laid his jacket and briefcase on the X-ray machine conveyor belt and walked through the metal detector. On the other side, he retrieved his things and walked to the reception desk where he gave his name and the purpose of his visit to a young Turkish woman.

"Doctor Dolan, welcome to Red Fig. Mister Aslan is expecting you. He will be here for you momentarily. You can wait over there if you like." She pointed to three red, oddly shaped chairs nearby.

"They're figs," she said to him.

"Excuse me?" asked Dolan.

"The chairs," she responded. "They're shaped like figs. You know, because *Red Fig*." She tilted her head to the side and smiled.

He smiled back. *I don't see it*, he thought. "I'll just wait here, thank you."

After a few minutes, he recognized Ahmet Aslan descending the curved staircase from the second floor to the lobby. Dolan walked to him, and they exchanged greetings.

"Unfortunately, Yusuf has been called away for an emergency," Aslan told him as they climbed the stairwell, "so we won't be having lunch with him today. He sends his apologies."

Aslan handed Dolan an envelope with his name scrawled in cursive on the front. "From the Minister," he said.

Dolan belied his disappointment. "It's understandable. He has a lot on his plate." He put the envelope in his pocket.

"That he does," Aslan agreed. "But you can be certain you will get the best possible tour of our facilities today. The main building is five stories high with over two thousand employees. We have six other, smaller buildings on the campus. And we generate our own electricity, did you know that? Our solar array is two kilometers away…"

The tour took two hours. To say it was impressive would be an understatement. Dolan had never been to the main Apple or Google campuses, but he imagined this was probably what they were like. The amount of money flowing through this company must have been astronomical. It was unfortunate Dolan wouldn't have another chance to glean more from a second meeting with Solak. He would get what he could, however, from Aslan.

Back at the top of the staircase, Aslan seemed ready to say goodbye.

"Since we're not going to have lunch, perhaps we can have a drink instead?" Dolan suggested.

Aslan hesitated, then smiled warmly. "I do have pressing work I must get to; however, I could use one myself. I have something in my office. Let's go there."

He led Dolan away from the stairs to the end of a wide hallway. His was the northeast corner suite. Aslan used his security badge to open the door and they walked inside. It wasn't lavish, but it was spacious and comfortable. Both outward-looking walls were floor-to-ceiling plate glass and gave him a good view of the north side of the campus. The two opposing, interior walls were bare.

"I'm a simple man, Michael," he said as he poured their drinks. "This office, I can take it or leave it. When I was selected as Chief of Technology, Yusuf gave me an office on the fifth floor. It's much nicer than this. I turned it down."

It sounded like virtue signaling to Dolan. "Why?"

"Because I wanted to stay closer to my employees. The work, and my workers. That is what I love, not things. All my directors have offices on this level. I could drive a Porsche, or a Lamborghini even, but I drive a Citroën. Driving fast doesn't matter to me. Getting there safe and reliably, that's what matters. Those are things that make people happy. To be free from worry. Have you heard of eL8?"

Dolan sipped from his glass and nodded. "Yes, it's the happiness app. Pretty successful, from what I've been told."

Aslan smiled. "My baby. I spent three years studying what makes people happy. Before I even began to code the app. I wanted to make sure I got it right. I think I did. Over six-hundred thirty million users agree with me. It's what got me where I am today." He gave Dolan a wink.

The number struck a nerve. Dolan had a sudden urge to wrap it up and get back so he could talk to Freeman. "Congratulations on eL8, it's an amazing accomplishment. Have you had a chance to look at it yet?" Dolan pointed to his thesis lying on the table next to Aslan's desk.

"No, not yet," Aslan replied. "I need to bring it home so I can read it when I have some spare time. Thank you again for the signed copy."

"My pleasure." Dolan stood up then, walked over to the table and picked it up, then sat back down. "I need to check something."

Aslan gave him a curious look. "Please."

Dolan then placed his briefcase on his lap, opened it, and pulled out another copy of his thesis. He made a point of holding a copy in each hand, as if comparing them. "Just as I thought."

"What?" Aslan asked.

"I accidentally gave you one of the older copies. The first print run had several missing pages. The publisher gave me the lot and reprinted. I was going to have them all destroyed, but some of them got commingled with the second print run."

He put Aslan's copy in his briefcase and handed him the other. "I'm glad I was able to make that right. This one is also signed."

Aslan took the book and raised his glass. "Well, thank you. I am fortunate you suggested having a drink!"

Dolan raised his as well. "As am I."

CHAPTER TWENTY-NINE

Back at the hotel, Dolan spent Saturday afternoon and part of the evening summarizing what they'd learned in a draft report. Dittrich had called him three times in the past two days, but he wasn't ready for that conversation. They were close, but still not there. He called Bolden in Berlin to get an update.

"Tell me some good news, Stan."

"Hi Michael. I wish I had more, but as you know I only started working this yesterday. I have a couple of folks here at the station helping. For now, I can tell you that the phone looks like a dead end. We haven't identified any texts, emails, or phone calls that I would call red flags. We're not done with it yet, but it looks like Duman is legit. He's an equity finance professional. Before he started his own firm, he was with Denizbank. Looks like he's on the Hypotherion Board for his expertise and nothing else. No other direct business ties to Red Fig."

"Well, that's unfortunate," Dolan replied. "Keep digging. And the recordings from Aslan? Anything there?"

"Thomas didn't send me the recordings, just the machine translated transcripts. I went through those myself last night. Lots of phone calls. Unfortunately, Aslan isn't a fan of using speakerphone, so we didn't get whatever was said on the other side. There were two, though, where he was most likely speaking with Solak. He received a call late Thursday and you were mentioned, it was about setting up your tour at Red Fig Headquarters. Nothing suspicious about that one. The second one, however, was interesting. Aslan called someone I presume to be Solak to inform him of the physical breach in Selçuk. The translation contained a lot of nonsensical language, so I asked Thomas to send me the original audio of that one file to see if one of our linguists could improve on it. You can hear what sounds like Solak on the other side yelling, but we couldn't make out what was said. Basically, Aslan mentioned the fence, cameras, and roof, and that he didn't yet know if any data had been compromised on the server. He made no mention of Thomas' malware, so I don't think, as of the time of the phone call, that it had been noticed. But it's probably just a matter of time."

"Hmmm," Dolan responded. "OK. We knew it wouldn't take long for them to notice. It's why Solak skipped out on lunch, I bet. He's doing damage control. Alright. Thanks Stan, this is helpful."

"Sure thing boss," replied Bolden. "Do you need me to come down there? I'm busy, but if I'm being honest, I'm not too busy to check out of here for a week. It sounds like the three of you have your hands full."

Dolan quickly weighed the pros and cons. Yes, they had too much to do and too little time. But too many boots on the ground would increase their risk of exposure. With the MIT on their scent, it was all they could do to stay one step ahead.

"Sit tight," he responded. "I may push a few more things your way. Depending on how my call with Dittrich goes, we might have to make a quick exit. I'll let you know."

"Understood," Bolden replied. "Stay safe."

"You too Stan."

Dolan ended the call and exhaled. He was tired and edgy. He hadn't had any physical activity at all since arriving in Turkey. He needed to declutter his mind, and nothing did that better for him than a good workout. He sent a text to Haddad to let him know, then changed into his running gear.

He left the hotel and crossed the street into Kurtuluş Park. It was the only good option, otherwise he'd be stopping and starting at every intersection through the middle of the city. He set his Garmin and sprinted off. It wasn't nearly big enough for his liking, but he could run loops in the park until he was finished. His mind raced as he pushed himself, nearly oblivious to the trees and long shadows cast across his path. He made seventeen full circuits, running right by the place where Andy was shot. Seventeen times. Each time he passed it, he was hit by a pang of guilt and sadness. Over and over and over. It felt like a penance of sorts. But with each repetition, it hurt a little less. By the time he finished, he was able to put his emotions in better perspective. Or at least he thought so.

After showering, Dolan checked the time. It was still early in northern Virginia. He was loathing the call he was about to make. He just couldn't put it off any longer. They'd gathered enough intel at this point to be able to pass everything off to Ankara Station. Dolan surmised that either way, Dittrich would probably be sending them home.

Before he made the call, however, he would check one last time on a reply from Yuri. He powered up the burner and logged in. As luck would have it, there was a new email in the inbox. The subject line read *Now You Owe Me 2*. All the adrenaline he'd burned off in Kurtuluş Park came roaring back, and then some. He opened it and scanned the text.

Nobelium. This is all I can give you. I've put myself at risk looking into it. If they were to be successful in this, it could benefit us, TBH. But only in the short term. It could hurt us greatly down the road. Stay safe.

The opening line was followed by a list of IP addresses and a lot of other technical data he didn't understand. He remembered Yuri's warning about how to save the data from the email. It required seven screenshots to capture all the information, which he texted to his work cell. He waited to see the texts were received, then deleted the images on the burner. He logged out of the email account, removed the battery, and broke the phone and the SIM card in two. After forwarding the texts to Freeman, he called him.

"Hello?"

"Check your cell. You were right, it's Nobelium."

Freeman was eating a sandwich, watching college football on one screen while working on the other. He paused the game and looked at the text.

"Michael... Where did you get this? How?"

"Never mind that," Dolan told him. "Is that something you can work with?"

"Well, I don't know. I'll need verification. What's your source?"

"Like I said, don't worry about it. The source is good," Dolan assured him.

"OK, but you know I can't just start hacking into servers without knowing what they are, who they are. Where they are. There's a protocol for this."

"Holy hell, Thomas. I just told you, it's Nobelium. Forget the protocols. We're not going to get any other verification. There is none. And we're running out of time. Can't you just go in, poke around, and verify for yourself?"

Freeman paused to think. "Yes, I suppose I can. But..."

"Just do it. And get back with me as soon as you do, OK?"

"Sure Michael. I'll get on it right now."

"Thanks."

Dolan hung up. He felt better now about his next call, though he wished like hell he could wait until after Freeman had dug into it. But he was out of time. He dialed Dittrich.

"It's about Fucking time," Dittrich answered. "Give me a minute. I'm just getting into the office."

Dolan listened as he closed his office door, walked across the room, and rearranged some of the files on his desk.

"Alright, I'm back. Why the hell have you been ignoring me?"

Dolan took a breath before answering. "We've been in the field. It's been nonstop through today. I'm doing what you told me to do."

"I see," Dittrich replied. "Not good enough though. You promised me to keep me informed on this one. It's too sensitive. Remember?"

It was true. "I remember. Yes, I should have gotten back with you earlier. The truth is, I didn't want you to make any decisions about pulling the team out before we figured out what's going on here."

"Have you?" Dittrich snapped back.

"It's definitely a puzzle. We've put all the edge pieces together. A picture is beginning to form." Stolen from Fitzhenry. Dolan didn't think he'd mind.

"That's a vague pile of nothing, Michael. Tell me what you know. Skip the puzzle crap."

Dolan was already exasperated. "I was setting the scene, Phil. Calm down. Solak is using a seventh server in Selçuk to hide a huge database of personal data, over six hundred million people. It includes financial information, usernames, passwords, even demographic data. And it's growing by the second. I think he and Red Fig have been stealing it from the users of their apps."

"That may not even be illegal, though," Dittrich countered, "depending on what the EULA says."

"I get it. But the data itself, it's atypical. A lot of it is banking information. In other words, it looks like usernames and passwords for their bank accounts, and the names of the banks. Not the kind of information they'd need for app accounts. In fact, it's way out of bounds. Thomas imaged everything. He should be writing up a summary of what he found today. But that's not even the big news."

"What is the big news, then?" Dittrich asked.

"I've been informed by a very good source that the Russian hacker group Nobelium collaborated with Red Fig on the HIVE software development project in Niamey."

"Seriously? SolarWinds Nobelium?"

"Yes."

"Seriously?" Dittrich replied.

"Yes. We have their IP addresses. The Nobelium engineers. We can target their systems. Whatever they were planning to do, we might be able to shut it down. Assuming they are hosting the application and not Red Fig. Even if they're not, we can still hurt them. I just sent all the information over the Thomas."

"Holy shit, Dolan. How on Earth did you manage that? Who's the source?"

Dolan took another breath. "Yuri Kuznetsov."

"From the GRU? From Berlin? Are you out of your mind? Michael, that was a terrible mistake. I know I told you a few years ago that we might be able to use him down the road, but that was before Ukraine. The state of things has changed drastically since then. You could be putting your team in serious jeopardy. How much did you tell him?"

"Just enough," Dolan answered. "Listen, I understand it was a risk. But I went with my gut, and I think I was right. He asked for nothing. I was able to convince him that what Nobelium was up to would be detrimental to the Russian Federation. He agreed with me. That means they've overstepped their bounds, and he's punishing them for it. Listen, we've made a lot of progress the past few days, and we're at the point where we have actionable intelligence. Before long, we should know what Solak and Red Fig are planning and we can decide what to do after that. But for now, I need you to give me more resources. Thomas needs help. I've got Stan doing phone forensics and translation services, for God's sake."

"Michael, I don't know how to tell you this any other way," Dittrich began, "so I'll just say it. I'm bringing you back. The Director told me to pull the plug. He has no choice, it's too political. Take a day to type up your reports and come home. If what you got from Kuznetsov pans out, I'll put the UMBRAGE team on Nobelium. No matter what happens, we are going to find out who was behind Andy's murder, and when we do, we'll decide how to respond. But that's out of your hands. The powers that be, right now they don't want to hear about how one of Avci's ministers might be breaking the law here and there to gain an industry advantage with Red Fig, or with Hypotherion for that matter. Everyone's in love with Hypotherion. The entire world is in love with Avci. The President doesn't want us touching Turkey right now. It's kryptonite. That's it."

Dolan could feel the world crumbling down around him as Dittrich spoke. They were *so close*. He couldn't shake the feeling that what Solak had put in motion here was far more sinister and far-reaching than anyone could have imagined. The evidence was piling up. Dittrich was telling him to ignore it, to let it evolve, because the President and Secretary of State and whoever else were petrified of disrupting the diplomatic status quo.

"Are you at least planning to give what we've uncovered to Ankara Station?" questioned Dolan.

"That remains to be seen," Dittrich replied. "We'll review your reports. In all likelihood, it will be a very narrow, targeted subset of what you've found that we'll pass on to them. It will take some time to analyze everything first."

"I met with Solak, by the way. In Istanbul," Dolan told him. "He wanted to meet me. He's familiar with my work on the spread and containment of epidemics. Said Miltner's math from our model inspired him. I have an in with him. There's so much more I can do…"

"You never cease to amaze me, that's for sure," Dittrich responded. "I'm impressed. But like I said, this is beyond my control. You'll have to shut it down and pack out."

Sir, I can't disagree more with this decision," Dolan stated forcefully. "It's the wrong play."

"Your opinion on the matter is noted," Dittrich shot back. "It's over. Come home." Then he hung up.

CHAPTER THIRTY

The next morning found Dolan, Haddad, and Welker huddled around the safehouse dining room table with Freeman conferenced in. Dolan began by bringing them up to speed on his phone conversation with Dittrich the night before.

"So, we've been shut down," Dolan concluded. "But…that doesn't necessarily mean we can't tie up a few loose ends as we head out of town. Dittrich gave us a day to finish our reports. So, let's do that. If one day stretches into two, I'll beg for forgiveness later. I want to make sure we capture absolutely everything before we leave. Thomas, I told Dittrich about the Nobelium server information, but I didn't tell him you were going to hack in. What did you find?"

"I'm glad you asked," Thomas responded ceremoniously. "Those IP addresses you gave me were the real deal. There's a whole trove of data, malware, exploits, you name it on those Russian servers. Dittrich told me to pass the info you gave me to UMBRAGE, which I did, but not before I found FrankenHIVE and made a copy. I've had some time to study it, and I learned three very important things. One, the server it is running on appears to be one of the three that were communicating with the server in Selçuk. It looks like FrankenHIVE is selectively grabbing information from the database in Selçuk, which I was pushed out of by the way, using an algorithm that has commonalities with…drum roll…the Miltner-Dolan Model."

"Bullshit," Welker blurted out.

"Thomas, what are you talking about?" Dolan asked incredulously. "How could my model possibly help in any way with a cyberattack? And no offense, but what made you come to such a conclusion?"

"*You* made me think of it, Michael," Freeman replied. "When you told us Solak was inspired by your model. Remember when I told you that some of the changes made to the original HIVE looked algorithmic? I put two and two together. Anyway, from what I can tell, the purpose of FrankenHIVE is to steal money from people and businesses, all over the world. That algorithm seems to be in place to decide which accounts to attack, and which ones to leave alone. What I can't figure out is, how are they getting the personal and financial information in the first place, and when they execute the application, where all the money will go. Most likely into crypto wallets controlled by Nobelium."

"Or…into Hypotherion?" Dolan questioned.

"Um, maybe?" Freeman answered. "I suppose that's a possible theory, but that level of criminal activity, on such a scale…for what is essentially a globally benevolent organization. It wouldn't make any sense. Someone would find out; they are too public."

"I'm thinking outside the box," Dolan countered. "And honestly, I don't think it's a stretch. It's all connected somehow. OK, what else?"

"Also, I think we found Demir's model. I'm not positive, as I've had very little time to look at it, but it's possible. It was saved on one of the thumb drives you found at his house. I'll let you know for sure when I can, but now that I'm off the case, it may be a while. That's it for now.

Dittrich told me to pause everything at my end and help UMBRAGE build an exploitation plan. I've already started with that."

Dolan was visibly upset. He needed Thomas for at least another day.

"It's Sunday. They have you working on this *today?*" asked Dolan.

"Of course—it's too big. We must move on it now," Freeman replied.

"Do me a favor first," Dolan said. "Wipe FrankenHIVE off the server. Do it now. It could go live at any moment, and I don't think anyone at Langley realizes how big the impact could be."

"Michael, I can't, you know that. It will alert Nobelium immediately, they'll know they've been hacked, they'll shut everything down and migrate to new servers. We won't have another shot at it. I'll be fired, for God's sake."

"You won't be fired, Thomas. I might be fired, but not you. This is on me. I'll tell you what, just wipe all the servers. Image what you can and destroy everything on all the servers."

Welker shot Dolan a sideways look. "Um, boss, not a good idea."

Dolan sighed. They were right. This was something he couldn't order Thomas to do based on a hunch.

Silence on the speakerphone.

"OK, OK OK," Dolan conceded. "Never mind any of that. Do what you need to do for UMBRAGE. But…what if you were to sabotage it, to prevent FrankenHIVE from working? Could you do that, without them noticing?"

There was a pause before he answered. "Er, maybe. There are several ways to do something like that. The trick is to do it in a manner that is difficult to find. Make it look like a coding error they made themselves. A team like Nobelium would be able to fix something like that quickly. But if they can't find the defect…"

"Alright. Try that then," Dolan instructed him. "Let me know when it's done, OK? Also, since I'm losing you, send all the data we got from the Hypotherion Exchange over to Stan. Let's see if he can data mine anything. And send me the folder path and filename of Demir's model."

"Sure thing," Freeman responded. "If and when Nobelium tries to go live with the cyberattack, they'll notice immediately that it's not working and try to fix it. We'll be monitoring the whole time though, and we'll never let them get to the point where they can fully implement it. You're right, Michael, about this being huge. The sheer number of accounts it could affect...hundreds of millions. It's staggering. It could tank stock markets worldwide, overnight. If enough accounts from a single bank were affected, it could cause them to go under. If too many banks in the U.S. were hit hard all at once, it could undermine the FDIC's ability to insure them. And even if they could, the limit is $250,000 per depositor, per account. Any amount over that would be lost."

"I'm putting all my money under my mattress," quipped Welker.

Haddad and Freeman laughed. *At least we know it won't be deployed now*, thought Dolan. He wondered what else he could do in the day or two they had left. Instead of gaining resources, he was losing them. The 'powers that be' weren't going to go after Solak or Red Fig. Instead, they would shift their focus to a palatable enemy so they could still feel good about themselves without having to blame the real villain.

"Thomas, thanks so much for all your work on this. Let me know what happens with FrankenHIVE, OK? I'll work directly with Stan on the Exchange data."

Freeman acknowledged and hung up the call.

Dolan looked at Welker, then at Haddad. "We have one last ace up our sleeve."

"What's that?" Haddad asked.

Dolan reached in his pocket and pulled out the envelope Aslan gave him the day before and opened it.

"This," Dolan held out the card, "is a formal invitation to a VIP event at the Beştepe Complex tomorrow night. From Solak. He'll be there, some of the other ministers. Industry leaders. And President Avci. Solak felt bad he couldn't be there to meet me for lunch yesterday at Red Fig Headquarters. Black tie."

"You gotta be shittin' me," said Welker incredulously.

"I'm not," replied Dolan.

"You're not going to go, though, right?" Asked Haddad cautiously.

"I wasn't. But I think now, I am. We're all supposed to leave tomorrow. I can't ask either of you to stay behind for this, and honestly, I'm not sure there's much you'd be able to help with anyway. Dittrich is going to be pissed. I recommend you fly home."

"He's going to be pissed because you're not going to tell him about it?" Welker asked.

"If I tell him about it, he'll order me not to do it," Dolan stated flatly.

"True. You know me. I'm in," said Welker.

Haddad sat there for a moment, contemplating his decision. "If you don't think I can really help, and you don't mind, I'll head back."

"Not a problem, Omar," Dolan replied. "But do me a favor. Don't tell Dittrich. I'll tell him about it myself, soon enough."

"Sure, OK," Haddad replied.

"So, what's the plan?" Welker asked eagerly.

"I'm still working out the details. One way or the other, though, I think it involves a conversation between me and President Adem Avci."

CHAPTER THIRTY-ONE

The next morning, Haddad said his goodbyes and grabbed a taxi to the airport. Dolan RSVPd for that evening and met with Welker at the safehouse to refine their plan. Then he headed out to get fitted for a tux, returned to his hotel, and went for another long run in Kurtuluş Park. Just as he was about to step in the shower, his cell rang. It was Freeman.

"Look at the news. It's all everyone's talking about. There was a deep selloff right at the opening bell in New York. They had to stop trading. Michael, they had a second copy of FrankenHIVE, and they deployed it…"

Dolan dropped his towel. "Shit. How bad is it? Is it still going on, the cyberattack?"

"That's just it, no," responded Freeman. "I sabotaged the Nobelium application like you said, and early this morning they tried to go live, and couldn't of course. Talk about good timing. But about three hours later, alarm bells started going off everywhere. Banks all over the world were being hacked. Remembered the Aslan recording in English where we thought he might be talking to the Russians? Where he mentioned a copy, and that under no circumstances would he launch from there?"

"I remember. So, Nobelium notified Solak that they had a problem and couldn't go live, so he decided to do it on his own. Shit."

"Yes. It made sense they would try to execute the attack from Red Fig Headquarters. It took me about an hour, but because I'd already collected a trove of information from the Berlin and Selçuk servers, and because I had an image of FrankenHIVE, I was able to pinpoint where it was and hack in. Turns out it was the second of the three servers that the Selçuk server was constantly communicating with. Right there at Red Fig. And get this, that server is *also* the operations and maintenance hub for all the eL8 app accounts, worldwide. Michael, they were using eL8, their happiness app, to phish financial account data from over six hundred million people..."

"Alright," Dolan interrupted. "You have my attention. What's the damage? Were you able to stop it?"

"Yes. But not until after it had processed over fifteen million transactions. It was happening so fast. I didn't want to delete it, because it's evidence, and people will want a way to get their money back. But I couldn't leave it running, either. So, I wiped the server. Two birds with one stone."

"I knew that eL8 app was fishy," Dolan remarked. "But you know, Aslan invented it. He didn't strike me as the type who would be involved with trying to rip off the entire world. Some people are just difficult to read I guess..."

"I'll take your word for it," Freeman replied.

"Sure. Nice work, Thomas. Do we know where all the money went?"

"That's just it. I have no idea. And I wiped the server, so I can't find out. The only way to know would be to do forensics on the integration of Nobelium's FrankenHIVE. But that's a delicate operation because we can't tip them off that we're in their servers..."

"Does Dittrich know?"

"He's about to. I haven't had time to loop him in. I wanted you to know first."

"I appreciate it, Thomas. Anything else?"

"That's it for now. I'm exhausted, I haven't slept for two days. I'm going to call Dittrich now. Then I need to bring the UMBRAGE team up to speed."

"Understood. Take care." Dolan hung up.

Dolan checked the news on his cell phone. The DOW lost almost three thousand points in the first fifteen minutes, at which point they halted trading. International markets experienced similar declines. There were initial estimates rolling in on the total amount of money that had 'disappeared' around the world, hundreds of billions, trillions. No one knew for sure. Dolan scanned several news articles and found one that listed the countries that had been hardest hit. The United States topped the list, which wasn't surprising. But two countries lower on the list *were* surprising: the Russian Federation and Turkey. Why would Nobelium get involved at all if they knew they'd be hurting Russia? Why did Yuri say that the hack could help Russia in the short term? He must not have understood the true scope of the attack. More importantly, why would Solak and Red Fig screw the citizens of their own country? It couldn't be for the money. It made no sense.

He checked his Breitling. He had about an hour to finish getting ready before heading to the event. As he showered, he tried to predict how the CIA and the President would react to all of this. Would they confront Avci, share the intelligence, force him to shut Solak and Red Fig down? Give all the money back? What would happen to Hypotherion? The best course of action, if they were to reimburse those whose money was stolen, would be to know where it went before that confrontation. Or, would they blame it on Russia? Dolan was betting that was a big part of the exploitation plan Freeman was helping UMBRAGE with. Blame the whole thing on the Russians. The idea made him feel sick inside. Politics was a dirty business.

Once in the cab, Dolan texted Welker, who replied right away.

OMW

Copy

About halfway to the complex, he received a call from Bolden.

"Hi Stan, what have you got for me," Dolan asked.

"I'm surprised I go a hold of you," he replied. "Figured you'd be on a plane right now."

"Not yet. What's up?"

"Well, I did some preliminary work on the mountain of data Thomas sent me from the Exchange. I'm getting help from one of our analysts; there's still a lot of work to do on it. But we came across something interesting I thought you'd like to hear."

"Go ahead, spit it out Stan."

"Right. We decided to focus just on the larger investments, a hundred thousand euros and up. There were no red flags in the past six months or so, in fact, there weren't a significant number of transactions in that category during that span. Not compared to before that period, anyway. Going back five years, there were just over twenty-two thousand transactions that were over that amount. And some of them were much, much higher. When we looked at who they were coming from, we noticed a few patterns. In most cases, the investments were made by an individual, or a company, or an investment firm. On the surface, those seem to pan out. About thirty-five percent of them, though, had no name or company associated with them, only routing and account numbers. Forty-seven accounts, to be exact.

"Those forty-seven accounts each made numerous deposits over the five-year period. We began checking on them, and get this, all forty-seven are closed. The accounts don't exist anymore. But here's the kicker. Eleven of the routing numbers are banks in Panama where Hakeem Lefebvre kept his money, and we confirmed at least three of the account numbers were his."

Dolan glanced at his driver to make sure he wasn't listening in, continuing in a whisper. "Holy shit, Stan, this is incredible news. It ties Solak directly to Lefebvre and the AMA. All the other circumstantial evidence we've uncovered now falls neatly into place. Solak was hiding him because Lefebvre was pumping cash into Hypotherion. And I'll bet more than three of those accounts were Lefebvre's."

"Yup," Bolden replied. "They couldn't possibly all be his, though. The amount is just too big. But it lends credence to the theory that when Lefebvre's cash ran out, Solak outed him and kept the money. Are you in a car?"

"Yes, I'm in a cab," Dolan responded. "Listen, keep digging through that data. Build the case. Don't tell anyone about it yet, though. OK?"

"Sure Michael. But that's not all. And this one is really weird. Back in March there were thousands of transfers that were made, all at once. Within a four-day period, there were over a hundred thousand transactions that moved a total of one point five trillion euros out of the bank. When you add up the nameless deposits I mentioned, it's almost the same amount. And they were all the same transaction type. *NFT payout.*"

"Non-fungible token," Dolan said. "Hypotherion's carbon offsets. Huh. All at the same time. It's an astronomical amount; it doesn't add up. Does the data show where those transactions went? Who got paid?"

"Nope. That's it. Poof."

"OK, I'm almost at my destination. Stay on it, I'll get back with you later tonight, or early tomorrow. Nice work!"

"Thanks, take care." Bolden ended the call.

A dark, foreboding feeling engulfed him as they drove on. Dolan again thought of his discussion with Fitzhenry. Dolan didn't tell him at the time because he didn't want to encourage Fitzhenry further, but he'd read Revelation. Back when he was in high school. And with his photographic memory, he still remembered most of it. If John of Patmos wrote Revelation to foretell of the events unfolding all around him now, it made sense that the book was so full of vague imagery and symbolism. There was no way he could have understood back then how technology would evolve; what dangers would exist in the world two thousand years later. Could a cyberattack be interpreted as a plague? Could the red horse and its rider, which 'takes peace from the Earth,' represent Red Fig? Who were the other three horsemen of the apocalypse? Solak had only been partially successful, thanks to REVENANT. Was it enough to forestall global financial catastrophe and all that might follow? Dolan's gut told him yes. If so, this was no apocalypse. Unless what Solak had unleashed was just enough to set the world on a path to inevitable destruction. It could be this was just the beginning. Or, the whole Revelation thing was just hogwash.

Dolan smiled to himself. In the end, it didn't matter. For him, it was simple. He would do what he could to protect America and Americans from those who sought to hurt them. Right now, that meant holding Solak accountable.

CHAPTER THIRTY-TWO

The sprawling Presidential Complex was in the Beştepe section of Ankara, inside the Atatürk Forest Farm. The main palace was flanked by two support buildings. Including the mosque, guesthouses, the botanical garden, and various bunkers and communications and security buildings, the entire estate covered 300,000 square meters and was constructed at a cost of over 100,000,000 euros.

He paid the driver and walked through the open gate, showing his invitation and ID to the guards. Several people in front of him were waiting to enter the palace. Once inside, he was asked to surrender his phone, but he'd decided earlier to leave it with Welker. He was certain it would be compromised if he handed it over to their security. Dolan wouldn't be able to communicate with Welker, which was concerning. But even if a situation arose where Dolan needed his help, Welker wouldn't be able to get inside. Welker's role was simple—keep an eye on the gate and make sure the car was ready for him whenever he came out. If Dolan didn't play his part perfectly, Welker might just have to watch instead as he was led to a police van in handcuffs.

After passing through the metal detector, he walked into the main hall where everyone was gathering. As he worked his way toward the middle of the room, a waft of delicious smells met him emanating from several long tables against the far-right wall laden with traditional Turkish foods and delicacies. Sharply dressed waiters stood at the periphery of the crowd with silver trays of champagne and fruit juice. Dolan scanned the crowd and noticed at least twelve security personnel stationed around the room. There were probably many more than that.

It was a night for the elitest of the elite. Ministers, defense and IT company CEOs, Mullahs, and movie stars. In any other situation, Dolan would have been honored to be invited to such an event. He grabbed a flute of champagne and moved closer to the stage. He wasn't sure about the schedule of tonight's events, other than President Avci would be speaking, among others. He needed to position himself perfectly. He would only get one chance at it.

Dolan made a point of introducing himself as a guest of Minister Solak to a handful of people right in front of the guards stationed closest to the stage. He continued to mingle nearby. Twenty minutes later, the lights dimmed, and the master of ceremonies walked across the stage to the podium. He spoke first in Turkish, then in English as he introduced Solak, who emerged from behind the right-side edge of the towering crushed red velvet curtains. A spotlight followed him to the podium amid a round of applause.

Just as his announcer had, Solak spoke first in Turkish, acknowledging a handful of high-ranking members of the government in attendance, including the President. Dolan watched and listened to the crowd as they reacted to his commentary that followed, first with disdain and chaotic side-chatter, and then, nearly all at once, with cheering. Many were elevating their glasses in the air. Then he began in English.

"Ladies and gentlemen, you have no doubt by now heard of today's global cyberattack. This was a truly evil act perpetrated against the people of the world for no other reason than greed. Those who did this cared not for the well-being of those they stole from, nor for the terrible effect on international financial markets, which has a secondary negative effect on the people themselves. There will be tertiary damages as well. This is far-reaching and will take years to recover from. I am speaking to you today to let you know that the Turkish government will not stand by. In coordination with President Avci, I have spoken with the Board of Directors at the Hypotherion Bank and Exchange, who held an emergency vote earlier today. I created Hypotherion years ago with the idea that catastrophic events such as this can be mitigated, and even reversed with carefully managed resources of a benevolent organization. Hypotherion is beholden to the needs of the people of the world. As such, the Board voted to fully reimburse all Turkish citizens who have been affected by this attack. There will be a public announcement made soon that details how each citizen can apply. Hypotherion will also lower its already very low interest rates and work hand in hand with the World Bank to immediately help those countries whose federal financial institutions are to the point of breaking. Turkey will not stand by while the world suffers around us."

As Dolan listened his blood began to boil. This man must be held accountable. Politics or not, this was someone who must be removed from power and punished. It made sense to him now why Solak did not exclude his own people from the attack. By including them, it threw the scent off. In the current political climate, anyone investigating where the attack came from wouldn't think to suspect Turkey. It also explained why Russia was not excluded; Nobelium didn't want Russia to be suspected, as the cyberattack could be traced back to them. Solak wouldn't want that either, as it could then lead back to Red Fig.

If *every* country was attacked, the attack could have come from *any* country. And the evil genius behind it all, Yusuf Solak, just announced to the world that he would reimburse his own people and lend money to the attacked countries using the very funds that he stole from them in the first place.

Solak continued. "Additionally, I've instructed my Technology Chief at Red Fig to assemble a team to investigate who is responsible for the attack. We will do everything within our power to bring these criminals to justice."

The crowd applauded and cheered again. Solak then introduced President Avci. The noise reached a crescendo as the most popular man in the world came to his side and thanked him. Solak moved to the side of the stage as Avci spoke, adding to his commentary and thanking him, Hypotherion, and Red Fig for their compassion and charity. He made other comments about the state of the country and its future, in new context of course, then wished everyone a good evening before walking towards Solak and the stairs to the main floor.

Dolan immediately began to move toward them with a smile on his face. As he approached, the two nearest security guards immediately tensed, their eyes focused on him like lasers.

"Minister Solak! Hello, what a wonderful speech. I enjoyed it thoroughly," Dolan said loudly as he extended his hand.

The two guards quickly moved between Dolan and the President, who appeared curious as to who this American might be.

Solak recognized him right away and held out his hand. "It's OK, it's OK. This is Doctor Michael Dolan, from American University. He is my guest."

They shook hands as the President smiled and began to turn away. The security agents loosened up but remained between them and Avci who was beginning to walk away.

"Minister Solak, could you possibly introduce me to your President?" Dolan entreated him.

Solak was momentarily irritated at the request, then thought better of it and smiled. "Of course. Wait here."

Solak quickly intercepted Avci and spoke briefly with him and the two guards. Then, the four approached together. All the while, the party continued all around them. A traditional Türkü band was setting up on the stage. One of the guards approached him, patted him down quickly and inspected his hands while the other eyed him suspiciously.

When the guard was finished Solak held out his palm towards Dolan with a flourish. "Mister President, may I present Doctor Michael Dolan. Doctor Dolan worked with the famous mathematician Philip Miltner to develop the Miltner-Dolan Model, which accurately predicts the spread of viral and other types of outbreaks and plagues. Our own Ministry of Health has used his model to reformulate our national epidemic response plan. Doctor Solak, Adem Avci, President of Turkey."

Avci and Dolan stepped toward each other and shook hands.

"It's a pleasure to meet you, Mister President."

"The pleasure is mine, Doctor Dolan." Avci smiled warmly. "Your great contribution to epidemiology is impressive and appreciated. What brings you to Turkey?"

"I am doing research for my work at American University in Washington, D.C.," Dolan responded. "I was attending a personal and health information study at the Ankara Center for Crisis and Policy Studies, and Hypotherion's blockchain summit in Istanbul. Both were very informative."

As he spoke, the guard who'd been eying him moved closer to Dolan. The expression on his face had morphed slowly from suspicion to great concern. Suddenly, he stepped between Avci and Dolan.

"Minister Solak," the guard blurted urgently. This man was with Demir and the American. I recognize him. He is not who you think he is."

President Avci was shocked at the sudden breach of decorum. The second guard stood there, looking back and forth between Avci and Solak, unsure of what to do in such a public space. Solak was shocked as well.

"Dogan, stop!" Solak commanded. "This is unacceptable. You don't know what you're talking about. You are relieved." He turned back to face Dolan. "Please accept my apologies, Doctor Dolan. I…"

Dogan bolted towards Dolan, drawing his weapon and grabbing Dolan by the arm. "Sir, Mister President, I apologize but I must confine this man for questioning. You must take my word. This man works for the CIA." He tugged on Dolan's arm, directing him through a doorway near the stage. The second guard stood by, ready to do whatever Solak recommended. Both Avci and Solak were visibly irate and followed Dogan through the door with the second guard and three others who'd caught wind of the commotion. No one seemed to notice what was going on as the Türkü band played on.

Once all were inside the room, the door was closed. All five guards had drawn their handguns, held ready at a forty-five-degree angle to the floor in front of Dolan. Dogan looked at the President and Solak, standing together a safe distance away and surrounded by the guards.

"Mister President, I implore you to leave. You are not safe. This man works for the CIA, I am sure of it. Minister Solak, *he is Individual One*." He held Dolan's arm behind his back and his weapon to Dolan's side.

Dolan realized at that moment that this was this man who had murdered Andy. There was no other explanation. His plan had fallen apart in spectacular fashion. Whether or not Solak and Avci believed what Dolan was saying, it wouldn't take them long to learn the truth. He could not risk being taken into custody.

At that moment, Dolan made a fateful decision, risking everything. With his free hand he knocked Dogan's pistol away from his ribcage and twisted his body while grabbing Dogan's arm and moving behind him. In less than half a second, Dolan had reversed places with his captor and was now holding the gun to Dogan's head. The four other guards immediately leveled their weapons. Avci and Solak were in shock.

"President Avci," Dolan stated immediately and loudly. "If you ever listened carefully and openly to anything in your life, listen to me now. Minister Solak and Red Fig were behind today's cyberattack. Minister Solak masterminded the whole thing, and I have proof. Yes, you are in danger, but not from me. The man hurting you and your administration is standing right next to you."

No one moved. Avci continued to look at Dolan, mouth agape. Solak took a step forward and was stopped by one of the guards. "Arrest this man. You are right, Dogan. He is not who I thought he was. Mister President, we must get you to safety."

"Yes of course," said the President. He turned toward the door.

"Mister President!" Dolan yelled louder, exasperated. "Yusuf Solak killed your wife."

At that Avci turned quickly back, the color drained from his face. "What did you say?" he asked venomously.

"Yusuf Solak murdered your wife and unborn child." Dolan said in a lowered voice. "He did it to make sure you won the presidential election. I have the proof with me. It's in my right jacket pocket. Minister Solak created an algorithmic model to predict the outcome of your election and it said you were going to lose. He changed the algorithm to include what would happen if your wife died just before the election. He assumed correctly that the sympathy of the Turkish people for your loss would turn the tide in your favor. He murdered your wife. The algorithm he created is in my pocket. This man," Dolan shook Dogan, "murdered Demir and my friend to prevent Demir from giving us the model. But we got it anyway."

The color was now drained from Solak's face. "Shoot this man. He is a terrorist. Solak lunged toward Dolan, clawing at his jacket.

"Yusuf, stop," Avci ordered. He looked to the nearest guard. "See what's in his pocket."

The guard nodded and approached the two men cautiously.

"Go ahead. Take it. Give it to the President," Dolan said to him.

The guard felt inside Dolan's jacket and pulled out a thumb drive as Solak looked on. Solak then lunged at the guard and attempted to grab the drive, but was rebuffed. "This must be confiscated. How did security not find this at the gate? You will all be fired." He was beginning to foam at the mouth. The guard handed the drive to Avci, who looked at it carefully, then put it in his pocket. Then he looked at Solak.

"You and I need to talk," Avci told him.

The color drained from Solak's face, but he kept his cool. "It's all a lie, Adem. I would never do such a thing. This man is a terrorist."

Dolan removed the barrel from Dogan's head. "I'm placing my weapon on the floor and releasing this man. I will go into custody peacefully."

He placed the handgun on the floor and let go of Dogan's arm. As the other guards converged, Dogan swiftly picked up his weapon and struck Dolan hard on the head. His world faded to black.

CHAPTER THIRTY-THREE

Dolan awoke to a raging headache. He touched his temple where Dogan
hit him and winced. His fingers came away red with blood. His vision
was blurred. Dolan was in a small, square room. The walls were plain
and gray, the floor was concrete. One door. He was seated, handcuffed
to a metal bar affixed to the middle of a heavy stainless-steel table. There
was a large one-way mirror on the wall in front of him and a camera
mounted in the upper left corner.

He sat there for what felt like hours before the door finally
opened. A well-dressed man entered holding a glass of water, which he
placed on the table. He reached in his pocket, withdrew a key, and
removed Dolan's cuffs. Dolan slumped back in his chair.

The next four hours were textbook interrogation. He was
threatened. They gave him food and took him to the restroom. They
showed him photos of Dolan entering the palace and mingling in the
crowd. They told him they knew all about him and why he was in Turkey.
That he'd violated international law, and that he had no diplomatic
immunity. That he would die in prison. Much of it was speculation on
their part, Dolan knew. Regardless of how much they really knew,
however, it was all somewhat close to the truth. By the fifth hour he'd
resigned himself to a dark fate. He'd never see the light of day again.

He'd be tortured. Dolan had no regrets, though; he'd do it all again. Perhaps with a few changes to his original plan, in hindsight. He hoped Welker hadn't tried anything stupid when he never came out...

At the end of the day, he was cuffed again and left in the dark. He tried to sleep but found it impossible. The night wore on. Eventually, the lights came back on, the door opened, and President Adem Avci walked in accompanied by a security guard.

"Take those off," Avci instructed.

The guard did as he was told.

"Now leave us," he said.

The man nodded. "Yes, Mister President."

After the door closed, Avci sat in the chair opposite him. "You, Doctor Michael Dolan, are an intriguing man. Most in your profession choose to remain in the shadows. It's a necessity, really. Well respected in the halls of academia and science. You're a celebrity of sorts, wouldn't you say?"

"I wouldn't say that, Mister President," Dolan responded.

"Nonetheless, you're in a spotlight. It must be difficult to tread that path, a tightrope really. To do what you do."

Dolan remained silent.

"Listen," Avci continued, "I don't want to make things more difficult than they already are. The reason I am speaking to you right now...the reasons are complicated. But I need certain assurances from you. But first, I owe you my gratitude, Michael. Someone I never thought would do anything to harm me..." He stopped, holding off emotion. "Someone, my best friend and closest confidant, hurt me more than anyone ever could. And you brought that to my attention at great risk to yourself. I apologize for how you've been treated, but you must understand we had to check you out. There was a lot to do and investigate, and we had to do it quickly."

Dolan only nodded cautiously, not knowing what to say.

"You will be returned to the United States, Michael," Avci assured him. "But first, like I said, I need assurances from you."

"Mister President," Dolan responded, "You reviewed the model then? You saw what I was saying was true?"

"No, we didn't look at it. Minister Solak took it from me last night and crushed it with the heel of his shoe. It was irreparably damaged. But his behavior caused me great concern. I picked up the pieces and told him later our engineers were able to retrieve the data on the drive. That's all I had had to say. He broke down and admitted everything. He begged me for mercy. We've been friends since we were children, you see. Aside from the day I lost my wife, this is the most painful thing I've experienced in life. And Yusuf was responsible for both. But knowing the truth of what happened is of immeasurable value to me. Things must be set right."

Dolan couldn't believe what he was hearing. It was as if divine intervention were a real thing. He smiled at the thought. "President Avci, what assurances do you require from me?"

Avci leaned forward across the steel table. "I know you are aware that there is more to all of this than the revelation my best friend could have done something so reprehensibly evil."

That word again, thought Dolan.

He continued. "You said it yourself. The cyberattack. This is something that affects the entire world, and it has set in motion an international financial calamity that can only be assuaged by undoing what was done. I still know very little of the details, but we are investigating thoroughly. I have spoken with your President. The resolution of this will be executed at a very high level, and there will be very few people involved. The truth of how it all came to pass can never be made public. If that were to happen, it would undermine confidence in the very fabric of every nation's political and financial institutions. The people of the Earth could very well enter a new dark age. It's impossible to predict, for sure. But your President agrees with me on this. My country will make things right, to the best of our ability. But we must be allowed to do so without conspiracy or resistance to our efforts. Can you promise me that your organization will follow this path? That you, Michael Dolan, will adhere to this plan?"

Dolan regarded Avci with open skepticism. This was not at all what he expected to hear from him. He was surprised Avci was even discussing it, and suddenly wondered if he'd been in on it all along. That he would be totally unaware of any part of Solak's plans and activities was already an improbable assumption. But Dolan was just a cog. What did Avci think he might do? Go to the press with his story? His job was to do, and not ask why. Though he hadn't historically been very good at it. Questioning authority and the reasons behind what he was ordered to do had led him to the place he was today. His gut had never let him down.

"Mister President," Dolan answered, "it is not my position to understand or try to influence what goes on at such a strategic level. I have my own opinions. I know what is wrong and what is right. And I know there has been a lot going wrong within your administration. My job was to address it somehow before it became a problem that affected *my* country. I did my best and believe I was at least partially successful. Whatever plan you and my President have hatched to try and undo what Yusuf Solak and Red Fig have done, that's between you and him. I do understand the sensitivities. A lot more is going to come out, you will undoubtedly hear it from my President, but I'll let you know this. On top of everything, it was none other than Minister Solak who was hiding Hakeem Lefebvre on that plantation in Niger. Lefebvre was paying him off by boosting investment in Hypotherion over several years. Billions of euros. When his money ran out, Solak had him eliminated by giving up his location."

Avci looked dumbfounded. "That's impossible. I don't believe it. I can't."

"It's true," Dolan replied. "You'll receive proof of it. Now, back to your request. I agree to it. I won't say anything. I can't. But I do have a request of my own, and it's not negotiable."

Dolan could see Avci struggling with the Lefebvre bombshell.

"What is it?" he asked hesitantly.

"The security guard, Dogan," Dolan replied. "The only way he could have recognized me was if he saw me with Murat Demir and my colleague the morning they were both shot. Dogan murdered them both. Demir wanted to expose the truth about what happened to your wife and unborn child. In that respect, what he tried to do was no different than what I did. Solak used Dogan to murder him and Andy to keep that truth from coming out. Andy was a good man. A husband and a father. Dogan must be punished. Promise me this."

Avci, still processing everything Dolan had told him, sat back in his chair, nodding. "I promise you Michael, Yusuf Solak and Dogan will both be held accountable for what they have done. The wheels of justice have a way of turning faster when I'm involved. You have my word."

"Thank you, Mister President."

"Of course," he replied. "We should get you cleaned up, fed, and ready to go home. I'll have a doctor look at your head." He stood up and reached into his pocket, holding something out to Dolan. A flat, round stone painted black on one side, and white on the other. "I want you to have this."

Dolan took it from him, turning it over in his palm. "What is it?"

"It's a Kirmizi-beyaz stone. It means 'red and white.' A children's game. Yusuf preferred black over red. When faced with certain decisions, he would flip it. Like a coin. I have my own, in fact, though mine is the traditional red and white."

"This was Solak's?" Dolan asked.

"Yes. Consider it a gift. A trophy. A symbol of my commitment to make things right.

Dolan placed it in his pocket, nodding thoughtfully as he did so.

"Thank you, Mister President."

CHAPTER THIRTY-FOUR

"I waited all night, and the next day as well," Welker laughed. "I finally left. Dittrich was calling your phone about every hour. Then he started calling me. I went back to the safehouse and took a shower. I didn't know what else to do, so I called Dittrich back and let him know everything. The shit really hit the fan at that point of course, everyone was called in. I've never experienced anything quite like it. Fucking amazing."

Welker arrived separately in D.C. ahead of Dolan earlier that morning. They were sitting in the reception area of Dittrich's office. He'd already spoken with the rest of the team.

"Sorry Howard," Dolan replied. Things didn't go as planned, obviously. But in the end, I think it all worked out OK."

Dittrich's executive assistant Mary caught their attention. "Gentlemen, you can go in now."

"Sit down," he told them as they walked in. Dolan closed the door.

"Never in my life have I been party to such a massive fuckup," he began. He pointed at Dolan. "You disobeyed my direct order. I couldn't have made it clearer. You were supposed to close up shop and come home. The mission was over. And you," he pointed to Welker, "went along with it knowing full well it wasn't sanctioned."

Both men remained silent.

"The President has my ass in a sling. The Director is on this twenty-four seven doing damage control. All thanks to you two. Michael, what could you have been thinking? A public and very dangerous confrontation with the president and minister of a foreign nation?"

Dolan and Welker still said nothing.

"Well, what do you have to say for yourselves? What am I supposed to do with you? With REVENANT?" This is an international incident of biblical proportions."

Dolan smiled inwardly at the term, but Dittrich caught it.

"That's not hyperbole, Dolan!" Dittrich yelled. "What the hell. Why did you do it?" he asked.

"Sir," he replied, "it was the right thing to do. And I think we can all agree that things worked out as well as they could have, given the circumstances. We got the bad guy. We stopped the attack. We shut down Nobelium; we've been trying get to them for years. Andy's killer is being held accountable. And now Avci and Turkey are beholden to the United States, instead of the other way around. All in all, that's a big win in my book."

Dittrich looked exasperated. "Despite what you believe to be true, the strategic costs incurred are significant. We were working on a plan, one that would have, ultimately, smoothed things over. Fixed everything behind the scenes. Prevented international political chaos. You unilaterally coopted that plan. Yes, there was information we were lacking, but your rogue mission was not the way to get it. It's literally unconscionable that something like this would ever happen on my watch."

Dolan regarded him stoically. "I'd do it all again. It was the right thing. I have no doubt the outcome would have been far worse had I not done what I did."

"You have no way of knowing that Michael!" Dittrich snapped. "You got lucky. You have no idea... The only reason you're not already fired is, Avci took a shine to you. He asked the President to go easy on you. So fucking lucky..." he was shaking his head. "What about you, Howard. Do you have anything to say?"

"Nope," Welker stated flatly. "Michael's right."

Dittrich rolled his eyes. "Ok well, you are both suspended pending investigation. Stay in the D.C. area. I need a couple days to figure out how to address this mess, then the three of us are going to have a very long discussion. Don't go anywhere; I don't want to have to go hunting you down. Dismissed."

Welker looked at Dolan sideways, grinning sardonically as they left through the door.

◆

"Fill me in," Dolan told Freeman. They were seated at the bar of a small watering hole in Georgetown. "What happened with UMBRAGE and Nobelium? Did you figure out where all the money went?"

Freeman cast him a sideways look. "We can't talk about that here. You know that."

"No one is listening, Thomas. Give me the broad strokes."

"OK," he relented. "Well, we captured everything off their servers. There were quite a few pieces of new malware they were working on that we'll now be able to defense and exploit. As for HIVE, we studied the integration. It was difficult to figure out, because we didn't want them to realize we were in there, but all signs point back to

Hypotherion. My theory is that Red Fig was doing a lot of backdoor mining for years. Making it look like coins were being mined traditionally when in fact they were just creating them out of thin air. All those coins generated millions of carbon credits with real value. They accelerated that process in the leadup to the attack. But you still must have investment. The money must come from somewhere. They had a lot of legal investment of course, but not nearly the amount Hypotherion was reporting. They had to drive the value up, which the backdoor mining did for them. But they couldn't get investors fast enough. It looks like almost a third of the total value of the exchange came from Lefebvre. He needed a safe place to keep his money. We were locating his accounts and freezing his assets. Why not do it in a place where he was guaranteed to make a profit, all the while completely hidden from public view? There was no way for anyone to know, not even us. It's not a normal bank. It was all sheltered."

"Holy cow," Dolan exclaimed. "I'm amazed that something this big, this complex, could have gone this far without someone noticing. It's mind boggling."

Freeman looked at him and smiled. "We noticed."

Dolan smiled back. "Yeah. We noticed."

"Once Solak had all Lefebvre's money, he hid all of it," Freeman continued, "making it all look like carbon credit payouts. That created a huge void in their accounting, one they had to cover up for a while. But that was all part of the plan—fill the void with money they got from the FrankenHIVE attack. Then they would lend the money back to countries they stole from, who now needed a loan to stay afloat, and at a profit of course. Solak said as much the night of your international incident… Nobelium would have received a percentage; there was evidence of that on their servers. But again, we can't trace *exactly* where the money went. The coding was truly amazing."

"There 'was' evidence on the servers?" Dolan asked.

"Was, yes. Once we decided we'd gotten everything useful that we could from their servers, we fried them."

"Good," Dolan responded. "I was worried the management was going to want to play games, let them stay up and running for a while."

"Nope," Freeman replied. "So, what now? Are you going to be OK?"

"Dittrich suspended me. And Welker. There's going to be an investigation."

"Shit," Freeman said under his breath. "I don't think he realizes yet how bad this would have gotten had you not intervened when you did. I still have to brief him on the details of the cyberattack and everything our team did to shut it down. He'll come around."

"I don't know," responded Dolan. "He said I was lucky. I don't believe in luck…"

Freeman laughed. "You should. That algorithmic model you gave Avci?"

"Yeah?"

"It wasn't the one Demir was trying to pass to us. The death of his wife and sympathy effect variables were not coded into it. It was just one of the regular social media models his team had worked on. If Solak hadn't smashed your thumb drive…"

"*Good God*," Dolan replied. "You have to be kidding…"

"I'm not. So yeah, you were very, *very* lucky."

"I guess I was," Dolan conceded.

"And then," Freeman went on, "there's the Miltner-Dolan Model."

"What do you mean?" Dolan asked.

"FrankenHIVE. Remember, I told you it looked like Red Fig used elements of the math from your model? After further inspection, we think we know what for."

"And?" Dolan pressed.

"To choose which accounts, from which regions, and in which countries to steal from. And to determine the sequencing and frequency of the individual hacks. The algorithm they coded was one intended to predict how to exact maximum economic impact on a national level for each country, adjusting in real time as it executed."

"Wow, are you sure? That would make sense if it's true. Almost like the spread…"

Freeman cut Dolan off. "Of a virus."

"Yeah," Dolan said, shaking his head in disbelief. "Like the spread of a pandemic."

"What are you going to do now?" Freeman asked.

"Good question." He took Solak's Kirmizi-beyaz stone from his pocket and tossed it in the air into his open palm. *White.* "I have some things I need to do, people to see. Here, take my secure cell." Dolan pocketed the stone and extended his phone to Freeman.

He regarded Dolan quizzically. "Why? You should keep it. Have you even been debriefed yet?"

"Not yet. Just take it," Dolan replied. "Where I'm going, I don't want to be bothered. If Dittrich calls, tell him I'm taking some down time. Just a couple days. I'll get it from you when I return."

With that, Dolan finished his beer and left a twenty on the bar. Then he got up, winked at a confused Freeman, and walked out.

CHAPTER THIRTY-FIVE

"I have to admit, I'm surprised to see you here," remarked Fitzhenry. "Water?"

"Sure," Dolan replied as he sat down."

"Aren't you supposed to be in D.C.?" he asked pointedly.

"Yes," Dolan acknowledged. "I'm already on Dittrich's shit list. There are some things I need to take care of though and talking with you is one of them."

"We could have done that on the phone," Fitzhenry noted as he took a seat opposite Dolan.

"Says the man who made me fly here from Turkey."

"Touché."

"Revelation. You know, I've read the book," said Dolan. "When I was a kid. I remember it. After everything, in hindsight, I can't say I agree that what happened is related to what we discussed. This wasn't an apocalypse. Unless you think this was only the beginning or something. Even then, I don't see it. That said, I was unable to prove my null hypothesis. That what was going on in Turkey had nothing to do with Revelation."

Fitzhenry took a swig from his water bottle. "You know, the most common misconception about Revelation is that it's just a prophecy concerning the end of days. That it foretells the end of the Earth, and that's it. It does do that, but it is also more than that. It's a book of hope."

"Hope?" asked Dolan.

"Yes. At the time John the Disciple wrote it, Christians were being persecuted. The visions he had and recorded revealed that there will, from time to time, be someone in power who is evil. Someone who will oppress them for what they believe. And that as long as they keep their faith, even as things get worse, they can still have hope. He was telling them to hang in there because God always wins. If you look at it that way, well, you could say this was one of those times. Just because the world didn't end, and because you and REVENANT were able to fix things before they got too bad, it doesn't mean that what is foretold in Revelation didn't actually happen. The bottom line is, Revelation is not just a prediction of a single, cataclysmic event. It is a prophecy of something that has happened over and over throughout history and will continue to do so until *THE* end. Nero, Hadrian, the Ottomans, the Bolsheviks, Hitler, Khrushchev... It's a long list. In a way, you could say there were many antichrists. And there will be more."

"But Solak was indiscriminate in his attack. He wasn't going after Christians," Dolan countered.

"Wasn't he?" Fitzhenry responded. "While you were locked up, a lot of analysis was done on the demographics. It was made to look indiscriminate, but a vast majority of the money was stolen from western, traditionally Christian countries. Muslim and other nations got off easy. It wasn't even close."

"I see. One other thing. Do you think Avci was involved? Do you think he was part of all this? The attack? How could he not be?"

Fitzhenry looked up at the ceiling. "Who's to know. It's difficult to believe he knew nothing. But at the same time, everything we know about Avci tells us he is a decent and fair man. It's why we ignored the fact Solak was bending the rules with Red Fig to get him elected. He has faults, like anyone else, but there are worse world leaders out there. We may never know the truth."

"Well, I guess that's all then. Thanks for your help."

"You're welcome," said Fitzhenry. "So that's it? You came all this way for this?"

"Don't flatter yourself," Dolan responded. "You're not the only reason I'm here."

"Right. Listen, Michael. You did it the right way. Don't worry about Dittrich. He has one foot in the Agency and the other in the White House. I wouldn't have done anything differently myself."

"Thanks Fitzy. I appreciate that."

♦

Dolan struck the door three times with the wrought iron knocker. The small wooden sign still hung there, *Petit a petit, l'oiseau fait son nid.* Little by little, the bird makes its nest. It was faded now. He grabbed the knocker again just as the door opened. Anne stood there then, a surprised smile on her face. The sun shimmered across her auburn hair.

"Michael!" she exclaimed as she sprung forward and enveloped him in her arms. "Come in, come in! Once again, you show up unexpected. Twice in two weeks! How did you know I would be here?"

He held her at arm's length. "I have my sources."

"Yes, you do, don't you," she said playfully. "Come inside. Can you stay?"

Dolan followed her inside. They sat next to each other on her living room couch.

"I'm leaving tomorrow. I have to get back to D.C. I'm not even supposed to be here, to be honest."

She touched his hand. "Yes, you are."

"Yes, I am," he conceded.

"*Listen you…*what are you doing, what is going on Michael? Is everything OK?" she asked.

"Yes, everything is fine, Anne," he assured her. "In fact, things have never been better. I've been doing a lot of thinking. These past few years have been difficult. Difficult for you. For us. I can't live my life this way anymore, and it's unfair to ask you to do it, either."

Anne moved away suddenly, apprehensively. "What are you saying?"

Dolan stood up then and looked down at her. "Love…is a difficult thing. What I mean to say is, there will never be a good opportunity for us to be together, to have a normal life together. This, what we've been doing, the way we've been doing it. It's not healthy for either of us."

Anne immediately put her face in her hands and began to cry.

"No, no, no, Anne, that's not what I mean!" he said as he quickly dropped to his knees in front of her. He carefully pulled her hands away and held on to them, looking straight into her soul.

"Anne Bernard, will you marry me?"

Anne's eyes went wide, her crestfallen expression changed in an instant to one of joy. She gripped his hands tightly. "Oui, oui, *a thousand times oui*, Michael Dolan! There is nothing else in life I want more."

They embraced again, and Dolan laughed quietly. "I don't even have a ring. I only decided to do this last night."

"It's doesn't matter," she replied. "You can get me one later. A nice one!"

"A nice one," he replied.

They kissed. A long, deep, sensual kiss. Then she pulled slowly away.

"What about your job, Michael? It's what has always come between us. It's what kept us apart all these years."

"Don't worry about my job. If they want to keep me now, they'll have to do it on my terms. From now on, *we* are my number one priority."

Anne kissed him tenderly on the cheek. "I love you, Michael," she said, tears still streaking her face. "Forever."

"I love you too, Anne. I love you too. Forever."

ACKNOWLEDGEMENTS

I wrote the first fifty or so pages of *Devolution* in the summer of 2013. At the time, it was the seed of an idea for a spy thriller series with a flawed main character who was very gifted in certain ways, but considerably challenged in others. That character was Michael Dolan.

To make things interesting, I decided that Dolan wouldn't begin as a CIA officer; that he would instead be identified and 'used' by the Agency for an ongoing black operations mission that was going sideways. Over time, the strength of his successes would overcome his miscues, leading to his promotion as a full member of the team and eventually as the leader of REVENANT.

But I was unhappy with those fifty pages. It was my first attempt to write a book, and the sheer volume of work required to do it well left me discouraged. So, I put it away to try my hand at poetry. Two years later my first book *Raw Thoughts: A Mindful Fusion of Poetic and Photographic Art*, was published. I couldn't have completed that project without photographer Scott Hussey. Scott also took the photos for all three covers of *The Devolution Trilogy*. Thank you, Scott.

Riding the high of being newly published, I went back to *Devolution*. I rewrote the beginning and pitched it to my publisher, who gave me a three-book deal. Thus began the journey that ended with my completion of *Revelation*, over nine years later. Along the way, I found that my experience working for the Defense Intelligence Agency and in other diplomatic and foreign affairs capacities was not sufficient. Consequently, there was an incredible amount of research involved in completing the series, and quite a bit of help from others.

After reviewing the manuscripts and my pitch, the Central Intelligence Agency Public Affairs Office agreed to meet with me to add legitimacy to certain aspects of the series. That collaboration led to recommendations that made the storyline more realistic and credible. The CIA has my gratitude for working with me to make each novel a better story.

My good friend and colleague Otto Habedank, who is an avid reader and one of the smartest people I know, was a willing and able pre-reader who had no problem telling me when I'd written something that needed improvement. Additionally, Otto gave me ideas that added quality to the trilogy. There is another pre-reader out there whose name and employer I cannot reveal who provided very useful guidance and constructive criticism. Thank you both.

Revelation required more research than *Devolution* and *Evolution* combined. This was due in part to the fact most of the story takes place in Turkey. I am blessed to have friends like Ferhat Ozturk and Melih Morgan who provided innumerable recommendations that enhanced the cultural authenticity of a story that unfolds in a country I've never been to.

Furthermore, I decided that the threat in *Revelation* would be a cyberattack, but I was lacking in the knowledge necessary to pull it off. Otto came through for me once again. His close friend Eric Waxvik is a cybersecurity expert who works for Amazon. Eric gave me great ideas in my search to create a very complicated, hi-tech scheme that would pass the smell test, even by IT professionals at his level. Jeff Prevost, a cryptocurrency and blockchain technology expert, gave me additional help in that respect. I'm indebted to you both, as your contributions enabled me to create a convincing scenario with Red Fig, the eL8 app, the intricate inner workings of Hypotherion, and with various aspects of Nobelium's role in the cyberattack.

Finally, the most difficult part of writing Revelation was integrating the theological subplot in a nuanced way that made good sense and truly added value, without overpowering the plot. Dan Schlueter, a noted theologian and author from San Antonio, walked me through it and made sure I didn't make any mistakes. I can't overstate how important his contributions to *Revelation* were—thank you so much, Dan.

ABOUT THE AUTHOR

JOHN CASEY is a novelist and Pushcart Prize-nominated poet from New Hampshire. *Revelation* is book three of *The Devolution Trilogy*. *Devolution* and *Evolution* are books one and two of the psychological spy thriller series. He is the author of *Raw Thoughts: A Mindful Fusion of Poetic and Photographic Art* and *Meridian: A Raw Thoughts Book* as well. A Veteran combat and test pilot with a Master of Arts from Florida State University, Casey also served as a diplomat and international affairs strategist at U.S. embassies in Germany and Ethiopia, the Pentagon, and elsewhere. He is passionate about fitness, nature, and the human spirit and inspired by the incredible spectrum of people, places, and cultures he has experienced in life.

For more on John Casey and his writing, visit **johnjcasey.com**, or use this QR code:

Made in the USA
Columbia, SC
27 November 2022

71969416R00148